THE PLAGUE OF GHOSTS

AND

OTHER STORIES

RAFAEL SABATINI

Contents

THE RISEN DEAD

Sir Geoffrey Swayne was hanged at Tyburn.

A merry, reckless, roaring soul had been Sir Geoffrey, and if it was said of him that in ten years he had never gone sober to bed, yet was it confessed that he was a pleasant, humorous gentleman in his cups, just as he was a pleasant, humorous gentleman in all the other traffics that made up his rascally life. If he lost his money at the tables, he did so with an amiable smile in his handsome eyes and a jest on his lips. If at intervals, more or less regular, he would beat his wife, periodically kick his servants down stairs, and systematically grind the faces of his tenants, yet all these things he did, at least, with an engaging joviality of demeanour.

In short, he was a very affable, charming scoundrel, and all England was agreed that he richly deserved his end. And yet, the humour of the thing – and it was just such a jest as Sir Geoffrey would have relished had it been less against himself – lay in the fact that although none of the rascally things he had done could be considered by the law of England reason enough for hanging him, the crime for which he was hanged – that of highway robbery – was the one crime it had never occurred to him to commit.

The thing had fallen out in this wise:

Sir Geoffrey, riding Londonwards, from his home near Guildford, one evening in late March, had been held up on Wandsworth Common by a cloaked figure on a huge grey mare. The failing light had gleamed from the barrel of a pistol, and the highwayman's tone had been one that asked no arguments, admitted of no compromise. But Sir Geoffrey in the course of his blustering career had become a useful man of his hands. One blow of his heavy riding-crop had knocked aside the highwayman's pistol, another had knocked in the highwayman's head and tumbled him headlong from his saddle.

Sir Geoffrey was master of the situation, and, mightily pleased by it, he bethought him of the spoils of war, which were his by right of conquest. Without a qualm – nay, with a laugh and the lilt of a song on his lips – Sir Geoffrey had dragged the stricken tobyman into the shelter of a clump of trees, and exchanged his own spavined horse for the fellow's splendid mare, on which he had blithely pursued his road.

But before he had gone a couple of miles he had caught the sounds of a numerous party galloping behind and rapidly gaining on him. Now Sir Geoffrey's conscience – if so be he owned one – was at rest. He had done no wrong, leastways no wrong that should make him fear the law, and so he rode easily, never thinking of attempting to outdistance the party which came on behind – a thing he might easily have done had he been so inclined, bravely mounted as he was.

So the others came on, hailed him, and when he paused to ask them what they craved, came up with and surrounded him.

'We have you this time, "Scudding Tom",' they cried, and fell to ill-using him, pulling him down from his horse, and bestowing upon him epithets for which he was utterly at a loss to account. But he was not a patient man. He had been assaulted, and it was a thing he would not suffer, although, as he plainly saw, they were sheriff's men that had set upon him. So he blithely laid about him, and contrived to crack a couple of heads before they had bound him and flung him, helpless, down upon the road, livid, blasphemant, and vastly furious.

A stout rubicund gentleman, in black with silver lace, who had stood well apart whilst the fighting had been in train, came forward now, swelling to bursting point with his own importance, and denounced Sir Geoffrey for the tobyman who had robbed him an hour ago. He was, he said, Sir Henry Talbury of Hurlingston, in the County of Kent, one of his Majesty's Justices of the Peace. He had been to collect certain sums of money in London, and was returning with a leather bag containing a hundred guineas, of which this ruffian had relieved him.

Sir Geoffrey heard him, and having heard him realized the situation, spat from his mouth the filthy rags with which he had been gagged, and spoke—

'You pot-bodied fool,' said he, for he had a rare virulence of tongue upon occasion. 'You gross, beer-fattened hodman, let me free of these bonds, and get you back to your pigs at Hurlingston ere I have you flayed for this business. I am Sir Geoffrey Swayne, of Guildford, as you shall learn more fully to your bitter sorrow.'

The little man's fat face lost some of its plethoric colour, but it was in rage that he paled, and not in any fear that Sir Geoffrey – being tightly bound and helpless – might inspire him.

'Are ye so, indeed,' he snapped, and his little eyes looked evil as a rat's. 'I have heard of ye, for a gaming, dissolute scoundrel.'

'Oh 'sblood!' panted Sir Geoffrey, writhing in his bonds. 'You shall be spitted for this, like the Christmas goose you are.'

'And so, 'tis to highway robbery that your debaucheries have brought ye?' The little man sniffed contemptuously. 'I'm nowise surprised, and ye shall hang as a warning to other scapegraces.'

And hang he did as Sir Henry promised him. Under the flap of his saddle they had found a bag with Sir Henry Talbury's name upon it and the hundred guineas he had mentioned contained in it. It was in vain that Sir Geoffrey told the true story of his meeting with the tobyman, thus explaining how he had come by the grey mare – which had proved his undoing, for it was the mare, not the man, that had been recognized. The fellow who rode that great, grey beast was known to the countryside as 'Scudding Tom', and nothing more, his identity never having been revealed. The court, whilst praising his ingenuity, laughed at his tale. They realized that he was Sir Geoffrey Swayne – he had brought a regiment of witnesses to swear it – but they were no less satisfied that Sir Geoffrey and 'Scudding Tom' were one and the same person. It sorted well with his general reputation, and besides Sir Henry swore to him as being the man who had robbed him, and whether he swore in good faith or out of revenge for the things Sir Geoffrey had said to him when he was overpowered, it might be difficult to say.

But Sir Geoffrey was hanged, and the world was done with him, although Sir Geoffrey was nowise done with the world, as you shall hear. His lands – or what was left of them out of all that he had gamed away – were forfeit to the Crown, and his widow stood thus in peril of destitution. Not even his handsome body did they leave. For when it was cut down, still warm, from the gallows, it was sold to Dr.

Blizzard, a ready purchaser of such commodities for dissecting purposes.

But the old doctor had bought more than he knew of this time, for upon the insertion of the knife into one of Sir Geoffrey's legs – the point at which the doctor had elected to start his work – Sir Geoffrey had suddenly sat upright on the slate table, stretching his limbs, and letting forth a volley of blood-curdling imprecations, which all but slew the doctor by the fright they gave him.

Then, memory of past events returning to his wakening mind, the rake had checked himself, blenched a little and looked awesomely about him. The doctor, quivering in every nerve, his teeth rattling in his head, vainly sought to crush himself behind a tallboy, to protect himself from the material, and pattered long-forgotten prayers to heaven for protection against the immaterial – for, scientist though Dr. Blizzard was, he could not here discriminate with which he might have to do.

'Rat me!' spluttered Sir Geoffrey, still looking about him, 'and is this Hades?' He shivered, for he was naked. 'It is colder than I would have credited from what they told me,' said he. He caught sight of the doctor's scared, grey face, horn-rimmed spectacles, and wig gone rakishly awry in the efforts the man made to conceal himself.

'Faith!' he pursued with a chuckle, 'but it's a place of surprises. You've a monstrous mild look, sir, for Satan – neither tail, nor cloven hoof, nor pitchfork? Gad's my life! but you're a disappointment.'

He swung himself down from the table, and found his limbs so cramped that he howled a second in pain.

At last, perceiving what manner of resurrection was this, the doctor took heart and came forward. 'God 'a mercy!' said he, 'I've heard of such things, but I'd never have believed it.'

'You've an odd turn of speech, old Lucifer. Are you a devil, or are you not?'

'I'm no devil,' the doctor answered testily.

'Then who the devil are you?'

'Man, you were hanged at Tyburn this morning,' quoth the doctor a trifle irrelevantly.

'Was I so? Egad! I was coming to think that I had dreamed it.'

'Oh, it was no dream. You were hanged. You are Sir Geoffrey Swayne.'

'Then I'm in Hades, after all. But of your pity lend me a cloak, for it seems I'm more in danger of being frozen here than burned.'

The doctor gave him the garment he craved, and explained the situation. Sir Geoffrey was incredulous. The doctor heaped up arguments, cited precedents.

'It is recorded,' he said, 'of a woman, in the reign of Edward III, regaining consciousness after having hanged for four-and-twenty hours, and of another woman at Oxford a hundred years ago who came to life again after having hanged for half-an-hour, besides other instances I've read of, yet discredited until now.'

The doctor was waxing excited, and Sir Geoffrey had much ado to restrain him from running out to tell all London of this resurrection.

'I'm dead,' he told the doctor, with a grin, 'and dead you'll leave me, or, by heaven, it's dead you'll be yourself. I was hanged, and there's an end to it – leastways until I've had a talk with that Kentish lout they call Sir Henry Talbury.'

He told the doctor the true circumstances of his case, and he so succeeded in convincing him of the truth of it that the old man was won over to befriend him, and put him in the way of having justice done him after all. But that night Sir Geoffrey sickened of a fever, and was forced to keep his bed some days, so that a week had passed before he was able to leave the doctor's house, and make his way to Hurlingston.

Blizzard lent him ten guineas and made him a present of a suit of black Camlett, a hat, and a brown *roquelaure*, his own clothes having been reduced to rags by the violence that had attended his arrest. Thus equipped, Sir Geoffrey arrived at Maidstone at six o'clock in the evening of the first Monday in April. From Maidstone to Hurlingston was a distance of some four miles, which Sir Geoffrey covered afoot, reaching Hurlingston Manor as dusk was falling.

He stepped briskly up the long white drive that wound its way between regiments of trees, to the clearing that fronted the grey, severely architected house. From long French windows to the left a shaft of light, emerging through half-drawn curtains, fell with a golden glow upon the lawn. One half of the window itself stood open, for it had been warm as a day of summer. Sir Geoffrey paused, and his eyes roved towards that glowing aperture. He hesitated in his original intention of boldly asking for Sir Henry. He turned aside, and still pondering, he drifted rather than walked, until he was in line with the opening, and able to look into the room. A second he stared with dilated eyes, then with a sharp indrawing of breath he sped forward, nor stopped until he was crouching at the window, peering into the room.

Within sat the Justice of the Peace, like a toad with its legs wide, and his wig on his knee. He was sucking contentedly at a long-stemmed pipe, and at his elbow was a decanter and a half-filled glass of sparkling yellow wine. His huge dome-like head shone in the light of a pair of candles that stood in their massive silver sticks on either side of the papers spread out in front of him.

Before him stood a woman all in black – a tall, nobly-proportioned woman, with a high nose and a handsome, high-bred face. She was speaking, and her fine eyes were full of supplication. Sir Geoffrey drew nigh and listened as he deemed he had the right to, for the woman was Lady Swayne.

'Sir,' she was saying, 'of your charity I do implore you again that you investigate this matter, and as sure as you're sitting there you shall discover that Sir Geoffrey was no robber, whatever may have been his sins. Sir Henry, you have made a widow of me. Do not make me a beggar also. I ask for justice – tardy justice – that my husband's estates be not confiscated from me.'

Sir Henry withdrew his pipe from his gross lips.

'Madam,' said he, 'your husband was found guilty by judge and jury. He was "Scudding Tom", the highwayman – there's never a doubt of it.'

The curtain rings rang harshly on the ensuing silence. The woman turned her head and screamed; the man looked up and gasped for breath. His face blenched, the pipe dropped from his nerveless fingers and broke into a dozen fragments on the floor; for there, between the dark green curtains, the lamplight falling full upon his face, which gleamed a ghostly white against the black background of the night, stood the wraith of Sir Geoffrey Swayne.

He stood there, enjoying the sensation his advent had created, a sardonic grin on his white face, a glitter mighty evil in his bold, black eyes.

The woman was the first to gather sufficient courage to address the apparition. Sir Henry had a desire to crawl under the table, and if he did not indulge it, it was because his limbs, palsied with fright, refused their office.

'Is that you, Geoffrey?' the woman whispered hoarsely, craning forward, her face white to the lips. 'Speak!'

And then a cunning notion shot through Sir Geoffrey's subtle mind. Of what avail to protest his innocence? What proofs had he? A judge and jury had found him guilty; the thing was done with. He must play a subtle game if he would retrieve his lands from confiscation, and the nature of it was at once apparent to him.

He stepped airily forward a pace or two, and the curtains fell together behind him with a shudder.

'My name, madam, is not Geoffrey. It is Jack – Jack Haynes, better known to the vulgar as "Scudding Tom", gentleman of the road. Your servant, madam, and yours, sir.' He made a leg first to the lady, and then to the knight.

Sir Henry's colour was returning. It came back in a flood until it seemed as if he were doomed to apoplexy. A grunt escaped him. He sought words in which to utter his amazement, his perplexity and his dawning dismay. But the woman was beforehand with him. She had stared a moment at her husband in unbelief. Then, as if convinced – and well she might be, knowing Sir Geoffrey hanged – she swung round upon Sir Henry, her arm dramatically outstretched.

'You have heard him, Sir Henry,' she cried. 'You have heard what he says. Will you believe me now, when I tell you again that you were mistaken? Here is the proof I needed. Will you do me justice now?'

'Wait, madam,' growled the knight. Then to the man: 'What brings you here?' he demanded.

'I am tardily come, sir,' answered the other, 'but I could not come before. I – I was detained. Yet am I here now, and, it seems, still in time to do some good. I am come to tell you that it was I who robbed you of your hundred guineas, and not Sir Geoffrey Swayne, whom you have hanged for the deed. 'Tis said that I resemble him, and indeed it must be so since you swore to him as being the man who robbed you. 'Twas an unlucky thing for him that when I held him up he should have knocked me from my mare and bestridden her himself, for the mare was well known – and belike 'twas the mare convinced men so easily that he was "Scudding Tom". So much for the ways of justice!'

Sir Henry stared at him with fallen jaw, and his thoughts were far from pleasant. This fellow was indeed the very image of Sir Geoffrey, so like in figure, feature and in voice, that neither he nor the man's own wife could have sworn that he was not Sir Geoffrey himself, but for the unquestionable fact that Sir Geoffrey was hanged a week ago. The sight of that incredible likeness convinced him of the error there had been. The man he hanged was the very counterpart of this one. Small blame to him, then, for having sworn away the other's life. Yet a sudden choler stirred the fat old knight, as much against himself for the life he had sworn away, as against this fellow for having been the cause of it.

He heaved himself to his feet, acting upon a sudden impulse. His neglected wig tumbled from his knee and lay on the ground beside the pieces of his shattered pipe, whilst its owner lurched across the room in the direction of the bell-rope.

'Whither away, Sir Henry?' came Sir Geoffrey's voice suavely; and, moved to look over his shoulder, the knight's progress was arrested, and his heavy underlip shuddered in affright against his teeth, for he was staring into a levelled pistol. 'I have not walked into the lion's maw without precautions, sir,' said he. 'I'll trouble you to sit.'

But the woman, who had been considering him with scrutinizing eyes, raised a hand and waved it imperiously to Sir Henry.

'Ring the bell, sir,' she bade him briskly.

'Madam,' smiled Sir Geoffrey, 'be not harsh with me. Besides, upon what charge would you have me taken?'

'Upon the charge of highway robbery,' thundered the knight. Nevertheless he sat down, as he was bidden. 'By your own confession, it was you who robbed me on Streatham Hill.'

'Bloodthirsty tyke,' returned the other. 'Have you not hanged one man already for that deed? Gads, my life, sir, you may not hang two men in England for one man's offence.'

Sir Henry considered him a moment, writhing under the insolence of the fellow's tone. 'Your resemblance to the late Sir Geoffrey is very thorough,' said he drily. 'It is little blame to me for my mistake. But if we have hanged one man for your robbery of me, yet there are counts enough besides, against you on which to hang you as well.'

'Maybe; but you'll drop the subject, or there'll be one count more – the death of Sir Henry Talbury.'

His lips smiled, but his tone was resolute, his eyes alert. Sir Henry, finding the subject as little to his own taste as it was objectionable to his visitor, dropped it there and then. Sir Geoffrey crossed to the door and turned the key.

'Sir,' said he, 'and you, madam – for Sir Geoffrey I am sorry, though the world has it he was a nasty rogue. But I am here to prove that, at least, he was not the thing for which they hanged him. He was no robber. Restitution must be made to his widow. I have his death upon my conscience. I'll not have more.'

'Why, there we are at one,' Sir Henry agreed. 'Since I have seen and heard you, it is my wish, no less than yours, that Lady Swayne should not suffer more than already she has done. Will you depose?'

'Let me have pen, ink and paper, and it shall be done at once.'

Sir Henry supplied his needs, and Sir Geoffrey sat down to write.

'You'll be so good as to sit there – as far from the bell as the width of the room will allow,' he bade the knight. 'Make an attempt to have me apprehended, and I shall take a look at the colour of your brains – if so be you have any.'

'Damme, you knave—'

'Peace, sir. Do you not see that I write?'

They left him to it, Sir Henry and Lady Swayne sitting silently in his presence, whilst his quill scratched its way across a sheet of paper, his pistol beside him on the table ready to his hand.

At last the confession that should save Sir Geoffrey's lands, now that it could no longer save his life, was accomplished. When it was done, he rose and went to ring the bell, then admitted the servant who answered the summons, and relocked the door when he was inside. In the presence of the magistrate, the lady, and the lackey, he swore to and signed his depositions, and they appended their signatures as witnesses. He emptied the sand-box over it, and, bowing to them, his bearing grave, his lips mocking, he strode off in the direction of the window by which he had entered. He paused, his hand upon the curtains, and looked back over his shoulder.

'Lady Swayne,' said he, 'I have done you some service this night. Let your gratitude see to it that I may go my ways without fear of pursuit.'

She nodded her assurance. His roving eye smiled a moment on the knight.

'Good-night, old beer-barrel,' said he, and so leapt out into the darkness, and was gone.

Lady Swayne shivered a little, and, moving to the table, took up the paper he had written and studied it a while. The bewildered lackey unlocked the door and departed at a curt nod from his master. A thin smile parted the lips of the woman, it was almost as a faint reflection of the smile that had haunted Sir Geoffrey's face.

'Madam,' said Sir Henry, with a rough attempt either at seeking or at giving consolation, 'you'll bear me no deep ill-will for my error. I deplore it grievously. I shall ne'er forgive myself. And yet, madam, the estates shall remain yours – have no doubt of that; and if all they say be true, belike you'll enjoy them better alone than in Sir Geoffrey's company. He was no over-pleasant mate for any woman; a bullying, drunken, wife-beating scoundrel, who—'

'Sir,' she broke in, 'he was my husband. Will you be so good as to ring? I'll be departing now.'

♦   ♦   ♦   ♦   ♦

It was a week before Sir Geoffrey found his way home to Guildford. He had tarried by the way until the last of Dr Blizzard's guineas was exhausted. One night, at last, he strode, as bold and debonair as ever, across the threshold of his home and bade a servant, who was new to him, to conduct him at once to Lady Swayne.

He stood in his wife's presence, the door closed; they two alone.

'Helen, my girl,' he cried – for on occasions he could be a very lover to the wife he had so often beaten – 'you played your part bravely at Hurlingston. It is as much to you, sweetheart, as to myself that I owe this re-unition. I'm with you again, my girl; and if I may not safely live in England, we'll sell the old home and begin life anew in a new world.'

She let him say no more. She had risen, and was regarding him from under knitted brows, her lips compressed, her bosom heaving under its black satin bodice.

'Mr. Haynes,' said she, at last, 'have your wits deserted you?'

His jaw fell, the boldness left his air and glance. 'God 'a mercy!' he gasped. 'Were you deluded too, then? Did you not recognize me? Helen, I am Geoffrey Swayne.'

'Go tell it to fools, man,' said she. 'Geoffrey Swayne was hanged at Tyburn, as all the world knows.'

'Aye, hanged was I, and yet I came to life again.'

'A likely story – such things are common happenings,' she smiled ironically.

He took a step forward, his brow black as thunder now. 'Madam,' he snarled, 'you are fooling me. You know me, yet will not own to me. Saw you not the writing of my depositions? Knew you not the hand? And if that were not enough to convince you, look you on this.' He thrust back the hair from his brow, revealing a long livid scar above the temple. But the sight of that identifying mark left her unmoved.

11

'Sir Geoffrey had just such another scar,' said she quietly. 'He came by it in this very room, one night when he was drunk. He had raised his whip to strike me, but lost his balance and fell, cracking his head against that hand-iron. Aye, your likeness to Sir Geoffrey is very amazing, yet are you not Sir Geoffrey,' she continued. 'You are Mr Haynes, known to the vulgar as "Scudding Tom", gentleman of the road, against whom there remains sufficient to hang you. Bear you that in mind,' she added impressively, 'nor push me too far, lest I forget my gratitude.'

He was upon her like a panther. He caught her wrist until it seemed he must snap it, all the blackguard in him risen like scum to the surface of his vile nature.

'Madam, you shall be whipped,' he promised her through his teeth. But the bell-rope was within her reach. Too late he sought to drag her from it. She had caught it in her free hand, and his dragging her sent a clanging peal reverberating through the house.

He let her go, and fell back quivering with rage, his face ashen. She recovered, and spoke coldly to him.

'Mr Haynes,' said she, 'I will forgive you this out of consideration for the service you have rendered me. I will even do more. You spoke just now of seeking your fortune in the New World. I counsel you to follow so excellent an intention. In England you go hourly in danger of capture, and "Scudding Tom" will unquestionably hang if he be taken.'

The door opened, and a servant stood before her. She bade him wait outside until she summoned him again. Then, to her husband, she continued:

'So follow my advice, and get you to America, as you proposed. In return for the service you did me by your depositions, I'll pay you half-yearly the sum of fifty pounds for life, so long as you remain out of England; and here you have your first six months' pension, which will enable you to get you beyond seas. Go now, and God be with you, and lead you into better ways of life. You have widowed me by your evil courses, and a widow I'm like to remain.' Her tone was full of a meaning he did not miss. He stared a moment, then his eyes moved to the roll of notes on the table before him, where she had placed them.

12

Fury had failed him; he sought to cajole.

'Helen, my girl,' he began. But the heart of the too-often beaten wife had been broken overlong ago to be still sensible to prayers of his.

'Robert!' she called, raising her voice, and instantly the servant reappeared. 'You will re-conduct this gentleman, and lend him a horse to ride to Bristol. Give you good-night, sir.'

With distorted features, Geoffrey Swayne turned to fling out of the room. But she called him back. 'You've forgotten something,' said she, and she pointed to the notes upon the table. A moment he looked at her almost furtively, a suggestion of crouching in his attitude, something akin to that of a hound that had been whipped. Then he took the notes and thrust them into his pocket.

In silence he went out of the room, and so out of her life.

THE BARGAIN

Mr Hawkesby stirred in his great chair and, half awake, opened his eyes to blink at the fiery reflection of the evening sun, which glared at him from the glass of his tall, well-furnished bookcase. Incuriously he looked round to see what had disturbed his slumbers, then he leapt wide awake to his feet, so violently that a little shower of powder rained from his carefully dressed hair to settle upon the neck and shoulders of his velvet coat.

Leaning against the solid mahogany table, midway between the open window and the chair in which Mr Hawkesby had rested, stood a man, a stranger, in a suit of homespun the worse for wear, ragged stockings, and a pair of silver-buckled shoes all spattered with mud and dirt. Hawkesby's face paled, for nature had not made him overvaliant. His first thought was that he had to do with a thief – and a thief who knew what he was about, for in the handsome, inlaid secretaire yonder reposed a bag containing three hundred guineas – rents collected that morning by Mr Hawkesby's bailiff.

The stranger raised a hand in a mild gesture of supplication.

'I beg that you'll not be alarmed,' said he, his manner that of a gentleman. 'I'm no robber. You'll be Mr Hawkesby?'

'I am,' answered the man of the house, his voice sharp. 'How came you here?'

The stranger waved a white, slender hand, a hand at odd variance with his clothes, in the direction of the open window and the blossom-laden trees of the orchard beyond. 'That way,' he said.

'Oh, that way?' Mr Hawkesby mimicked him; for, seeing him so tame, his own courage was returning fast. 'And what may you be wanting with me, my man?'

The other left his position by the table, and took a step towards the young squire. Mr Hawkesby retreated towards the bell-rope.

'Keep your distance, my man,' said he, his tone less arrogant.

'Don't ring, Mr Hawkesby!' cried the other in a tone of such sudden alarm that Hawkesby paused, his fingers on the rope. 'I've come to ye for shelter. 'Tis a hunted man I am this day.'

'You're glib enough with my name,' said Hawkesby. 'What may yours be?'

'Look me in the face, sor, an' ye'll never need to ask,' answered the other with a smile that was between sorrow and jauntiness. Hawkesby looked as he was bidden, and he saw that the man wore his own hair, black as coal and tied in a queue, from which a few escaping strands had matted themselves about his brow. It was a fine, distinguished countenance, but Hawkesby was not aware that his eyes had ever encountered it before. He said so, and a whimsical smile lifted the corners of the intruder's close-lipped mouth.

'Black hair, black eyes,' he recited, 'arched eyebrows, hooked nose, thin lips, sallow complexion, a mole on the right of the chin, and a scar over the right temple' – he pushed back his matted hair, and showed a milk-white line – 'stands five foot ten, and is of a slender shape. Have ye read that description nowhere of late, Mr Hawkesby?'

Hawkesby fell back a pace.

'Egad!' he exclaimed, and then again, 'Egad!'

'Just so,' said the Irishman, with a shrug.

'Then you're—'

'Miles O'Neill, your most obedient, Mr Hawkesby,' said the Irishman, making a leg.

In a quiver of apprehension, not of the man but of the things that might result from the man's presence, Hawkesby now approached his visitor.

'In Heaven's name, why are you here, Mr O'Neil?' quoth he, and his face was pale, his blue eyes wide with horror.

'I lay at Appleby last night – at Mr Robertson's,' said the fugitive. 'He tould me that should I need shelter farther south, I'd find it at your hands. I was for rachin' Lancashire, and I'd niver have throubled ye, but that from Orton hither I have been followed.'

'Followed?' cried Hawkesby in alarm. 'Followed hither? And by whom?'

'By a dhirty rogue who caught a glimpse of me as I was lavin' Orton. Shure, an' he dodged me footsteps ivery moile of the foive. Half a moile from here I led him through a confusion of lanes, and lost him. Glory be to God! There's a thousand guineas on my head, but the earning of them'll not be his, the dhirty shpy.'

'How knew you this to be my house? How knew you me?'

'More by luck than controivance, faith! I was hidin' in the orchard there, and seein' a window convaniently open, I bethought me that beloike I'd find closer hiding-room within doors. By your coat-of-arms over the fireplace yonder I saw that I'd found luck for the first toime since I joined the Prince's banner.'

Hawkesby looked at him out of eyes that did not exactly beam with welcome. He had contrived to keep the Tories in ignorance of his connection with the Cause, for all that it might be a matter of common knowledge in the ranks of Charlie Stuart's followers. His had been but a half-hearted devotion, for he was by no means a man of rash impulse. His head governed his heart always; it governed it now, and he misliked the risk he might be running in harbouring this notorious rebel.

Still, the man before him looked in sore need of aid. His face was pale, and there were black lines beneath his eyes that lent them a haggard look. In what sorry condition were his garments we have already seen. Yet he bore himself with a certain jauntiness; when he spoke of being hunted he did so with a devil-may-care manner that should have earned him sympathy from a stone image. Hawkesby was not altogether insensible to this, and he felt, too, that he would be for ever shamed did he turn this fugitive out of doors without more ado. So, however reluctant he may have been at heart, outwardly at least he made a decent show of befriending O'Neill. He invited him to rest in the great easy-chair, whilst he went in quest of food and wine.

'For, I take it, you'll welcome refreshment, Mr O'Neill,' said he.

'It's little enough of it I've had since the shlaughter at Culloden,' laughed the Irishman as he dropped into the great chair and stretched his dusty legs luxuriously.

Hawkesby fetched him some cold pigeon-pie, a loaf, and a flask of French wine, and, setting the things before him on a small table, he bade his visitor fall to. O'Neill did so with a will, and when he had eaten he turned a scornful eye upon the slender, lily-shaped glass his host had set before him.

'Have ye no such thing as a bumper, now, about the house, Mr Hawkesby?' quoth he. 'There's a health I'd be after dhrinkin' with all me heart.'

Hawkesby rose with a shrug of impatience to fetch the thing his guest craved. O'Neill filled it to the brim, and emptied it twice in brisk succession – thereby exhausting the flask. He drank first to Mr Hawkesby's long life, and next to the Duke of Cumberland's short shrift. Hawkesby fetched more wine – a brace of flasks this time. The rebel's eyes sparkled at sight of them.

''Tis a power of dust gets in your throat a-walkin',' said he. 'Aye, an' the weather's hot an' all. Here's long loife to ye agin, Mr Hawkesby.' And again was a bumper poured down that amazing gullet. 'Ye're not drinkin' yerself,' he expostulated, making himself mightily at home.

'If you'll pardon me,' said the other stiffly, 'it is not my habit of an afternoon.'

'By me sowl, ye should acquire it, thin,' was the laughing answer, and O'Neill emptied the second flagon into his tall glass. 'Ye're missin' a power of loife!'

Hawkesby sat himself on the arm of a chair, and craved news of the Prince.

'Where left you his Highness?' quoth he. 'Is he still in the heather, know you, or has he contrived to ship for France?'

But the question did no more than suggest a fresh toast to the rebel. He raised his glass to the light, and eyed the blood-red colour of the wine with a fond glance.

'Here's a health to his Hoighness, where'er he may be!' He drained his bumper. *'Super naculum!'*, he laughed, as he turned it up, and made a bead on his thumbnail.

'You've a fine thirst, sir,' said Hawkesby a trifle tartly.

'An' it's yourself would have the same, bedad, if ye'd run with the Scots from Culloden. But it's an iligant wine,' he added politely as a further reason.

'The battle should never have been delivered as it was,' said Hawkesby, who, like many another, could criticize what he could never have had a hand in doing. 'The Prince should have fallen back behind Nairn Water.'

'Maybe,' quoth the Irishman pensively. 'But ye'll allow it's an ill thing to fall back on water or behind it.' And he reached for the wine, to add point to his meaning. 'I'll give ye the sow's tail to Geordie!' said he, and with that the flagon was emptied.

Hawkesby affected not to notice that again the wine was done, lest hospitality should force him to fetch more. A gallon of good French claret should be, he thought, enough for any man; and Hawkesby was careful by nature to the point of stinginess. Once more he sought to draw his guest into talking of the Cause, and he did so with moderate success for a little while. But presently O'Neill sank back in his chair and fetched a sigh.

'Shure, talkin's dhry work,' said he, and he held a flask to the light to make certain it was empty.

The hint was over-broad to be ignored. Hawkesby fetched another brace of bottles from his cellar, swearing to himself, however, that they should be the last. He was beginning to dislike his guest exceedingly. There were more toasts when he returned. If O'Neill had been half the fighter that he was the drinker, surely the side he fought for should have been victorious at Culloden. He pledged all manner of men and all manner of events; it was 'long loife' to this, and 'bad cess' to that, until his last bumper stood before him and he appeared at a loss for a subject. Indeed, there was by then an ominous flush to his cheek and a sparkle in his eye that had not been there when first he had clambered into Mr Hawkesby's room.

Hawkesby began mightily to fear for him now – and more for himself. Here was a plight! The man was a rebel with a thousand guineas on his head; he had been recognized and followed from Orton to this neighbourhood. What if he were to become too drunk to move, and so were to be found in Mr Hawkesby's house? He began to expostulate with his guest. He spoke of caution, and as politely as he could he suggested to O'Neill that there was danger for him in drinking as he was doing. He went so far even as to seek to remove the last bumper. But O'Neill's hands shot out at that sign of danger, and his fingers encircled the glass in a resolute clutch.

'Bedad!' he hiccoughed. 'The man was hanged that left his dhrink behind him.'

'I'm thinking, sir, that should the same fate overtake you it will not be from the same cause,' was Hawkesby's irritable answer. But the Irishman was not to be offended. He emptied his glass, and got unsteadily to his feet. His wits were surely all soaked in wine by now, for he waved his hand in the air and broke suddenly into song.

It's Geordie he came up to town, Wi' a bunch o' turnips in his crown; Aha, quo' she, I'll pull them down, And turn my tail to Geordie!

'For Heaven's sake, sir!' gasped Hawkesby, in very real affright; 'You'll have the house about my ears. Silence, man, if you value your life at a farthing! Are you not afraid?'

'Afraid?' roared O'Neill; and it almost seemed for a moment that he was offended. Then he laughed aloud and long, and for an answer broke into another Jacobite ditty—

O that's the thing that ne'er can be, For the man's unborn that'll daunton me! O set me once—

Abruptly his song ceased. His mouth remained opened – nay, fell wider – and his eyes stared with a sudden look of horror past his host at the window to which Hawkesby had his back. With a premonition of what was afoot, Hawkesby swung round, then stood, his face livid, scarce breathing in his affright.

Leaning on the sill of the open window was a man of swarthy complexion, whose face was rendered villainous now by the leering grin with which he surveyed the room's occupants.

A three-cornered hat was set rakishly upon his loose, untidy hair, and he wore a scarlet riding-coat of velvet, very soiled and frayed, with tarnished gold lace and dirty, torn ruffles. Seeing himself observed, he waited for no invitation to enter, but set his hands upon the sill and vaulted lightly into the room. He was a tall, powerfully built man, and he flourished a long, gleaming pistol.

'Mr Hawkesby, your servant, sir,' he leered, with an ironical bow. 'Mr O'Neill, your very humble servant.' And coolly stepping aside he locked the door.

Hawkesby looked askance at O'Neill. The Irishman's knees had been loosened, either from drink or from fright, and he had sunk limply to a chair, where he sat staring foolishly at the intruder.

'Bedad!' he muttered at last in a thick voice. 'Ye're as persevering as a shpider. I t'ought I'd losht ye, me friend.' And as he spoke his hand went fumbling towards the breast of his coat. The bully's weapon came level with his brows.

'I'll trouble you to put that pistol on the table,' said he, with a snarl; and O'Neill sheepishly relinquished the weapon he was slyly drawing.

Hawkesby stepped to the bell. His was the courage of despair. He braced himself, and...

'What do you want, my man?' he demanded, with pretended firmness.

'Just your friend, O'Neill, yonder,' said the fellow, with a grin. 'He's worth a thousand guineas to me.' Hawkesby laid a hand on the bell-rope. 'Oh, ring away, Mr Hawkesby; ring away!' the ruffian airily encouraged him. 'Fetch in your servants; fetch in the whole town to see how you shelter and befriend a rebel.'

Hawkesby's hand fell back to his side. The affair looked ugly. He turned to O'Neill to see how the rebel took matters, hoping in his heart that the fellow would surrender before more harm was done. But O'Neill made no shift to move. Instead, he was settling himself more comfortably in his chair. He eyed the spy with a from-head-to-foot glance of contempt.

'An' who the dickens may you be, me man?' quoth he.

'I'm a loyal subject of King George's.'

'Bedad, ye look it, sor,' answered O'Neill, as bold as brass; 'ye look it; and ye look, too – if one may judge by externals – as if there moight be a price on your own dhirty head.'

Hawkesby, watching the bully, saw the shot strike home. The fellow's eyes dropped uneasily, he shuffled where he stood, and there was a pause before he answered, still truculent, but with half the assurance gone out of him:

'You'll be leaving my affairs alone, and you'll be treating me respectfully. The constable'll be none too inquisitive if I hand over to him the notorious Mr O'Neill.'

'Maybe; but Mr O'Neill'll be after arousin' the constable's inquisitiveness,' said the rebel, with an ugly look. It was plain he saw the weak spot in his opponent's hide. Hawkesby was thinking briskly. An idea had come to him – an inspiration. He had accounted himself lost, for the sheriff would want to know where O'Neill had been captured, and the bully, not a doubt of it, would inform him. He was cursing the hospitality he had extended to this drunken fugitive; he had begrudged it when he saw how dear it was like to cost him in wine; how much more, then, did miserly Mr Hawkesby not begrudge it now that he saw how dear it was like to cost him in good gold guineas? – for clearly this fellow must be bought off. His voice, cold and precise, cut into the momentary silence.

'It is quite clear,' said he to the spy, 'that you are in no condition yourself to approach the constable. You'll need to go before the sheriff, and there'll be awkward questions asked.'

'I'm no fool,' snapped the spy, 'and you'll not make me one. They'll welcome me very cordially when I take them Mr O'Neill. They'll not ask many questions – saving, perhaps, as to whereabouts I came upon him. Why, if they had a grievance against me – which I'm not saying that they have – this day's work should earn me a pardon.'

'That's as it may be,' sneered O'Neill.

'Just so; but you'll not alter it with talking.'

'I might alter it with something else,' interpolated Hawkesby, in a tone that drew the brisk attention of the others. 'Listen to me, now. If you yield up Mr O'Neill, and even if no questions are asked concerning yourself, the Government's a mighty slow paymaster. You may wait a long time for your thousand guineas.'

'True,' the man confessed.

'Will you strike a bargain with me, now? What'll you take, money down?'

The fellow looked up, licking his lips – it was a lick of anticipation.

'You speak me very fair,' said he, his head on one side, his glance shifting from one to the other of the men. 'I'll take five hundred guineas for my bargain.'

'Don't listen to the thafe!' said O'Neill contemptuously.

'You shall have a hundred,' was Hawkesby's answer.

The man laughed scornfully. 'You're jesting,' said he. 'Come, now; say four hundred, and Mr O'Neill may go his ways for me.'

'One hundred,' repeated Hawkesby doggedly. It was in all conscience money enough to pay for having entertained O'Neill. More he would not give, betide what might. But neither would the other abate further. Seeing Hawkesby resolute:

'Come, Mr O'Neill,' said he at last, his pistol raised to enjoin obedience, 'we had best be moving.'

'Aye,' said O'Neill gloomily, 'I'm thinkin' we had. I'm much obliged to you, sor—' he began, turning to Hawkesby. But Hawkesby broke in excitedly:

'No, no! You must not go.'

'Well, well,' said the bully, 'you shall have him for three hundred guineas. Now that's reasonable. He's worth a thousand to any man. Three hundred guineas, money down, and he's yours.'

Hawkesby stood with his shoulders to the mantelshelf, his face very white, his lips very tight. He must clear himself from this position. His neck would certainly be stretched if O'Neill were taken in his house. Yet, three hundred guineas was a deal of money! And then the devil – or else something that the spy had said – breathed a wicked suggestion into his miserly soul.

'Three hundred guineas is all that I have by me,' said he, in a hard voice. 'Yet you shall have the money.' And thus the bargain was concluded, and Hawkesby took a heavy bag from the secretaire, where it was locked, and banged it on the table. The spy peered at the yellow contents, weighed it appreciatively in his hands.

'I'll take your word for the amount,' said he, and with a flourish of compliments he took his leave, and departed by the way he had come. Hawkesby, meanwhile, turned a deaf ear to O'Neill's warnings. At last, when the man had disappeared, the rebel leapt to his feet. In his excitement he seemed completely sobered.

'Mr Hawkesby,' said he, 'I'm eternally your debtor. Yet forgive me if I tell ye ye've done a mad thing.'

'How?' asked Hawkesby, his eyebrows going up and his hand toying idly with the pistol O'Neill had placed on the table when the spy had bidden him.

'In allowing that ruffian to depart with the money. You should have kept him here till I was gone. It is odds he'll go fetch the constable, and still seek to earn his thousand guineas.'

'Aye,' said Hawkesby, with a singular smile. 'It is odds he will.'

'Then, bedad, give me the pishtol, and let me after him before he's clear of the orchard.' And, making shift to go, O'Neill held out his hand for the weapon. Instead, the muzzle was presented at his head.

'Stand where you are, Mr O'Neill,' said Hawkesby, in a voice of steel. There was no timidity about him now. He was safe and brave behind his pistol. He backed across the room, the weapon levelled at the rebel, who eyed him with fallen jaw. For the third time in that afternoon Hawkesby's hand went to the bell-rope. This time his fingers closed upon it, and peal after peal went reverberating through the house.

'What are ye doin'?' gasped O'Neill.

Hawkesby showed his teeth in a ghastly smile, his face livid.

'Mr O'Neill,' said he, and his voice was crisp and cold, 'if that ruffian fetches the constable, he'll be too late. You heard what he said. You are worth a thousand guineas to any man. You are worth that sum to me. I've bought you, and I'm – going to sell you again. I've driven a shrewd bargain in you.'

The rebel stared at him a moment, unbelief in his face. Then he drew himself up, the last vestige of his drunkenness departed, and a singular smile – a mocking, cynical, yet exultant, smile – upon his hawk face.

'So that is your loyalty to the Cause; that your devotion to the Prince?' said he. 'Bedad! If ever Charlie comes to his own he shall hear of this. But since it's so – why I'm glad it's so. You are mighty well served, Mr Judas Iscariot Hawkesby; three hundred guineas is a mort of money to lose over any man.'

'It's hardly lost,' sneered Hawkesby. Then, as O'Neill moved to the window, 'Stand, or I fire!' he shouted.

'Foire, and be hanged,' said O'Neill. And Hawkesby, angered and desperately afraid of losing his prey, fired one barrel after the other. But the only sound that broke the stillness of the room was the click of the hammer on the empty pan and O'Neill's soft contemptuous laugh. The pistol was not loaded.

There came a sound of feet, and a knocking at the door.

With a last laugh O'Neill dropped from the sill and sped through the orchard like a hare, to vanish in the twilight. Hawkesby, shaking in every limb with the fear that had come upon him born of an awful thought that had arisen in his mind, sprang to open. In flowed a stream of servants, and after them, walking briskly, stained with dust, came Mr Robertson of Appleby. At sight of him, Hawkesby checked the words that were on his lips. He caught his visitor by the lapel of his coat and drew him aside. His habit of caution was with him now, excited though he was.

'Did Miles O'Neill lie at your house last night?' he whispered.

Robertson stared at him a moment. 'No,' said he at last; 'but it is odd you should ask, for I came to tell you that Miles O'Neill was taken last night at Penrith. I heard of it this morning.'

'I have been robbed!' screamed Hawkesby. 'Robbed of three hundred guineas.'

They saw the disorder of the room, with its strewn flagons, and they opined him drunk. By the time he had convinced them he was sober it must have been too late, for his ingenious visitors were never taken.

THE OPPORTUNIST

To follow the early career of Capoulade down its easy descent of the slopes of turpitude were depressing and unprofitable. He had reached the stage at which he pocketed his pride and – like the adaptable opportunist that he was – passed from the artistic plane of swindling to the clumsier methods of purse-cutting and housebreaking. The pursuit of the latter brought him one night into the domicile of Monsieur Louvel.

Old Louvel was a man of fortune and the owner of an unique collection of old Italian jewels, and this was the lure that attracted Capoulade. Did rumour prove well founded he hoped to derive enough profit from this night's work to enable him to lead, hereafter, a life of ease and honesty in some foreign land; for Capoulade was disposed enough to be honest once it should cease to be worth his while to be dishonest.

He stood in Louvel's room at dead midnight, facing the press which he had been at considerable preliminary pains to ascertain was the repository of the treasure that was to make him honest – a treasure useless to Louvel, a mere hoard of artistic miserliness. Six steps across the room; twenty seconds to cut a panel; five minutes to secure the booty and make good his retreat – that was all that he now asked of Fortune to the end that his salvation might be wrought. Yet niggardly Fortune denied him even that little.

For even as he took his first steps towards the press a loud knock fell upon the street door. It reverberated through the silent house, it found an echo in Capoulade's heart, and sent an icy chill through the marrow of his spine.

The knocking was repeated, vigorous and insistently; and Capoulade groaned to reflect how soundly they must sleep, how fine and rare the opportunity that was being ruined for him.

Then came other sounds – shuffling steps of slippered feet descended the stairs; the street door was opened. Voices sounded awhile, then the slippered feet reascended, accompanied now by a heavy, booted tread.

Physically Capoulade was a coward, but morally he possessed the courage of ten men. So averse was he from going empty-handed from that treasure-chamber that he decided at all costs – despite his thudding heart and chattering teeth – to remain until this newcomer should have gone either to bed or back to the streets from which he had been so inopportunely admitted.

A moment later he repented this decision in a passion of alarm. The steps were approaching the very room in which he stood. A shaft of light entered under the closed doors and thrust out along the gleaming parquet to Capoulade's feet. Swift and silent as a shadow, he crossed to where a curtain masked an alcove, and there he hid himself, prayers on his lips and a knife in his hand, desperate and vicious as a cornered rat.

The door opened, and old Louvel, in nightcap and white quilted dressing-gown, advanced, candle in hand. He was followed by a tall, showily dressed young gentleman, Theodore Louvel, his son, who filled in Lyons the high office of agent to M. Turgot, the Comptroller-General.

In silence the old man crossed to the press, unlocked the double doors and threw them wide.

'There,' he exclaimed, anger quivering in his voice, 'let the evidence of your own eyes satisfy you.'

He held the candle aloft, so that its light shone upon rows of shelves – all empty.

His son took a step forward, staring. From behind his curtain Capoulade stared, too, in amazement and chagrin.

'But what does it mean?' cried Theodore at last. 'What, then, has become of the treasure?'

There was a dry, contemptuous laugh from his father.

'Ask yourself rather than me,' he croaked. 'You have not by any chance kept an account of the sums of which you have drained me in the last two years? When I remonstrated with you, you laughed. When I sought to restrain you by refusing you the money which you demanded, then, like a dutiful son, you threatened my life. Thus, you said, you should inherit that which I withheld.'

He turned his vulture face upon his son, and a smile of mockery, ineffably bitter, twisted his lipless mouth.

'I have given you the rope you needed, and you have hanged yourself. In two years you have had from me five hundred thousand livres – and all is gone. I sold my treasures little by little, and there is nothing left.'

'I'll not believe it!' cried Theodore.

Louvel shrugged his narrow shoulders.

'Believe it or not, it is true. There is nothing for you. You may kill me now, if you will. I have seen to it that my death, at least, shall not profit you.'

With black, scowling brows Theodore faced his father, pondering him as if he would read the mind behind that cynical old mask.

'It is a lie!' he said at last, between his teeth. 'How do you live if you have nothing – eh? Answer me that.'

The old man leisurely closed the press and placed the candle on the table.

'You would, perhaps, deprive me of the little I have retained to ensure me from perishing of hunger?'

'Ah! You confess, then, that all is not as you represent it?' was the quick retort. 'You can save me from this ruin that impends – and save me you shall – you must! Do you hear? You must!'

'You had better kill me, and take what you can find,' the old man mocked him. 'I would as soon perish by your hand as starve. The deed, too, would set a fitting climax to our relations.'

'Will you not understand that it is but a loan that I require?'

'It has always been a loan.'

'This time I will repay – I swear it.'

'You swear it? *Farceur!* Out of your beggarly salary from the Comptroller-General?'

Theodore took a turn in the room, his face as white as his powdered hair, his eyes anxious. At length he paused.

'It is but ten thousand livres I need, and it is the price of my salvation from ruin and shame.'

'So has it always been,' sneered his father.

'But I will repay you, I say!' was the vehement, almost frenzied answer. He plucked a paper from his pocket. 'Listen!' he insisted. 'You are acquainted with Madame Lobreau?'

There was nobody in Lyons to whom that lady's name was not familiar. Under years of her capable management the Grand Theatre of Lyons had been raised from a mere puppet-show until it might have rivalled the most brilliant playhouses of the capital, not excepting the famous Comédie-Française.

'Do you propose to murder her in her bed and steal her jewels?'

Theodore swore furiously under the spur of this sarcasm.

'Will you listen to me seriously?' he demanded. 'This lady holds her managerial privilege from the Comptroller-General, in whose power it lies to deprive her of her theatre. I am the Comptroller's agent in Lyons, and it lies within my power to dispossess her. Now, it has occurred to a certain Monsieur de Noirmont that, considering the handsome yields of the Grand Theatre, it should be worth his while to deal liberally with me to the end that I might enable him to step into Madame Lobreau's shoes. I trust I have made myself clear?'

'Yes, yes.'

Old Louvel was always ready to be interested in schemes that promised profit. The proposal to dispossess Madam Lobreau of the fruits of her labour and talent was a rascally one. But at heart old Louvel himself was a rascal, worthy father of his worthless son.

'Then listen to this,' rejoined Theodore. He unfolded his paper and read aloud:

In consideration of the Grant Theatre of Lyons being placed under my control and management, I hereby agree to pay the Sieur Theodore Louvel the sum of 10,000 livres, and further to allow him an annuity of 8,000 livres for as long as the said Grant Theatre shall continue under my management. Henri de Noirmont

Old Louvel, who had stood hand on ear while his son read the agreement, pursed his lips like one in thought.

'Let me see it,' he requested. His son delivered him the paper, and the old man examined it, assuring himself of its genuineness. Then he pondered again.

'Very well,' he said slowly at last. 'You shall have the ten thousand livres by tomorrow evening as a loan, but this agreement remains in my hands as security until I am repaid.'

Theodore protested blusteringly. But his father held so stubbornly to the condition that the Comptroller's agent was forced in the end to submit.

'But I must have the money early in the morning. Monsieur – er – the man in whose debt I stand has given me until noon tomorrow to find the money.'

'If by noon tomorrow Madame Lobreau is no longer manager of the Grand Theatre the money will be at your disposal. Tell me,' he added, 'how soon may I expect to be repaid?'

'I shall place M. de Noirmont in possession of the theatre in a fortnight. I dare not do it sooner, for the sake of appearances.'

'Very well.'

The old man locked away the document in a secretaire, took up the candle, and re-conducted his son.

After Capoulade had heard the street door close upon the departing Theodore and the old man mount the stairs on his way back to bed, he crept out of his alcove.

His feelings were those of a man who has been swindled. He had come there at the peril of life and limb to possess himself of old Louvel's collection of Italian gems, only to learn that these had already been sold to pay the gaming debts of that villain Theodore. He was naturally indignant.

He advanced moodily towards the window and opened it with caution. He paused in the act of bestriding the sill, and chuckled softly at his own inspiration. He took the night into his confidence.

'To make opportunity your slave is the whole philosophy of life,' he said.

◆   ◆   ◆   ◆   ◆

Next morning he waited upon Madam Lobreau at her residence, representing himself as an actor fallen upon evil days.

'You are come,' she greeted him, offering him a chair, 'to seek my help. Hélas, monsieur, you come too late!'

'Madame,' loftily answered that tatterdemalion, 'you are entirely at fault.' He sat down with the air of one who has the right to do so. 'I do not come to seek your aid, but to offer you mine.'

He stemmed her questions with a gesture which – were he the actor he had announced himself – might have made his fortune as *Sganarelle*. No man was ever more sensitive to his surroundings than Capoulade, and already he was saturated by the theatrical atmosphere in which he found himself.

'Madame,' he announced dramatically, 'you have been dispossessed of your theatre.'

'Is it known already?' she exclaimed.

'Not to the world at large. But to me – Capoulade – even the very reason of it is known.'

'Monsieur,' she protested, bridling, 'I have heard enough and more of these trumped-up reasons. A cruel, an infamous swindle has been perpetrated to rob me of my rights – the rights earned by years of labour.'

'Adversity, Madame, is blunting the edge of your judgement.'

And in lordly gesture he waved the dirty ruffles that hung like weeping willows over his dirtier hands.

'The reasons known to me are not the lying, trumped-up reasons expressed to you and to be laid before the Comptroller-General by your enemies. The reasons that I bring you are the real ones.'

And he proceeded to disclose to her the infamous compact existing between Louvel and a certain M. de Noirmont.

Madame Lobreau went white and red by turns as she listened.

'But yes,' she cried. 'It is no more than I might have suspected. You convince me that it is the truth. If we could but lay proof of it before the Comptroller-General, how I should trample upon those that would ruin me!'

Capoulade launched his thunderbolt.

'Madame,' said he, pulling a paper from his pocket, 'the proof is here. Listen to the agreement signed by Monsieur de Noirmont.'

She heard it in amazement, and, what time he was reading the terms of that scandalous contract, subconsciously she was taking stock of him, and neither his shabby raiment nor his keen, wolfish face was of a quality to inspire her with confidence.

'Monsieur,' she asked him, when he had finished reading, 'how does it happen that you are in possession of this document?'

He looked at her out of his keen black eyes, scenting the suspicion that was awake in her. He wisely deemed it a time for frankness.

'Madame,' said he, 'I am here to serve you – that is my guarantee that you will not betray me. I am not exactly an actor. Such parts as in my time I have played have been played upon that broad stage we call the world. In short, Madame' – and he dropped his eyes in a delicate assumption of shame – 'I am just a thief.'

'And you stole this paper from M. Louvel?' she asked.

He bowed.

'It occurred to me that by appropriating it I might at once perform a worthy action and compensate myself for my trouble.'

'But how compensate yourself?' she enquired, knitting her brows.

Capoulade explained that such a document should not be without its marketable value. She agreed, and offered to purchase it for a *louis d'or*. Capoulade gasped.

'Twenty francs, Madame?' Then he laughed. 'Perhaps it has not occurred to you that I might easily get a thousand times that sum from M. Louvel.'

'Then in your own interests you had best take it to M. Louvel,' was the uncompromising answer.

Capoulade rose with great dignity.

'I am an honourable man, Madame,' he informed her, 'and I prefer to be on the side of honour. Therefore I come to you, for I should prefer to deal with you.'

'But if you find me unreasonable you would no longer scruple to go to M. Louvel?'

'I should scruple, Madame, but I should go,' said Capoulade.

Thereafter they bargained for the best part of an hour, the negotiations being protracted by Madame's distrust of Capoulade. It was not until he rose to leave her that she made up her mind.

'Very well, sir,' she said. 'You shall have a thousand livres; five hundred now in exchange for that document, and my note of hand for the other five hundred, payable when I am once again in possession of the theatre.'

Capoulade considered.

'If I agree, Madame,' he asked, 'how do you propose to act?'

'Why, I shall go straight to Paris and place the matter before the Comptroller-General.'

'You might bungle the affair,' he objected, 'in which case I should lose five hundred livres. I insist, Madame, upon accompanying you, and you must consent to be guided by my advice.'

She made some demur at first, but ended by agreeing, reflecting that his advice might, after all, be useful.

Madame Lobreau took a post-chaise that very evening, and, accompanied by Capoulade, now in a suit of black and looking almost respectable, she set out for Paris.

She possessed some little influence, and by exerting it she obtained, three days later, an interview with M. Turgot, the

Comptroller-General. Accompanied ever by Capoulade, she was ushered into the great man's room in the Tuileries.

There, for once in his life, the little rogue was rather out of countenance. He was overawed by the splendour of his surroundings, and not a little scared by the elegant man with the weary face and wide-set eyes who sat at the ormolu-encrusted writing-table.

'I am come to tell you, monsieur, that your agent in Lyons is a rogue,' was Madame's uncompromising opening. 'He abuses the authority which you have vested in him by selling appointments for his own profit.'

Now, it happened that Monsieur Turgot placed the utmost confidence in Louvel. He flashed his searching glance upon the pair, and Capoulade shivered.

'You allude, Madame, to the revocation of your licence for the Lyons theatre,' said the Comptroller in a voice that was as weary as his countenance. 'My agent gives the soundest reason for the step, which I approve whilst deploring its necessity.'

Madame breathed gustily.

'May one enquire your agent's reason, monsieur?'

Monsieur took up a paper.

'Amongst others, Madame, he finds that a class of play is being encouraged in which the new and unhealthy doctrines of the rights of man, and the like, are being exploited.'

'But, monsieur, that is utterly false.'

'I must prefer my agent's judgement,' said that composed and weary gentleman.

Madame gasped as if for breath. Then:

'If I can lay proof before you, monsieur, that Louvel has dispossessed me so that he may earn a bribe, what then, monsieur?'

'Such an abuse of authority shall be punished.'

'Good,' said Madame, with satisfaction. 'Will you give yourself the trouble to read this?'

And she produced Capoulade's document.

Monsieur Turgot perused it with frowning eyes. He turned it about in his fingers.

'You pretend that this is genuine?' he said contemptuously.

'Certainly, monsieur,' snapped Capoulade.

The Comptroller's eyes were levelled upon him for a moment.

'Who is this?' he enquired.

'My secretary, monsieur,' replied Madame.

'Ah! And how does this document, if genuine, come to be in your hands?'

Again it was Capoulade who interposed.

'It – it was – procured, monsieur.'

'Procured, was it? Now listen to me, both of you. In view of your categorical accusation of Monsieur Louvel, I shall summon him to Paris. If he prove guilty he shall be fitly punished and your theatre shall be restored to you. But if, as I suspect, this document is a forgery, then the law shall deal with you both, and rigorously.'

Madame Lobreau was assailed by momentary panic, partly allayed, however, by Capoulade's show of confidence.

'Sir,' he said, 'may I, in the interests of justice, venture upon a suggestion?'

'In the interests of justice all suggestions are welcome,' replied M. Turgot sardonically.

Capoulade bowed.

'Then, monsieur, I would very respectfully submit to your consideration that not Monsieur Louvel's word but only the subsequent events themselves can prove whether this document is true or false, and I would suggest, again very respectfully, that you allow the events to speak.'

M. Turgot frowned thoughtfully.

'And how long do you suggest that the matter should lie in this suspense?' he asked.

'A fortnight, monsieur, should prove long enough,' said Capoulade.

The Comptroller pondered the matter yet a moment.

'Be it so,' he said, and upon that dismissed them.

The fortnight that ensued was for Madam Lobreau a period of considerable anxiety, which not all Capoulade's assurances sufficed to allay. When, at the end of it, there came a summons from Monsieur Turgot, that anxiety was converted into positive alarm. She obeyed it, nevertheless, and Capoulade went with her to the Tuileries once more.

Monsieur Turgot was very grave, and his manner less weary and sardonic than when last they had seen him.

'Madame,' he announced, 'I have here a letter from my Lyons agent, Theodore Louvel – a letter received five days ago – in which he announces to me that he has found in a certain Monsieur Noirmont your successor at the Grand Theatre.'

'Ah!' said Capoulade.

'Immediately upon receiving it I desired Monsieur Louvel to wait upon me. I judge no man unheard. He has just arrived, and is awaiting audience. I deemed it well that you should be present at the interview.'

Nervously Madame expressed her gratitude. Capoulade trembled a little.

Theodore Louvel was introduced – raffishly elegant and impudently at ease, no whit discouraged by the presence of Madame Lobreau, though guessing she was there as a plaintiff.

'A complaint has been lodged against you, monsieur,' said the Comptroller, when Louvel had made his bow and his compliments. 'It is alleged by Madame Lobreau that the reasons you urged for dispossessing her of the theatre are ill-founded.'

Theodore smiled deprecatingly.

'Of course, monsieur, but I can affirm that I had no interests to serve other than those of his Majesty.'

'Naturally,' said Monsieur Turgot. 'And yet Madame goes so far as to say that you were bribed by M. Noirmont.'

'That,' replied Theodore, 'is an obvious calumny.'

'True,' said Monsieur Turgot. 'And yet Madame's story is oddly circumstantial. She can even tell me the sum paid by this Noirmont. It was, she says, ten thousand livres.'

Louvel's aplomb fell from him for a moment. He stood chap-fallen, and his colour changed. But his recovery was swift. He repudiated the charge with all the heat of offended virtue.

'Look at this, monsieur,' said the Comptroller, 'and tell me if you have ever seen it before.'

He held out the document which Capoulade had sold to Madame Lobreau.

Louvel took it nervously, but as he scanned it he recovered his composure. He almost laughed when he placed it on the Comptroller's writing-table.

'An impudent and an obvious forgery, monsieur. Noirmont's very name is misspelt.'

'Yet,' was the slow answer, 'this document, if forged, as you say, is oddly prophetic. It has been in my hands a fortnight – a fortnight, do you understand? Can you explain how it came to foretell so accurately the name of the man to whom the control of the Lyons theatre has since been granted by you?'

'Why – why—' faltered Louvel; and there he paused, staring in dismay at the smiling Comptroller. He was utterly bewildered – utterly without answer to so incredible a statement. 'But that is not possible, monsieur,' he cried out at last.

'I tell you that it is so, monsieur. You cannot explain the circumstances, eh? It is at once mysterious and convincing – a remarkable combination. Be good enough to wait in the ante-room, Louvel. We shall talk of this again.'

The dumbfounded agent stumbled blindly out of the room in the wake of the servant summoned by M. Turgot. Then for some moments the Comptroller wrote rapidly, watched in silence by Madame Lobreau and Capoulade.

'There, Madame,' he said at last, 'is an order to my new agent in Lyons to restore you possession of your theatre. In all the circumstances I will ask no questions about this document you brought me. I confess that I am curious, but if I knew all perhaps my duty would not permit me to deal with you as generously as I desire to deal.'

Bewildered, but clear, at least, upon the all-important fact that she was once more in possession of her theatre, Madame Lobreau expressed her thanks and took her leave.

'What did he mean?' she asked Capoulade when they were outside the palace.

Capoulade grinned. In his immense relief he was proud of his exploit.

'Why, you see, Louvel was right,' he confessed. 'You see, that document – *enfin*, I wrote it as well as I could from memory, after hearing Monsieur Theodore read it to his father. I am afraid my spelling—'

'You wrote it?' Her voice became shrill. At last she understood. 'Then it was a forgery. Why, you have swindled me.'

'Ah, no, Madame. I undertook that your theatre should be restored to you, and I have your note of hand for five hundred livres payable when that shall be accomplished. It is accomplished, Madame. But,' he added, as an afterthought, 'I must improve my spelling.'

THE PLAGUE OF GHOSTS

Capoulade had made the discovery that honesty is the best policy. He was in hiding in an alley near the Carousel at the time, and in hourly expectation of capture and harsh treatment as an anti-climax to his three years' career of ingenious and successful crime.

He was persuaded that from this Paris, to which an evil hour had brought him, there could be no escape, for he was well-informed that M. de Sartines' ubiquitous agents were diligently seeking him. So he set his wits to work, and resolved upon a course whose boldness would have appalled a stouter but less ingenious spirit. If he would find safety he must look for it under the very wing of the Minister of Police. Such was the resolve he took. Dishonesty, he realized, was stale, it was failing him in his adversity, and he would mark his scorn of that fair-weather friend by abandoning its pursuit, and ranging himself hereafter on the side of law and order – always provided that M. de Sartines should prove the astute opportunist he was reputed.

The brilliant notion once conceived, he was not the man to delay its execution. The same spring day, whose waking hours had been devoted to its conception, saw him, towards noon, in the ante-chamber of the famous Minister. Thus far he had penetrated without hindrance, and he now sent M. de Sartines a message to the effect that a certain M. Quélaure, whose acquaintance with criminal methods was vast, sought to place his services at the Lieutenant-General's disposal.

From the ante-chamber to the chamber is but a step; yet it was the one step in his journey from the Carousel to the presence of M. de Sartines which Capoulade had expected to find fraught with difficulty. Instead, he found it astonishingly, discomposingly, easy. He had not been waiting more than a few moments when an usher approached him with the message that M. de Sartines would see him at once.

He took a deep breath, like a man about to plunge into deep waters, and he might have been observed to pale a little. Here was the situation he had boldly sought; yet, despite his unparalleled effrontery, he did not relish it now that it had arrived. The notion which had seemed a finely daring one two hours ago, seemed now incalculably rash, and he found himself wishing that he had given it longer consideration before so recklessly proceeding to act upon it.

Thus, feeling very much as the fly may have felt after it had accepted the spider's invitation to walk into its parlour, he stepped into the famous policeman's office. At a littered writing-table he beheld a richly apparelled gentleman, in the prime of life, with a hooked nose and a pair of eyes grey and wide-set that were submitting him to an undisguised and searching scrutiny.

'Monsieur Capoulade,' said that gentleman, in the most affable voice in the world, 'I have been expecting you for some days, although I had not presumed to hope that you would do me the honour of a spontaneous visit.'

Capoulade felt his knees sinking under him, as many another criminal had done in the presence of that dread man from whom nothing seemed concealed. 'Monsieur—' he gasped, and there he stopped, his cheeks blanched and his ferrety eyes as wide as he could make them. What, indeed, remained for him to say? Sartines laughed musically.

'You are surprised that I should know you?' murmured the Minister, with a lift of the eyebrows, and it flashed through the little rascal's mind that if ever he had need of effrontery, he had need of it now.

His aplomb returned. 'Immensely flattered,' he answered, with a bow.

Sartines' smile broadened. He liked self-possession, accounting it one of the qualities that make for worldly success.

'I understand from your message – although you sent it under a *nom de guerre* – that you are seeking service with me, and that you suggest that your acquaintance with criminal methods should render you a valuable agent?'

'Yes, monsieur,' answered Capoulade, a world of mingled hope and despair in his mind. 'I am sick of crime, and I have a mind not only to be honest, but to make war upon the dishonesty of others.'

Sartines settled himself comfortably in his chair, and for ten minutes Capoulade could make nothing of the conversation that ensued, which was now serious, now rallying on the Minister's part. Suddenly the Lieutenant-General asked a question.

'Monsieur Capoulade, are you interested in ghosts?'

Capoulade's eyes dilated slightly.

'Monsieur, I have never met one.'

'I can afford you the opportunity,' was the Minister's calm reply. 'If you care to avail yourself of it, I have employment for you, if not – there is always the Châtelet.'

Capoulade shuddered, and moistened his lips.

'I should have preferred, monsieur, that you could have entrusted me with some affair in which I should have to deal with ordinary mortals; but if you give me to choose between the Châtelet and the ghost, why, then, I must take the ghost.'

'Then it is settled. My information is that the Château de la Blanchette, in Maine, is infested by a plague of ghosts. You should be acquainted with the place, for I understand that you burgled it six months ago.'

'I knew nothing of the ghosts, or I should have hesitated,' rejoined Capoulade, with an effrontery that provoked a smile from Sartines.

'You know now,' said the Minister, 'and if you are anxious for an affair with ordinary mortals, you shall have that as well. A deal of spurious silver is circulating in Maine at present, and my agents trace its source to the town of La Blanchette. Since you are going there to rid the Château of its plague of ghosts, I will further entrust it to you to rid me the town of this plague of coiners. I should not be surprised if the elucidation of one mystery affords the explanation of the other. Former agents of mine have failed over this same task. To you shall belong the honour of succeeding. I may take it that you accept?'

Sartines was justified in his assumption, for poor Capoulade was between the sword and the wall, and must be content with any terms that were offered him. And so, entrusted with this double mission, he left Paris for Maine that very afternoon.

He travelled by post without incident as far as Chartres; and here his luck came signally to his assistance, thrusting him into conversation with a neighbour who had joined the coach at the post-house of that city. In itself this was a trivial matter, a daily happening among travellers; but in Capoulade's case it had this much of interest that ere they had been acquainted an hour the conversation between them had turned upon the supernatural. It was this new travelling-companion – a healthy, hearty, rubicund fellow, of some forty summers – who had introduced the subject. And Capoulade had not allowed it to be lightly thrust aside by other topics. Ghosts were concerning him very closely just then, and he was of a mind to discover all that he could concerning their habits. His companion seemed no less anxious to pursue the subject, with the consequence that Capoulade had presently mastered the facts – surprising by virtue of the coincidence they covered – that his name was Coupri, that he was the intendant of the Sieur de la Blanchette, and that he was on his way to the Château de La Blanchette to investigate a matter of supernatural apparitions with which the place was said to be plagued.

'Nobody has resided at the Château for the past five years with the exception of a Monsieur Flaumel and his son, who are acting as stewards. They are honest fellows both, and the estate has thriven under their rule, of which they render my master a six-monthly account. Of the ghosts they know nothing, and refuse to believe in their existence. But six months ago M. de la Blanchette's two children went down there with a nurse, intending to remain for the vintage. Three nights was all they could endure, and they were obliged to return to Paris lest the children's minds should suffer from the terrors to which they were nightly submitted. A month ago Madame de la Blanchette, herself, accompanied by a maid, went to Maine in consequence of her doctor having ordered her a few weeks in the country. She slept at La Blanchette one single night, and returned to Paris next morning, vowing that nothing would ever cause her to set foot again across that accursed threshold. It is in consequence of this that my master is sending me down to see what I can discover.'

Capoulade looked at his stolid, merry face, and envied the man his courage. 'You are not – not afraid?' he suggested.

'Afraid?' roared the other. 'Fichtre! I am taking a brace of pistols to bed with me. I promise you I shall solve this mystery.'

Capoulade sidled closer to him. Here, indeed, was the very comrade he needed. He put on a sober, mysterious air.

'I perceive that you are sceptical,' said he, a note of reproof in his voice. 'It is a dangerous attitude in which to approach the supernatural. Your patience, monsieur,' he cried, waving aside the other's threatened interruption. 'You are referring to matters of which my knowledge may be more extensive than your own. I am an investigator of the supernatural.'

'A what?' exclaimed Coupri, making of his companion a closer scrutiny than hitherto. There was about Capoulade, with his unpowdered black hair tied in a stiff queue, and his keen, sallow, almost wolfish face, an air that lent colour to his amazing statement.

'I am an investigator of the supernatural,' he repeated. 'I have made it the subject of some profound researches, which have taught me, at least, that it is an ill thing to approach such a task as yours in the spirit of mockery by which I deplore to see you actuated.'

Some of the high colour left Coupri's healthy cheeks.

'But, name of a name, monsieur!' he gasped, 'am I to understand that you believe – that your studies have made you a believer in such things?'

'A staunch believer,' said the rogue impressively, 'convinced against my will, converted by mortal terror from such unbelief as is inspiring you to make a jest of the matter. Your pistols are very well, my friend, if there is chicanery at work – and, indeed, I do not say that there is not. But such weapons will prove of little avail if it should be a question of – of the impalpable.'

In Coupri's eyes the matter of the ghosts of La Blanchette began to assume formidable proportions. He sat glum and silent for a moment; then he laughed, to convince himself that it was a laughing matter.

'Bah!' he scorned. 'All may be as you say, but at La Blanchette I am convinced that there is nothing but trickery, and I shall deal with it with powder and lead. They will prove great exorcisers.'

But despite this outward fanfaronade his mind was grown uneasy, and of this Capoulade was quick to detect the signs on the fellow's honest countenance.

'Monsieur,' said he, speaking very seriously, 'if I were not afraid of presuming upon our slight but interesting acquaintance' – here he bowed to his companion – 'I would suggest that you take me with you to La Blanchette. You might find the fruits of my studies of service.'

He had timed his proposal excellently, and it was pounced upon with flattering eagerness by his fellow-traveller. 'Together,' ended the honest Coupri, 'we cannot fail to solve this mystery, I with my natural weapons if the ghosts be flesh, you with your supernatural ones if they be spirits.'

Thus was the matter arranged between them, and Capoulade concluded from the adroitness with which he had worked to the end he desired, that M. de Sartines might congratulate himself upon his new agent.

They arrived at La Blanchette on the morrow, and Coupri made no secret of the business that had brought him, presenting Capoulade to the elder Flaumel as a fellow-servant who had been chosen to accompany him.

Flaumel frankly laughed at them.

'Come now,' said he, with scornful amusement, 'to what old wives' tale has the sieur been listening? There are no ghosts at La Blanchette. Jacques and I have dwelt here these ten years, and never sound nor sight of them has disturbed our slumbers. A night, a couple of nights at the most, will convince you, mon cher.'

'Madame de la Blanchette has ordered us not to stir from the château until I can present her with some explanation of these disturbances. I hope the ghosts will take an early opportunity of manifesting themselves, or my stay may be protracted. The sieur wishes to make holiday here with Madame. He considers that it is time he occupied this château of his. But Madame refuses to accompany him until the mystery has been cleared up.'

Flaumel shrugged his narrow shoulders.

'My explanation – the only explanation,' said he, 'is that Madame had the *migraine* when she was here.'

'But what of the nurse and the children?' cried Coupri.

'Pish!' he sneered. 'The nurse was no doubt frightening them with some ghost stories, and succeeded in frightening herself as well. The sleeping apartments are gloomy enough for the rest.'

And with fresh expressions of his scorn, the old steward passed on to other matters and asked for news of the sieur. Capoulade had been scrutinizing him closely, but had seen in his demeanour nothing to excite suspicion. Besides, why should the fellow have set himself wantonly to frighten women and children – assuming that he had a hand in the apparitions?

He was a slender man, whose countenance had been mellowed by age into a set of benignity, oddly contrasting with the villainous countenance of his son Jacques. Capoulade looked at the younger Flaumel's low forehead, flat nose, and eyebrows between which there was no division, and mentally pronounced him a knave to be watched.

He spent the remainder of the day roaming the grounds, where all was green with the fresh, pale green of spring, and Coupri went with him, but talked little. They supped with the two Flaumels – there was no woman at La Blanchette – and when they had supped, it was the elder Flaumel who lighted them to their rooms.

Coupri had insisted that he should lie in the chamber occupied by Madame during her recent visit, and he further insisted Capoulade should have a room in its immediate neighbourhood. To this Flaumel made no difficulty, and Coupri was conducted to the bedroom known as the sieur's chamber. It was a lofty apartment, panelled in oak to a man's height, and half-filled by the great canopied bed. Facing the bed, above the wainscot, stood a life-sized portrait of the present Sieur de la Blanchette's great-grandfather – a rakish gentleman of the time of the fourteenth Louis. Seen in the yellow, flickering light of their tapers, the apartment wore a sombre, gloomy air – in itself almost enough to complete the rout of Coupri's courage. Nevertheless, it was with a brave display of being at his ease that he drew the pistols from his bosom and laid them on a chair at his bedside.

'If any ghost disturbs me, my good Flaumel, I will see how it takes a charge of lead.'

Wishing him good-night, and still laughing over that last pleasantry, Flaumel withdrew, and escorted Capoulade to his room across the corridor. That done, he stepped back and rapped on Coupri's door. The intendant opened it at once.

'Monsieur Coupri,' said the steward, between seriousness and mockery, 'I must confess that, after all, I am not quite easy concerning you. You are sleeping so far from our apartments, my son's and mine. I am satisfied that you will not be troubled, and yet, perhaps it is best to be prepared for anything. If you will step down the corridor with me I will show you where Jacques and I are lodged, so that you may call us should you require anything.'

Troubled by this half-descent from his lofty scepticism on the part of Flaumel, Coupri went willingly with the steward, to be shown the whereabouts of the latter's quarters. That done, he returned to his chamber, closed and securely locked the door; then taking a copy of Monsieur Le Sage's droll story of 'Le Diable Boiteux' from his pocket, he flung himself, fully dressed as he was, upon his bed, his pistols within easy reach, and disposed himself for his vigil.

For best part of an hour he read undisturbed, and reassured by the peace of the room, his late qualms might have been dissipated but that whenever he looked about him, peering into the shadows that lay thick about the chamber, the gloom of the place chilled his courage anew.

Suddenly the stillness was broken. Reclining on his elbows he lay and listened, and he felt his flesh creeping as he did so. There was a sound as of someone faintly scratching on the wainscot opposite; and for all that his eyes were on the spot, he saw nothing.

'A mouse,' he sneered aloud, as if seeking to encourage himself with the sound of his own voice. 'What a poltroon I become!'

The next instant he had fallen back with a stifled scream. A rush of cold air had swept past him, extinguishing his candle in its passage. Again he strove to master himself, and for all that his pulses thundered fearfully, he put forth his hand and groped for his pistols. Clutching one of them, he sat up and waited, his teeth chattering in his head. He wished in a subconscious sort of way that Capoulade was nearer than across the corridor, and that there were no locked doors between them. Then he ceased to wish anything, ceased to think anything, as a grim horror took him and held him spellbound. Fronting the bed at a man's height from the floor, a white, luminous patch was spreading, like a phosphorescent cloud, and out of it boomed a horrid groaning sound followed by a shriek of hellish laughter.

The sweat stood in icy beads on Coupri's brow. He bethought him of prayers learned in childhood, and he pattered them in a frenzy. Then from out of the luminous cloud a form began to shape itself, a figure immensely tall, swathed in a winding sheet, and – horror of horrors – surmounted by a hideously grinning skull with eyeballs of glowing fire. And the shrieks of it filled the chamber and froze the very marrow in Coupri's bones.

Then in a flash his late scepticism recurred to him, and with it his resolve to test the ghost with lead. Mechanically almost he raised his pistol, and blazed with both barrels at the apparition. A burst of laughter answered him; next a glowing skeleton hand slipped from the cerecloth and held out two bullets which it let fall on to the parquet floor. Coupri heard the double thud of their fall, then, with a scream, he swooned.

When he recovered there were lights in his room, and Capoulade and the two Flaumels were at his bedside. Their questions as to what had happened he could but answer with entreaties that they should let him depart at once from that hideous chamber, and so in the end it was arranged that he should spend the remainder of the night in Capoulade's room and Capoulade's company.

But it was not until next morning, not until the comforting light of day had dispelled the horror of the night, that Coupri could be induced to tell his companion what had chanced. Capoulade listened attentively and very gravely, but when the end of the story came his glance brightened a little. After they had broken their fast, he took Coupri for a ramble through the grounds, and then it was that he communicated an idea that had occurred to him.

'Does it not seem somewhat strange that a spirit being a thing impalpable, a thing of no substance to be affected by bullets, should yet have the wherewithal to grasp those same bullets and fling them back?'

'Ask me not,' groaned the intendant. 'Who am I that I should explain these marvels? Never again will I doubt; never again will I mock.'

'My good Coupri, you go too fast. To doubt unreasonably is assuredly an ill thing, but in this case I will make bold to say that nothing has happened yet to warrant any change from your late scepticism.'

'Nothing?' gasped Coupri. 'Do you say nothing has happened?'

'I will add, Coupri, that, with your permission, it is I who will sleep in the sieur's bedchamber tonight – I hope to some purpose.'

Coupri, like the good soul that he was, sought to dissuade the young man; but Capoulade would not be dissuaded; he insisted that in the Sieur de la Blanchette's interests, it was Coupri's duty to further him in this last attempt to solve the mystery of this plague of ghosts; and Coupri let him have his way.

He had yet to contend with the opposition of the two Flaumels, when they met at supper. After last night's happening, following as it did upon the two former scares, they seemed, themselves, to have abandoned their scornful attitude, and they entreated Capoulade not to expose himself. But he was firm in his determination.

'I cannot believe Coupri's preposterous story,' was his astonishing declaration. 'The poor fellow has been the victim of a morbid imagination. The proof lies in the fact that we could find no bullets when we searched the chamber, although he swears he saw them cast there.'

Flaumel shrugged his shoulders, and Capoulade drawing a brace of pistols from his pocket proceeded to load them under the eyes of the company. He placed them on the table, and the talk proceeded desultorily until Flaumel rose to make fast the doors.

From the hall they heard him calling, agitation quivering in his voice, and Coupri and Capoulade started up and ran out to him. He was standing on the steps outside the door, and when they came up he told them of a white, shrouded figure that had passed round the corner of the house. They started in pursuit, but though they made the tour of the château they saw no indication of Flaumel's vision.

'Mon Dieu!' groaned the old man, as they were re-entering the hall. 'Am I too become a visionary, or is the place really accursed?'

Capoulade's answer was one of contemptuous incredulity.

'Monsieur Flaumel, for shame! I had thought better of you. You are becoming the victim of these old wives and their fancies. I am for bed.'

He re-entered the dining-room, passing the younger Flaumel, who was coming forth in quest of his father, and taking up his pistols, Capoulade accompanied the others to the floor above. At parting with Coupri, he exacted a promise that should he hear a shot he would at once repair to him.

'But,' he added, 'do not keep awake to listen for it; for the odds are greatly against your hearing it. I shall laugh at you in the morning.'

With that they parted, and Capoulade entered his bedroom and closed the door. He set the pistols he had carried on a chair, as Coupri had done the night before, and his candle beside them. Then he lay on the bed and waited.

Two hours went by, and Capoulade was beginning to fear disappointment, when, suddenly, there came, as on the previous night, the scratching on the wainscot to attract his attention. But instead of looking in the direction of the sound, he furtively peered behind him. He saw what he had expected. One of the panels of the wainscot at the head of the bed slid silently aside, leaving an open gap. Then came the rush of cold air which had so frightened Coupri, and Capoulade was in darkness.

He lay quite still and watched the luminous cloud appear, and as he watched his thoughts were very busy, but no thrill of fear unnerved him. The gibbering, howling skeleton grew clearer. Capoulade smiled grimly in the dark, and left the pistols on the chair untouched. From his breast-pocket he drew a fresh one, levelled it with a steady hand, and fired one barrel at the apparition.

A frightful scream rang through the chamber – no shriek of laughter this – and the ghost tumbled forward and down a height of some six feet, striking the floor with a thud.

In an instant Capoulade had his candle alight again, and he was leaning over the prostrate form, which had ceased to glow now that the candle's yellow light was upon it. He stooped and pulled aside the sheet, then rolled the figure over on its back and plucked away the cardboard death's head.

Beneath that mask the ashen face of the younger Flaumel was revealed, and in one of his clenched hands Capoulade found two bullets. Above the wainscot, where the Sieur de la Blanchette's portrait usually stood, a black gap now yawned.

In that moment the door opened, and Coupri, looking very white, stood on the threshold.

'*Voila!*' said Capoulade, pointing to the figure. 'I've laid the ghost. But he'll recover to answer M. de Sartines' questions yet.' Then, suddenly, his hand went up, levelling his pistol once more and covering the elder Flaumel, who entered. 'Throw down that pistol, or you're a dead man,' he commanded savagely, and the old man obeyed him.

When father and son were fast under lock and key, Capoulade added one or two words of explanation to make things clear to Coupri's slow mind.

'Last night, after you had laid your pistols down, Flaumel called you from the room on pretext of showing you where they lodged. Whilst he was doing this, his son was drawing the bullets from the charges of your pistols. They did the same by me tonight, when the old man led us round the château to hunt a spectre. But I had a third pistol in reserve to exorcize the ghost with.'

'But,' stammered Coupri, still bewildered, 'to what end should they have sought to frighten all who came to the château?'

'Who shall say? There are men whose minds never rise above childishness.'

But Coupri shook his great head. 'No, no,' said he, 'that is no explanation. It must be that, for some purpose, they wanted to have the château to themselves, as during the past five years.'

Capoulade looked at him, then he smote his thigh with his hand, and swore a great oath. 'You have said it,' he cried, for he had suddenly remembered his second task – the discovery of the coiners who were pouring spurious silver into Maine. He now recalled Sartines' words, that the elucidation of one mystery would probably afford the explanation of the other.

They made search in the château, and at last, in a secret chamber, to which they found access through the passage opened by the Sieur de la Blanchette's picture, discovered crucible and moulds and other implements of that nefarious craft, beside a quantity of base coin in bags. All this, together with their two prisoners, they conveyed to Paris.

M. de Sartines complimented Capoulade upon his address and definitely enrolled him in his army of secret agents. And if Capoulade kept back one of those bags of Flaumel's coins, to the end that he might obtain good value for bad money, it must be remembered that the transition from dishonesty to honesty is not accomplished all at once.

THE SWORD OF ISLAM

Ordinarily Dragut Reis – who was dubbed by the Faithful 'The Drawn Sword of Islam' – loved Christians as the fox loves geese. But in that summer of 1550 his feelings acquired a far deeper malignancy; they developed into a direct and personal hatred that for intensity was second only to the hatred which the Christians bore Dragut.

The allied Christian forces, under the direction of their emperor, had smoked him out of his stronghold of Mehedia; they had seized that splendid city, and were in the act of razing it to the ground as the neighbouring Carthage had been razed of old.

Dragut reckoned up his losses with a gloomy, vengeful mind. He had lost his city; and from the eminence of a budding Basha in the act of founding a kingdom he had been cast down once more to be a wanderer upon the seas.

He had lost three thousand men, and amongst them the very flower of his fiery corsairs. He had lost some twelve thousand Christian slaves – the fruit of many a desperate raid by land and water. He had lost his lieutenant and nephew, Hisar, who was even now a captive in the hands of his inveterate enemy, Andrea Doria. It is little wonder that he lost his temper, too. But he recovered it quickly, that he might set about recovering the rest. He was not the man to waste his days in brooding over what was done. Yesterday and today are but as pledges in the hands of destiny.

So he returned thanks to Allah, the Compassionate, the Merciful, that he was still alive and free upon the seas, with three galleasses, twelve galleys, and five brigantines; and bent his energetic, resourceful, knavish mind to the matter of making good his losses.

Meanwhile, he had been warned by the Sultan of Constantinople, the Exalted of Allah, that the Emperor Charles, not content with the mischief he had already wrought, had, in letters to the

Grand Signior, avowed his intent to pursue to the death 'the pirate Dragut, a corsair odious to both God and man.' He knew, moreover, that the emperor had entrusted the task to the greatest seaman of the day – to the terrible Admiral of Genoa, Andrea Doria, and that the Genoese was already at sea upon his quest.

Now, once already had Dragut been captured by the navy of Genoa, and for four years, which it afforded him little satisfaction to remember, he had toiled at an oar aboard the galley of the admiral's nephew, Gianettino Doria. He had known exposure to heat and cold; naked had he been broiled by the sun, and frozen by the rain; he had known aching muscles, hunger, and thirst; filthy, crawling things, and the festering sores begotten of the oarsman's bench; and his shoulders were still a criss-cross of scars where the bo'sun's whips had lashed him to revive his flagging energies.

All this had Dragut known, and he was not minded to renew the knowledge. It behoved him, therefore, to make ready fittingly to receive the admiral.

And by way at once of replenishing his coffers, venting a little of his vengeful heat, and marking his contempt for his Christian pursuers, he had made a sudden swoop upon the south-western littoral of Sicily. Beginning at Gergenti, he carried his raid as far north as Marsala, leaving ruin and desolation behind him. At the end of a week he stood off to sea again with the spoils of six townships and some three thousand picked captives of both sexes.

He would teach the infidel Christian dog to allude to him as 'the pirate Dragut, a corsair odious to both God and man.' He would so, by the beard of Mahomet!

He put the captives aboard a couple of his galleys, in charge of his lieutenant, Othmani, and despatched them straight to Algiers, to be sold there in the slave market. With the proceeds Othmani was to lay down fresh keels. Until these should be ready to reinforce his little fleet, Dragut judged it well to avoid encounters with the Genoese admiral, and with this intent he kept a southward course along the coast towards Tripoli.

Towards sunset of the day on which Othmani's galleys set out alone for Algiers, a fresh breeze sprang up from the north and blew into the corsair's range of vision a tiny brown-sailed felucca, as it might have blown a leaf in autumn. It was hawk-eyed Dragut himself who, lounging in the poop of his galley, first sighted this tiny craft.

He pointed it out to Biretta, the renegade Calabrian gunner, who was near him.

'In the name of Allah,' quoth he, 'what walnut-shell is this that comes so furiously after us?'

Biretta, a massive, sallow fellow, laughed.

'The fury is not hers, but of the wind,' said he. 'She goes wherever it blows her. She'll be an Italian craft.'

'Then the wind that blows her is the wind of Destiny. Haply she'll have news of Italy.'

He turned on his heel and gave an order to a turbaned officer below. Instantly the brazen note of a trumpet rang out, clear above the creak and dip of oars. As instantly the rowers came to rest, and from the side of each galley six-and-twenty massive yellow oars stood out, their wet blades glistening in the evening sunlight.

Thus the Moslem fleet waited, rocking gently on the little swell that had arisen, and its quality was blazoned by the red and white ensign charged with a blue crescent, which floated from the masthead of Dragut's own galley.

On came the little brown-sailed felucca, hopelessly driven by what Dragut accounted the breeze of Destiny. At last, when she was in danger of being blown past them, Dragut crossed to meet her. As the galley's long prow ran alongside of her, grappling-hooks were deftly flung to seize her at mast and gunwale, and but for these she must have been swept over by those gigantic oars.

From the prow, Dragut himself, a tall and handsome figure in gold-broidered scarlet surcoat that descended to his knees, his snowy turban heightening the swarthiness of his hawk face, with its square-cut black beard, stood to challenge the crew of that ill-starred felucca.

There were aboard of her six scared knaves, something betwixt seamen and lackeys, whom the corsair's black eyes passed contemptuously over. He addressed himself to a couple who were seated in the stern-sheets – a tall and every elegant young gentleman, obviously Italian, and a girl, upon whose white, golden-headed loveliness the corsair's bold eyes glowed pleasurably.

'Who are you?' he demanded shortly, in Italian.

The willowy young man answered for the twain, very composedly, as though it were a matter of everyday life with him to be held in the grappling-hooks of a Barbary pirate.

'My name is Ottavio Brancaleone. I am from Genoa on my way to Spain.'

'To Spain!' quoth Dragut, and he laughed. 'You steer an odd course for Spain, or do you look to find it in Egypt?'

'We have lost our rudder,' the gentleman explained, 'and we were at the mercy of the wind.'

'I trust you have found it as merciful as you hoped,' said Dragut. He leered at the girl, who, in affright, shrank nearer her companion. 'And the girl, sir? Who is she?'

'My – my sister.'

'Had you told me different you had been the first Christian I ever knew to speak the truth,' said Dragut, quite amiably. 'Well, well 'tis plain you're not to be trusted to sail a boat of your own. Best come aboard, and see if you can do better at an oar.'

'I'll not be trespassing on your hospitality,' said Brancaleone, with that amazing coolness of his.

Dragut wasted no time in argument. It was not his way. Of the grinning, turbaned corsairs who swarmed like ants upon the prow he flung a half-score down into the felucca. Brancaleone had time to stab but one of them before they overpowered him.

The prize proved far less insignificant than at first Dragut had imagined. For, in addition to the eight slaves acquired – and the girl was fit to grace a sultan's harem – they found a great chest of newly minted ducats, which it took six men to heave aboard the galley, and a beautifully chiselled gold coffer full of gems of price. They found something more. On the inside of the coffer's lid was engraved the owner's name – Amelia Francesca Doria.

Dragut snapped down the lid with a prayer of thanks to Allah the One, and strode into the poop cabin, where the girl was confined.

'Madonna Amelia,' he called softly, to test her identity. She looked up at once. 'Will you tell me what is your kinship with the Admiral of Genoa?'

'I am his granddaughter, sir,' she answered, with something fierce behind her outward softness, 'and be sure that he will terribly avenge upon you any wrong that is done to me.'

Dragut nodded and smiled.

'We are old friends, the admiral and I,' said he, and went out again.

A mighty Nubian bearing a torch – for night had now descended with African suddenness – lighted him to the galley's waist, where, about the mainmast, lay huddled the seven pinioned prisoners.

With the curved toe of his scarlet slipper the corsair touched Messer Brancaleone.

'Tell me, dog,' said he, 'all that you know of Messer Andrea Doria.'

'That is soon told,' answered Brancaleone. 'I know nothing, nor want to.'

'Therein, of course, you lie,' said Dragut. 'For one thing, you know his granddaughter.'

Brancaleone blinked, and recovered.

'True, and several others of his family. But I conceived your question to concern his movements. I know that he is upon the seas, that he is seeking you, and that he has sworn to take you alive, and that when they take you – as I pray God they will – they will so deal with you that you shall implore them of their Christian charity to hang you.'

'And is that all you know?' quoth Dragut, unruffled. 'You did not, peradventure, sight this fleet of his as you were sailing?'

'I did not.'

'Do you think that with a match between your fingers you might remember?'

55

'I might invent,' said the Italian. 'I have told you the truth, Messer Dragut. Torture could but gain you falsehood.'

The corsair looked searchingly into that comely young face, then he turned away as if satisfied. But as he was departing Messer Brancaleone called him back. The Italian's imperturbability had suddenly departed. Anxiety amounting almost to terror sounded in his voice.

'What fate do you reserve for Madonna Amelia?' he asked.

Dragut considered him, and smiled a little. He had no particular rancour against his prisoner; indeed, he was inclining to admiration for the cool courage which the man had shown. At the same time, there was no room for sentiment in the heart of the corsair. He was quite pitiless. He had been asked a question, and he answered it without malice.

'Our lord the Sublime Suleyman,' said he, 'is as keen a judge of beauty as any living man. I do the girl the honour of accounting her a gift worthy even of the Exalted of Allah. So I shall keep her safe against my next voyage to Constantinople.'

And then Brancaleone's little lingering self-possession left him utterly. From his writhing lips came a stream of vituperation, expressions of his impotent rage, which continued even after the Nubian had struck him upon the mouth and Dragut had taken his departure.

Next day a slave on Dragut's galley who had been taken ill at his oar was, in accordance with custom, unshackled and heaved overboard. Brancaleone, stripped to his delicate white skin, was chained in the fellow's empty place. There were seven men to each oar, and Brancaleone's six companions were all Christians and all white – or had been before exposure had tanned them to the colour of mahogany. Of these, three were Spaniards, two were Italian, and the other was a Frenchman. All were indescribably filthy and unkempt, and it was with a shudder that the delicately nurtured Italian gentleman wondered was he destined to become as they?

Up and down the gangway between the rowers' benches strode two Moslem bo'suns, armed with long whips of bullock-hide, and it was not long ere one of them, considering that Brancaleone was not putting his share of effort into his task, sent that cruel lash to raise a burning weal upon his tender flesh. He was sparingly fed with his half-brutalized companions upon dried figs and dates, and he was given a little tepid water to drink when he thirsted, which was often. He slept in his shackles on the rowers' bench, which was but some four feet wide, and, despite the sheepskins with which that bench was padded, it was not long ere the friction of his constant movement began to chafe and blister his flesh.

In the scorching noontide of the day he collapsed fainting upon his oar. He was unshackled and dragged out upon the gangway. There a bucket of sea-water was flung over him to revive him, and the too-swift healing action of the salt upon his seared flesh was a burning agony. He was put back to his oar again with the warning that did he permit himself a second time the luxury of swooning he would have the whole ocean in which to revive.

On the third day they sighted land, and towards evening the galleys threaded their way one by one through the shoals of the Boca de Cantara into the spacious lagoon on the north-east side of the Island of Jerbah, and there came to rest.

It was Dragut's intention to lie snug in that remote retreat until Othmani should be ready with the reinforcements that were to enable the corsair to take the seas once more against the Admiral of Genoa. But it would seem that already the admiral was closer upon his heels than he had supposed, and that, trackless as are the ocean ways, yet Andrea Doria had by some mysterious means contrived to gather information as he came that had kept him upon the invisible spoor of his quarry.

Not a doubt but that the folk on that ravaged Sicilian seaboard would be eager to inform the redoubtable admiral of the direction in which the Moslem galleys had faded out of sight. Perhaps even that empty felucca left tossing upon the tideless sea had served as an index to the way the corsairs had taken, and perhaps from the mainland, from Monastir, or one of the other cities now in Christian hands, a glimpse of Dragut's fleet had been caught, and Doria had been warned. Be that as it may, not a week had Dragut been anchored at Jerbah when one fine morning brought a group of friendly islanders with the alarming news that a fleet of galleys was descending upon the island from the north.

The news took Dragut ashore in a hurry with a group of officers. From the narrow spur of land at the harbour's mouth he surveyed the advancing ships. What already he had more than feared became absolute certainty. Two-and-twenty royal galleys were steering straight for the Boca de Cantara, and the foremost was flying the admiral's ensign.

Back to his fleet went Dragut for cannon and slaves, and so feverishly did these toil under the lash of his venomous tongue, and of his bo'suns whips, that within an hour he had erected a battery at the mouth of the harbour and fired a salute straight into the Genoese line as the galleys were in the very act of dropping anchor. Thereupon the fleet of Doria stood off out of range, and hung there, well content to wait, knowing that all that was now required on their part was patience. The fox was trapped, and the sword of Islam was like to be sheathed at last.

Forthwith the jubilant Doria sent word to the Emperor that he held Dragut fast, and he despatched messengers to the Viceroys of Sicily and Naples asking for reinforcements with which, if necessary, to force the issue. He meant this time to leave nothing to chance.

Dragut, on his side, employed his time in fortifying the Boca de Cantara. A fort arose there, growing visible under the eyes of the Genoese, and provoking the amusement of that fierce veteran, Doria. Sooner or later Dragut must decide him to come forth from his bottle-necked refuge, and the longer he put off that evil day the more overwhelming would be the numbers assembled to destroy him.

Never since Gianettino Doria had surprised him in the road of Goialatta, off the coast of Corsica, on that famous occasion when he was made prisoner, had Dragut found himself in so desperately tight a corner. He sat under the awning of the poop of his galley, and cursed the Genoese with that astounding and far-reaching fluency in which the Moslem is without rival upon earth. He pronounced authoritatively upon the evil reputation of Doria's mother and the inevitably shameful destiny of his daughters and their female offspring. He foretold how dogs would of a certainty desecrate the admiral's grave, and he called perfervidly upon Allah to rot the bones and destroy the house of his arch-enemy. Then, observing that Allah remained disdainfully aloof, he rose up one day in a mighty passion, and summoned his officers.

'This skulking here will not avail us,' he snarled at them, as if it were by their contriving that he was trapped. 'By delay we but increase our peril. What is written is written. Allah has bound the fate of each man about his neck. Betide what may, tonight we take the open sea.'

'And by morning you'll have found the bottom of it,' drawled a voice from one of the oars.

Dragut, who was standing on the gangway between the rowers' benches, whipped round with an oath upon the speaker. He encountered the languid eyes of Messer Brancaleone. The repose of the last few days had restored the Italian's vigour, and certain thoughts that lately he had been thinking had revived his courage.

'Are you weary of life?' quoth the infuriated corsair. 'Shall I have you hanged ere we go out to meet your friends out yonder?'

'You're very plainly a fool, Messer Dragut,' was the weary answer. 'Hang me, and you hang the only man in all your fleet who can show you the way out of this trap in which you're taken.'

Dragut started between anger and amazement.

'You can show me a way out of this trap?' he cried. 'What way might that be?'

'Strike off my fetters, restore me my garments, and give me proper food, and I'll discuss it with you.'

Dragut glowered.

'We have a shorter way to make men speak,' said he.

Brancaleone smiled, and shook his head.

'You think so? I might prove you wrong.'

It was odd what a power of conviction dwelt in his languid tones. The corsair issued an order and turned away. A half-hour later Messer Brancaleone, nourished, washed, and clothed, once more the elegant, willowy Italian in his doublet of sapphire velvet and in pleasantly variegated hose of blue and white, stepped on to the poop-deck, where Dragut awaited him.

Seated cross-legged upon a gorgeous silken divan that was wrought in green and blue and gold, the handsome corsair combed his square black beard with fretful fingers. Behind him, stark naked save for his white loin-cloth, stood his gigantic Nubian, his body oiled until it shone like ebony, armed with a gleaming scimitar.

'Now, sir,' growled Dragut, 'what is this precious plan of yours – briefly?'

'You begin where we should end,' said the imperturbable Genoese. 'I owe you no favours, Messer Dragut, and I bear you no affection that I should make you a free gift of your life and liberty. My eyes have seen something to which yours are blind, and my wits have conceived something of which your own are quite incapable. These things, sir, are for sale. Ere I part with them we must agree the price.'

Dragut pondered him from under scowling brows savagely. He could scarce believe that the world held so much impudence.

'And what price do you suggest?' he snarled, half-derisively, by way of humouring the Genoese.

'Why, as to that, since I offer you life and liberty, it is but natural that I should claim my own life and liberty in return, and similarly the liberty of Madonna Amelia and of my servants whom you captured; also, it is but natural that I should require the restoration of the money and jewels you have taken from us, and since you have deprived us of our felucca, it is no more than proper that you should equip us with a vessel in which to pursue the journey that you interrupted. Considering the time we have lost in consequence of this interruption, it is but just that you should make this good as far as possible by presenting me with a craft that is capable of the utmost speed. I will accept a galley of six-and-twenty oars, manned by a proper complement of slaves.'

'And that is all?' roared Dragut.

'No,' said Brancaleone quietly. 'That is but the restitution due to me. We come now to the price of the service I am to render you. When you were Gianettino Doria's prisoner, Barbarossa paid for you, as all the world knows, a ransom of three thousand ducats. I will be more reasonable.'

'Will you so?' snorted Dragut. 'By the splendour of Allah, you'll need to be!'

'I will accept one thousand ducats.'

'May Allah blot thee out, thou impudent son of shame!' cried the corsair, and he heaved himself up in a fury.

'You compel me to raise the price to fifteen hundred ducats,' said Brancaleone smoothly. 'I must be compensated for abuse, since I cannot take satisfaction for it as between one honourable Christian gentleman and another.'

It was good for Dragut that his feelings suddenly soared to a pitch of intensity that defied expression, else might the price have been raised even beyond the figure of the famous ransom that Barbarossa had paid. Mutely he stood glowering, clenching and unclenching his sinewy hands. Then he half-turned to his Nubian swordsman.

'Ali—' he began, when Brancaleone once more cut in.

'Ah, wait,' said he. 'I pray you calm yourself. Remember how you stand, and that Andrea Doria holds you trapped. Do nothing that will destroy your only chance. Time enough to bid Ali hack off my head when I have failed.'

That speech arrested Dragut's anger in full flow. He wheeled upon the Genoese once more.

'You accept that alternative?'

Brancaleone met his gaze blandly.

'Why not? I have no slightest fear of failure. I have said that I can show you how to win clear of this trap and make the admiral the laughing-stock of the world.'

'Speak, then,' cried Dragut, his fierce eyes kindling.

'If I do so before you have agreed my terms then I shall have nothing left to sell.'

Dragut turned aside and strode to the taffrail. He looked across the shimmering blue water to the fortifications at the harbour's mouth; with the eyes of his imagination he looked beyond, at the fleet of Genoa riding out there in patient conviction that it held its prey. The price that Brancaleone asked was outrageous. A galley and some two hundred Christian slaves to row it, and fifteen hundred ducats! In all it amounted to more than the ransom that Kheyr-ed-Din Barbarossa had paid for him. Yet Dragut must pay it or count his destiny fulfilled. He came to reflect that he would pay it gladly enough to be out of this tight corner.

He came about again. He spoke of torture once more, but in a half-hearted sort of way; for he did not himself believe that it would be effective with a man of Brancaleone's mettle.

Brancaleone laughed at the threat and shrugged his shoulders.

'You may as profitably hang me, Messer Dragut. Your infidel barbarities would quite as effectively seal my lips.'

'We might torture the woman,' said Dragut the ingenious.

On the words Brancaleone turned white to the lips; but it was the pallor of bitter, heart-searing resolve, not the pallor of such fear as Dragut had hoped to awaken. He advanced a step, his imperturbability all gone, and he spat his words into the face of the corsair with the fierceness of a cornered wildcat.

'Attempt it,' said he, 'and as God's my witness I leave you to your fate at the hands of Genoa – ay, though my heart should burst with the pain of my silence. I am a man, Messer Dragut – never doubt it.'

'I do not,' said Dragut, convinced. 'I agree your terms. Show me a way out of Doria's clutches, and you shall have all that you have asked for.'

Trembling still from his recent emotion, Brancaleone hoarsely bade the corsair call up his officers and repeat his words before them.

'And you shall make oath upon this matter,' he added. 'Men say of you that you are a faithful Moslem. I mean to put it to the test.'

Dragut, now all eagerness to know what plan was stirring in his prisoner's brain, unable to brook further suspense in this affair, called up his officers, and before them all, taking Allah to witness, he made oath upon the beard of the Prophet that if Brancaleone could show him deliverance, he, on his side, would recompense the Genoese to the extent demanded.

Thereafter Dragut and Brancaleone went ashore with no other attendant but the Nubian swordsman. It was the Genoese who led the way, not towards the fort, as Dragut had expected, but in the opposite direction. Arrived at the northernmost curve of that almost circular lagoon, where the ground was swampy, Brancaleone paused. He pointed across a strip of shallow land, that was no more than a half-mile or so in width, to the blue-green sea beyond. Part of this territory was swampy, and part was sand; vegetation there was of the scantiest; some clumps of reeds, an odd date palm, its crest rustling faintly in the breeze, and nothing else.

'It is really very simple,' said the Italian. 'Yonder lies your way.'

A red-legged stork rose from the edge of the marsh and went circling overhead. Dragut's face empurpled with rage. He deemed that this smooth fellow dared to mock him.

'Are my galleys winged like that stork, thou fool?' he demanded passionately. 'Or are they wheeled like chariots, that I can sail them over dry land?'

Brancaleone returned him a glance that was full of stupefaction.

'I protest,' said he, 'that for a man of your reputation you fill me with amazement. I said you were a dull fellow. I little dreamed how dull. Nay, now, suppress your rage. Truth is a very healing draught, and you have need of it.

'I compute, now, that aboard your ships there will be, including slaves, some three thousand men. I doubt not you could press another thousand from the island into your service. How long, do you think, would it take four thousand men to dig a channel deep enough to float your shallow galleys through that strip of land?'

Dragut's fierce eyes flickered as if he had been menaced with a blow.

'By Allah!' he ejaculated; and gripped his beard. 'By Allah!'

'In a week the thing were easily done, and meanwhile your fort there will hold the admiral in play. Then, one dark night, you slip through this canal and stand away to the south, so that by sunrise you shall have vanished beyond the skyline, leaving the admiral to guard an empty trap.'

Dragut laughed aloud now in almost childish glee, and otherwise signified his delight by the vehemence with which he testified to the unity of Allah. Suddenly he checked. His eyes narrowed as they rested upon Brancaleone.

''Tis a scurvy trick you play your lady's grandsire!' said he.

The Genoese shrugged.

'Every man for himself, Messer Dragut. We understand each other, I think. 'Tis not for love of you that I do this thing.'

'I would it were,' said the corsair, with an odd sincerity. And as they returned to the galleys it was observed that Dragut's arm was about the shoulders of the infidel, and that he spoke with him as with a brother.

The fact is that Dragut, fired with admiration of Brancaleone's resourcefulness, deplored that so fine a spirit should of necessity be destined to go down to the Pit. He spoke to him now of the glories of Islam, and of the future that must await a gentleman of Brancaleone's endowments in the ranks of the Faithful. But this was a matter in which Brancaleone proved politely obdurate, and Dragut had not the time to devote to his conversion, greatly as he desired it. There was the matter of that canal to engage him.

The Italian's instructions were diligently carried out. Daily the fort at the Boca de Cantara would belch forth shot at the Genoese navy, which stood well out of range. To the admiral this was but the barking of a dog that dared not come within biting distance; and the waste of ammunition roused his scorn of that pirate Dragut whom he held at his mercy.

There came a day, however, when the fort was silent; it was followed by another day of silence, in the evening of which one of the admiral's officers suggested that all might not be well. Doria agreed, laughing heartily in his long white beard.

'All is not at all well with that dog Dragut,' said he. 'He wants us within range of his guns. The ruse is childish.'

And so the Genoese fleet continued well out of range of the empty fort, what time Dragut himself was some scores of miles away, speeding for the Archipelago and the safety of the Dardanelles as fast as his slaves could row.

In the words of the Spanish historian Marmol, who has chronicled the event; Dragut had left Messer Andrea Doria 'with the dog to hold.'

Brancaleone accompanied the Moslem fleet at first, though now aboard the galley which Dragut had given him in accordance with their agreement. And with the Genoese sailed the lovely Amelia Francesca Doria, his chest of gold, the jewels, and the fifteen hundred ducats that Dragut – grimly stifling his reluctance – had paid him. On the second day after leaving Jerbah, Messer Brancaleone and the corsair captain parted company, with mutual expressions of goodwill, and the Genoese put about and steered a north-westerly course for the coast of Spain.

It was some months ere Dragut learnt the true inwardness of Messer Brancaleone's conduct. He had the story from a Genoese captive, the captain of a carrack which the corsair scuttled in the Straits of Messina. This fellow's name, too, was Brancaleone, upon learning which Dragut asked him was he kin to one Ottavio Brancaleone, who had gone to Spain with the admiral's granddaughter.

'He was my cousin,' the man answered.

And Dragut now learnt that in the teeth of the opposition of the entire Doria family, the irrepressible Brancaleone had carried off Madonna Amelia. The admiral had news of it as he was putting to sea, and it was in pursuit not only of Dragut, but also of the runaways, that he had gone south as far as Jerbah, having reason to more than suspect that they were aboard one of Dragut's galleys. The admiral had sworn to hang Brancaleone from his yardarm ere he returned to port, and his bitterness at the trick Dragut had played was increased by the circumstance that Brancaleone, too, had got clear away.

Dragut was very thoughtful when he heard that story.

'And to think,' said he afterwards to Othmani, 'that I paid that unconscionable dog fifteen hundred ducats, and gave him my best galley manned by two hundred Christian slaves that he might render himself as great a service as ever he rendered me!'

But he bore no malice. After all, the Genoese had behaved generously in that he had left Dragut – though not from motives of generosity – the entire glory of the exploit. Dragut's admiration for the impudent fellow was, if anything, increased. Was he not, after all, the only Christian who had ever bested Dragut in a bargain? If he had a regret it was that so shrewd a spirit should abide in the body of an infidel. But Allah is all-knowing.

The Poachers

They were a hangdog-looking pair as they rode into Liphook on that sunny morning of May. One was short and weedy, with bony shanks and a hungry countenance, the other was a little taller and a deal bulkier, but bloated of face and generally flabby. They were dressed in a soiled and tawdry imitation of their betters, and each looked every inch the gallows-bird that he was.

They drew rein on the little patch of rugged turf before the Lame Dog, and the portly Nathaniel, without dismounting, called for a nipperkin of ale, whilst the weedy Jake – who had received some elements of education, and was never weary of parading his scholarliness – became engrossed in the contents of a bill nailed to the post that bore the sign of the inn.

It had for title the arresting phrase, 'One Hundred Guineas Reward.' It began with WHEREAS, and ended with GOD SAVE THE KING, all in fat letters. In between there were some twenty lines of matter in smaller type, with the name of THOMAS EVANS boldly displayed amidst it.

Ominous as was this advertisement to the rogue who, under the style of Captain Evans, had now for some months been working the Portsmouth road, it nevertheless filled Master Jake with envy. It spoke of fame and success in his own line of industry, such as seemed far indeed beyond the reach of himself and his colleague.

They were a pair of London foists – to use the term of their own thieves' cant – a couple of sneaking pickpockets who never should have attempted to soar to higher things, and who were bitterly regretting their recourse to robbery in the grand manner. So far it had not proved profitable; at least, not commensurately with its perils. Yesterday evening, grown bold under the spur of necessity, they had attempted to demand toll from the London coach – thereby usurping the privileges of Captain Evans himself; but they had bungled the matter through inexperience, and had been ignominiously driven off by the guard's blunderbuss. Indeed, but that the guard himself was so scared that he could not keep his limbs from shaking, they might have brought away a charge of lead apiece for their pains.

You will now understand Jake's feelings of envy as he scanned that proclamation. He felt that it would be many a year before the justices honoured himself in like fashion, before his own unkempt head became worth a hundred pounds to any man who could come and fetch it.

In his nasal, sing-song, cockney tones, he proceeded labouredly to read the advertisement aloud for the benefit of his unlettered associate. He was interrupted by the advent of the ale. When they had paid for it, they had but fourpence left between them, and, unless fortune were singularly benign, they were very likely to starve. Sullen and downcast, they departed and rode on side by side with no word passing between them. For sixpence either would have cut the throat of the other that morning. They turned out of the highway into a pleasant, well-hedged by-road a little way beyond Liphook, and they ambled slowly forward in the dappled shade with the fragrance of hawthorn all about them. It was their unspoken hope that here they might chance upon some lonely wayfarer – preferably of the weaker sex, or at least someone who would give no trouble. And the very next turn in the road brought them face to face with one who, in the distance, looked a likely quarry. This was a slight gentleman astride of a tall, roan mare with a white blaze. He was dressed all in black, like a parson, yet with more worldliness and elegance than would have been proper in a parson. The three-cornered hat over his auburn bag-wig was pulled down to shade his eyes; for our gentleman was reading. The roan was proceeding at a walk, the reins loose upon her neck, whilst her rider, gripping her flanks easily with his knees, was deeply engrossed in the book he held, which was a translation of the diverting adventures of a Salamanca student named Gil Blas.

Our rascally twain sighted him from afar, and by common impulse drew rein, and looked at each other. Jake winked portentously. Nat nodded, and licked his lips. Then, again by common impulse, they quietly backed their screws round the corner they had just turned, and there, out of sight of that solitary and studious wayfarer, they waited. They had one pistol between them, and it was Jake – the gunner of the expedition – who had charge of this. He drew it, looked to the priming, breathed on the barrel, and rubbed it on his threadbare sleeve to increase its lustre.

Round the corner plump into that ambush rode our student, and—

'Stand!' thundered Jake, levelling his weapon.

The rider looked up, checking instantly as he had been bidden, and displaying a keen, wolfish face that did not seem to tone quite well with his studious habits and demure apparel. Indeed, a certain raffishness hung about him despite his clothes. He seemed compounded of an odd blend of courtier and lackey.

He considered the rogues who challenged him, and they found his expression disconcerting.

He displayed none of the sudden terror they had hoped and expected to inspire. Instead, his glance was vaguely contemptuous in its nice mingling of amusement and surprise. Calmly he closed his book and slipped it into his pocket, whilst from under his left arm he took the heavy riding-crop that had been tucked there.

'What's this, you rabbit-suckers?' he demanded.

Jake thrust his pistol a couple of inches nearer, as if to insist upon its presence.

'It's this,' said he, 'and it's your purse we want. Come, sir, deliver!'

'Now, here's impudence, ecod!' was the amusedly scornful answer. 'Am I to be hunted on my own preserves by a couple of poaching tykes?'

He moved suddenly. Swift and abruptly as a flash of lightning his heavily loaded crop smashed down upon the dirty hand that held the barker, and knocked the weapon into the dust. Then he had plucked a pistol from his own holster, and thus in the twinkling of an eye made himself master of the situation.

Jake nursed his injured hand, grimacing with pain. Nathaniel snatched up his reins, stricken with sudden panic. But his flight was arrested as soon as conceived.

'Stand, hog!' our gentleman summoned him; 'or I'll turn you into bacon with a bullet.'

They stood at his mercy, and he surveyed them with that sardonic eye of his.

'On my life, you're a fine pair of tobymen!' he admonished them. He read their true natures as easily as he had read the diverting history of the Salamanca student. ''Twas an ill hour in which you left your town kennels, you rats, to turn gentlemen of the pad and take toll in the heroic manner! Turn out your pockets, you cony-catchers, and let us see how you have thriven! Turn 'em out, I say, and hand over your poachings!'

They obeyed him with a ludicrous alacrity, and revealed the miserable state of their affairs. Our gentleman in black surveyed with an eye of scorn the copper coins in Nathaniel's dirty palm.

'How long have ye been poaching upon my preserves?' he demanded. Receiving no answer: 'Speak out, you muckrakes!' he bade them. 'I am no sheriff's officer. I am Captain Evans, of whom you may have heard.'

Jake needed but this confirmation of what already he had suspected. He fell to fawning upon the notorious gentleman of the pad, and proceeded to relate a moving tale of misfortune. The Bow Street runners had been on their trail in town, and they had taken to the country for a change of air and of method. So far, however, they had not prospered as highwaymen. They had robbed a parson two days ago, but his purse had held but three poor shillings, of which all that remained was the fourpence Nathaniel had displayed. Finally came the admission that they were hungry; and thus a business begun with a fiercely bellowed 'Stand and deliver!' ended now in a piteous whine for alms.

Captain Evans considered them. At length he addressed Nathaniel.

'Get down, pig-face,' he commanded, 'and fetch me that barker!'

Obediently Nathaniel dismounted, picked up the fallen pistol, and delivered it to the captain. Evans dropped it into his pocket. Then, restoring his own weapon to its holster, he took the heavy crop, and, tucking it under his arm again, he finally addressed these rogues.

'Ye inspire me with little confidence,' said he. 'Still, I have a better notion. If I were to toss you a guinea, you would be in no better case when that was eaten. I'll do better by you, and, meanwhile, I'll mend your emptiness. Follow me, but at a distance, for I'd not have it thought I keep such rat-bitten company!'

On that he wheeled his mare about, and rode off briskly along the road by which he had approached. The twain looked at each other. Nathaniel's prominent eyes asked an obvious question.

'Ay,' said Jake; and they set out to follow.

The captain led them a half-mile or so down that by-way, then for a short distance along a narrow, grassy lane to a cottage that stood back in a little patch of land – a little, white-washed house set in a miniature orchard, as innocent-looking a retreat as could have been conceived. Within the gate he waited for them to come up with him, and when the horses had been stabled in a lean-to, he conducted them within doors to what was at once the kitchen and the living-room. He bade them to table, and, having set meat and drink before them, took his own seat apart, and smoked thoughtfully while they noisily satisfied their hunger.

From time to time he would fling them a disdainful glance, and from time to time they would steal awed looks at him, noting his boots of fine leather and his silver spurs, the cut of his handsome black coat, and the extravagance of his ruffles – which, incidentally, were not as clean as they might have been, although that was too nice a point for our tatterdemalions.

Captain Evans was a man of ideas. It was not for nothing that he had been reading the adventures of Gil Blas that morning. He had been greatly taken with the description of the retreat of the robbers who captured the Salamanca student, and he was romantic enough to desire on a lesser scale to organize a somewhat similar band in the pleasant county of Hampshire – at least, the notion assailed him when he came to consider how he might turn these two starveling thieves to account. They were to form the nucleus of the band, which he would rule as captain absolute. Thus, you see, he was concerned with improving upon the heroic traditions of the high toby.

He unfolded his scheme to the twain, when at last they had fed. It was as yet a little vague and inchoate in its details, but the main lines it should follow were plainly indicated, and he expected it to be greeted with enthusiasm. At the conclusion he addressed himself more particularly to Nathaniel.

'Well, pig-face,' he questioned, 'how does it seem to you?'

'My name,' said the flabby rogue, 'is Nat.'

'Maybe, but pig-face becomes you better. Will ye work with me?'

And he looked from one to the other.

Jake agreed with alacrity to the plan, profoundly honoured to serve under so illustrious a leader. Nathaniel, more reluctant because resentful of the lack of respect shown him by the captain, required to be persuaded by his fellow. But in the end it was settled; the twain were to be enrolled under the captain's banner.

The nature of the active service upon which they were to adventure had yet to be considered, and the captain promised to consider it forthwith. Meanwhile, since they showed signs of slumber as a result of their gross overfeeding, he let them rest for today and recuperate their energies.

'Ye'll be snug and safe here, so that ye lie close,' he assured them, rising. Then he issued an order, 'Now that ye've eaten, clear the table and wash the platters clean. 'Twill be some employment for you while I'm gone. I shall be back tonight.'

With that he left them.

They heard the hoofs of the roan go padding down the lane, then at last Nathaniel loosed his pent-up wrath.

'I'll be triply durned,' said he, 'if I turn scullion to any ruffling cove of the pad! Wash the platters!' He snorted angrily. 'Skewer my vitals, do I look like a scullery wench?' He rose in his rage at the indignity. 'And he called me pig-face, the dirty thief! And – and you, Jake, ye fool, let him beguile you with his smooth cant into promising to serve with him! Fine service, i' faith! Us'll risk our necks while his lordship takes the plunder. If ye've an ounce of sense in your ugly head, ye'll come away with me this instant!'

Jake raised his weasel face, and looked at his fellow with shrewd, narrowing eyes.

''Tis the way o' fools and drunkards,' he moralized, 'that they must think all the world in their own case. Sit down, you cackling Tom o' Bedlam, and listen! I know ye're an unscholarly, ignorant cove that can't read for yourself. But didn't I read ye what it said on a paper outside the Lame Dog at Liphook this morning? Didn't ye hear that the Guvviment be offering a hundred guineas for the capture o' this ruffling cove?' He paused a moment to give more effect to what he was about to add. Then he closed one eye slowly. 'Us'll earn it,' he said softly.

Nathaniel stared, his mouth gaping, his eyes bulging. Then he smacked his dusty breeches, and again invited someone to skewer his vitals. Thereafter they discussed the matter.

Captain Evans returned towards evening, and he came at a breakneck gallop, which in itself might have warned his newly enrolled followers that something was wrong. He was breathing heavily when he entered the kitchen, where the twain awaited him, and his face gleamed white in the gathering dusk. He dropped to a chair, and mopped his face with a handkerchief; raised a wig, and mopped his cropped head as well.

''Od's life, my lads, a near thing!' he panted.

The sense of peril oozed from him like perspiration, and, catching the infection of it, they sat still, watching him, and awaiting his explanation.

''Twas that sleuth from Bow Street, Baldock – the shrewdest catchpoll in the country. He's been on my heels this month past and more. I fooled him once out o' sheer wantonness, and it is an unforgiving dog, without humour. But I'll fool him again ere all is done. He has never seen my face save once, and then it was so disguised that he'd never recognize it. Yet this evening he was within an ace of laying me by the heels. There was a trap set for me. I had taken a fat purse 'twixt this and Petersfield, and I was returning, when I stopped for a pint of claret at a roadside inn. But for a friendly ostler who gave me a hint, I'd have had more than my pint of claret, and 'tis odds ye'd never again have seen Captain Evans, unless ye went to his hanging.' He stretched his legs, and breathed more easily. 'Give me to drink, one o' ye. There should be ale in the cupboard there.'

It was Jake who did him the service he asked, and fetched a jar from the cupboard. There was little left in it, no more than a cupful, but the captain drained it gratefully. Then he fished out of his pocket a green silk purse with a glint of gold showing through the meshes – a purse which he had taken that afternoon.

'And now, my lads, we must part company,' he informed them. 'The sleuths are too hot upon the scent, and the moment were ill-chosen for the association we had thought of. If we stick together you will but increase my danger, whilst I shall bring danger upon you, too. I am for the West Country for a season, until the Portsmouth Road is clear of Baldock and his runners. 'Twas but to warn you that I returned tonight. You must fend for yourselves, my lads: and here's to help you on your way.'

On the word he flung the silk purse on to the table, where it fell with a mellow clink.

His generosity, both in this and in having taken risks to return to warn them, must have touched hearts less vile. Them, however, it left unmoved, save by greed and the sense of the need for urgent action. Jake fastened a lean claw upon the purse, and his eyes were two glistening beads.

''Tis very generous of you, captain,' said he; and it almost seemed that he sneered.

Captain Evans rose.

'And now, fare you well,' he said.

As he spoke the pair of them leapt at him. Taking him utterly by surprise, they bore him struggling to the ground under their combined weight. He was strong and agile, and almost a match for the pair of them – almost, but not quite. The fight that ensued was fierce and long-drawn. The captain writhed and twisted, grappled, kicked, and smote at them, and before he was overpowered that savage, silent scrimmage had swept across the length of the kitchen floor, raising a cloud of dust, knocking over chairs and table in its furious course. But in the end they had him helpless, bound hand and foot; sweating and panting from his exertions, wigless, dusty, and with disordered garments, glaring at them with furious eyes.

Nathaniel righted one of the chairs that had been knocked over. They forced the captain into it, and bound him firmly to it with cords which they had prepared. Thus powerless, his white face writhing with anger and contempt, he cursed them fiercely for a moment.

'What are ye at all?' he asked them thereafter. 'Could I be mistook? Are ye a couple of dirty catchpolls who have tricked me into believing ye are upright men?'

The flabby Nathaniel, who, winded by his labours, had dropped wearily to a chair, had a miserable pretext ready.

'Ye called me pig-face!' he said, with a show of being offended.

'I see,' said the captain. 'And it was that led you to remember that I am worth a hundred guineas to any that can take me.'

He was on the point of adding something more, but it occurred to him that invective was not likely to help him here, that never had he been in more desperate plight since once when the constables had actually fastened their talons on him. What saved him then was his presence of mind, his ready wit. And that was the only weapon that remained him now. He took their measure accurately. He saw that they would no more be loyal to each other than they had been to him did they perceive a course of profitable disloyalty. His first aim must be to separate them so that he might deal with each in turn. He threw back his head, and laughed – a thing so unexpected that it set them staring at him in alarm.

'Faith,' he said, 'the situation has its humour! I've been a fool, and I'm no such curmudgeon, after all, as not to know that a fool must blame only himself, and pay the reckoning.'

''Tis the proper spirit,' said Jake. And he proceeded diligently to empty the captain's pockets.

They yielded him another purse, a gold snuff-box with a jewelled crest, a watch, a couple of valuable rings, and, finally, a brace of barkers. He piled the plunder on the table, and Nathaniel fell to inspecting it, chuckling.

The captain watched them, his wits busy.

'Perhaps ye've chosen wisely,' said he presently. 'Ye make better thief-takers than tobymen. Ye'll turn king's evidence against me, thus save your dirty necks, and pocket the reward that Baldock covets. Ay, 'twas shrewdly thought.' He coughed. 'Gad, the dust is thick in my throat. Give me a drink.'

'The ale is done,' said Jake, who had his suspicions of the captain's amiable philosophy.

'Ay, plague on't,' growled Nathaniel, lifting the jar.

'True,' said Evans. 'I had forgot. But there's a bottle of brandy upstairs in my bedroom – in one of the drawers of my chest.'

Nathaniel's eyes glowed sombrely.

'Go fetch it, if ye will. Ye'll need to break the lock, maybe; for I cannot mind me where I left the key.'

Nathaniel departed without further persuasion. They heard him at work overhead, and the smash of woodwork told of the ardour of his search. Since, as a matter of fact, there was no such bottle as the captain suggested, that search was likely to be protracted.

The captain looked at Jake.

'Seize this chance,' he said softly. 'Set me free, and I'll pay you twice the sum the Crown is offering for me. More, Jake, I'll make your fortune ere all this is done.'

Jake scowled, displaying not the slightest sign of compliance. But then the captain had not expected any.

'And who's to warrant me that?' sneered the rogue at last, when he had overcome his surprise at the impudence of the proposal.

The captain nodded his head in the direction of the table.

'Why, there,' he exclaimed, 'you have a good two hundred guineas' worth at the least. 'Tis twice as much as the reward, and more easily earned. Sweep it into your pocket, man, and let us begone while that drunken fool is busy above stairs. Make haste, man! Cut me these cords!'

He watched the slow kindling of Jake's eye, the gradual loosening of his mouth, and he was satisfied that the rascally idea he had released was biting deep into the scoundrel's brain. Then followed precisely what the captain had expected. Jake moved furtively towards the table, his lips twitching, his whole countenance alert and somewhat scared. He swept the two purses and the rest of the plunder into his pockets. Then he took up the pistols and examined them. One was his own weapon, of which the captain had dispossessed them on their first encounter. It was loaded and primed, and so he dropped it also into his pocket. The other one was a barker that the captain had emptied that afternoon to scare the postilion of the gentleman he had robbed. It had not since been reloaded, and it may have been due to this that Jake laid it down again.

Then, without another word or so much as another glance at the prisoner, he stepped quickly and softly to the door.

Seeing this, the captain raised his voice in protest.

'Ye'll never leave me, Jake!' he cried, in simulated horror.

Jake leered at him over his shoulder in silence. Then he pulled the door open, passed out, and closed it gently after him.

The captain smiled to himself and waited. He heard Jake leading a horse into the open, while the fool above stairs continued his quest for the phantom bottle. In another moment hoofs went thudding down the lane, gathering speed as they receded. The captain laughed outright. So far things had sped excellently, and he was rid of one of his enemies. True, the thing had been achieved at considerable cost. But our tobyman was no niggard with the fruits of his ventures.

Minutes passed, then down the stairs, breathing noisily and swearing fluently, came Nathaniel.

'Skewer my innards,' said he, as he entered, 'I can't find no plaguey bottle.' Then he stopped short and looked about him. 'Jake!' he called. And then, 'Where's Jake?' he enquired.

'Gone,' said the captain.

'Gone!' echoed Nathaniel, uncomprehending. 'Gone where?' He rolled forward into the room.

'Why, to some stuling-ken, belike, to dispose of the plunder. He went off with it what time ye were rummaging for the brandy.' He laughed at the other's blank face. 'Ye're a confiding soul – nay, a durned confiding soul.'

Nathaniel rolled his eyes to the table, and saw its emptiness of all save the pistol.

'Ye don't mean that he's bubbled me!' he cried, on a whimpering note.

'What else?' wondered Captain Evans.

'That he's not coming back?' Nathaniel insisted, still disbelieving his senses.

'Oh, he may be coming back. But if I were you, I should pray that he may not, or at least I shouldn't stay for him.'

'What d'ye mean?'

'Gad!' said the captain. 'I vow ye're the flabbiest fool that ever cut a purse. What do I mean? Why, isn't it plain? If he comes back at all, he'll come back with Baldock, and take you together with myself, turning king's evidence against the pair of us, and thus making sure of the hundred guineas reward in addition to all the rest.'

It was a blow that winded Nathaniel. His face turned first purple, then pale. To express his amazement, his realization, and his poisonous rage, he swore with a most disgusting fluency. Then he paused.

'I'll not believe it!' he cried. 'He'll never be so dirty a tyke as that.'

'You've but to stay if you desire to ascertain precisely how far his villainy will go.'

'But, man—' Nathaniel checked. His eyes alighted on the pistol lying on the table. 'Nay, now. He'd never have left his barker if he meant such business as that.'

'The barker! Ha!' said the captain, with an odd inflection; and he added sharply, 'Look at it!'

Nathaniel snatched it up.

'Unloaded!' said he; and with that his last, lingering, hopeful doubt was dissipated.

Utter consternation invaded his soul, and overspread his face. To linger here now was to await certain capture, as the captain so shrewdly had warned him.

'Odds rot the plaguey thief!' he snarled. 'If ever I meet him ag'in, I'll—'

He stopped. He had no words in which to express the horrors he would perpetrate upon the person of his treacherous associate. Then, abruptly, he snatched up his ragged hat, pressed it upon his no less ragged head, and made for the door.

Now, this was not at all as the captain desired it. He did not himself believe for a moment that Jake would undertake any such desperate adventure as to fetch Baldock. He was convinced, in fact, that Jake would be perfectly and wisely satisfied with the result of his treachery to his comrade as it stood, and would avoid a risk in which he might well lose all, and find his way to the gallows in addition.

Nevertheless, he had no desire to be left pinioned there as he was. He had rid himself of one of his captors, and was about to rid himself of the other, and he flattered himself that he had contrived the thing with a rare thoroughness; but, before Nathaniel abandoned him, he must see to it that he was set at liberty.

'Hold!' he shouted. 'Are ye going to leave me here to fall into his hands?'

Nathaniel shrugged, and lifted the latch.

'Is this how you repay me for warning you? For you'll admit that but for my warning you 'ld never ha' smoked his full intentions. You'd ha' lain in Petersfield Gaol with me this night. And would ye desert me now?'

'Each for himself,' said Nathaniel callously, and opened the door.

Then the captain played his trump-card.

'Are ye going to put another hundred guineas in that weasel's dirty pockets?' he cried.

Nathaniel checked at that. He turned, his face grimly resolute.

'No, by gad! No, sink me!' he declared.

'Come, now, that is better. Besides, my friend, I can show you how to overtake him yet, and turn the tables on him.'

'How?' quoth Nathaniel, with fresh eagerness.

'How?' said the captain; and he smiled. 'Gad! There's not a drawer or ostler in an inn on all the Portsmouth Road but is my friend. They'll set me on his track, and when we've got him— But bestir, man; we'll talk of that as we go!'

Nathaniel produced a knife, and slashed away at the prisoner's bonds. Evans rose, and stretched himself, a little numb from the pressure of the cords upon his arms and legs. He straightened his disordered garments, and bent down to dust his breeches.

'Give me my wig, Nat,' he said, pointing to it where it lay in a corner of the room.

Nathaniel, unsuspecting, stooped to do his bidding, nor rose again. For, swift as a cat, the captain leapt upon him from behind, and bore him to the ground, wielding in his right hand the empty pistol which he had snatched up from the table.

Pinned there, prone, with the captain's knee in the small of his back, Nathaniel squealed like a stricken rabbit, what time the captain mocked him.

'You pig-faced foist!' he said. 'You to play the tobyman! You to rob in the grand manner! You to ruffle it on the pad! Odds my life, you dirty thieving dawcock, I hope this will cure you of all such vanity. And you thought you could hold Captain Evans – you! Bah!'

The captain tapped him sharply over the head with the butt of the empty pistol, and rose, leaving him stunned where he lay. Then he adjusted his wig, took up his hat and riding-crop, and left the cottage.

But in the lean-to an unpleasant surprise awaited him. The horses stabled there were the two screws upon which Nat and Jake had ridden. His own roan mare with the white blaze was gone, and he realized that it was Jake who had taken her. In an exceeding ill-humour, and breathing redoubled vengeance now that his chances of overtaking Jake to effect it were considerably diminished, the captain rode off on the better of those two sorry nags.

He made straight for Liphook and the Lame Dog, hoping there to pick up news that should set him on the track of the renegade. The news he found was of another kind.

'It is well for you, captain, that ye didn't come a half-hour ago,' was the greeting he received from Tom, the drawer.

And thereupon the fellow told his tale:

'There was a gentleman here who swore he had been robbed this very afternoon twixt this and Petersfield. With him was Baldock, the thief-taker, who swore 'twas yourself had robbed the gentleman, and likewise swore to lay you by the heels. And then, whilst they were in the taproom, up rides a down-at-heel scarecrow of a fellow on your own roan mare, captain. The gentleman who had been robbed was sitting by the window, and no sooner does his eye light on this traveller than up he jumps in a great heat, swearing that this was the man who had robbed him.

'"Are ye sure?" cried Baldock, all of a shake in his eagerness.

'"Certain sure," says the gentleman. "I couldn't be mistook; though the rascal's face was masked there was no mask on the nag, and I 'ld recognize that white blaze anywhere."

'That was enough for Baldock. He whistled, and in the twinkling of an eye they had that scarecrow off the mare, and they was going through his pockets. And there, sure enough, it seems, they found some rings and other things of which the gentleman had been robbed this very day.

'The rogue swore that he was not Captain Evans. He told a wild tale of how he had come by those trinkets. He protested that he had himself captured Captain Evans, and that he had him bound fast in a place to which he offered to lead Baldock. But the Bow Street runner laughed at him.

'"Ye've bubbled me afore, Captain Evans," says he, "and I'll be blistered if ye bubble me again! I have ye safe this time." And they carried the poor devil off to London.'

The captain's laughter pealed forth.

'I was sorry for the poor rogue,' said the drawer, 'and I might ha' helped him. But, o' course, it weren't for me to be doing that at your expense, captain.'

'Small need for sorrow on his account, Tom,' the captain assured him. 'The rogue is well served for his impudence in setting up for a ruffler of the pad. The high toby is a place for gentlemen, egad, and he was no better than a poacher. What of the mare, Tom?'

'They took her along.'

The captain sighed.

'I've paid dear for my folly. Still, when all is said— Bah! Give me a pint of claret, Tom, and lace it well with brandy. I am somewhat shaken by this adventure.'

THE SENTIMENTALIST

Captain Evans – to give him the rank he had assumed for decorative purposes and without having any real claim to it – rode out of Godalming alone and early one fragrant summer morning, leaving his younger brother, Will – in conjunction with whom he was in the habit of 'working', as the term was, the Portsmouth Road – snugly abed at the Black Boar Inn. He was bound for Petersfield, or, rather, for the Fox and Hounds, which invites custom a mile or so to the north of that prosperous little township, and he rode in answer to an urgent message from Tim, the ostler, whom he subsidized to keep him informed of such movements upon the road as it imported him to know in the way of business. Tim had bidden him to be at the Fox and Hounds not later than noon, intimating that he would then have an important communication for our captain. But the captain, having risen early, found himself breasting the slopes in the neighbourhood of Thursley by nine o'clock – as recorded by a watch which a week ago had been the property of the Bishop of Salisbury, and which could not, therefore, be suspected of inaccuracy.

It followed that the captain had an hour or so to spare over and above the necessary time in which to complete the journey without undue exertion, and no sooner had he realized this than he caught sight of a yellow chaise coming into view on the brow of the hill above him. A man of quick decision – which, after all, is the first essential of success in his difficult calling – the captain swung his mare to the right, and vanished down a narrow lane that opportunely offered itself. Fifty yards down this lane he halted, swung aside again, and, putting the roan at a low fence on his left, landed in a meadow. He rode gently back towards the road, took up a position behind a clump of trees, and waited, vigilant and invisible.

The carriage came lumbering down the hill, a two-horse post-chaise, yellow as a buttercup in the morning sun, betraying nothing of its contents. More pressed for time, the captain might have allowed the hired vehicle to go unmolested. It was not his way in these days to take risks where he was not sure of profit; but with an hour or so on his hands, and the very freshness of the morning stimulating his young blood to high adventure, he resolved to investigate at closer quarters.

Back he went by the way he had come, and along the lane out into the open road, there to turn and trot in the wake of the coach, which was heading for Godalming. At a pace that, without being hot enough to alarm the travellers, yet steadily lessened the distance between himself and the chaise, Captain Evans drew alongside. It was his intent – and in accordance with his usual practice – first to reconnoitre, and then, if satisfied, to ride ahead and turn to deliver the attack.

He was the last man to shirk a hazard, but he had long since realized that for success on the high-toby, as on the field of battle, prudence and the elimination of the unnecessary risk is as essential as courage. He had, you see, an orderly mind even in disorderliness, probably resulting from the fact – to be read in Mr Whitehead's 'Life' of him – that he had been bred up for the law by his father, a prosperous Welsh farmer. For the rest, he had found the law more amusing in the breach than in the practice, and the open road more attractive than a musty attorney's office.

He drew, then, alongside of the coach, and looked boldly in, as any other traveller might have done. Nor was there anything of the ruffian in his appearance to alarm those who might come under his inspection. He was dressed with sedate elegance in a riding-suit of grey, with silver lace, and the lustrous brown hair under his three-cornered hat was neatly clubbed.

To his vexation, he found that the curtains of the chaise were drawn, which would make his projected adventure more of a leap in the dark than ever. But even as he looked one of the curtains was whipped aside, and straining through the window came the head and shoulders of as delicious a piece of young womanhood as ever the captain – something of a dilettante in these matters – had contemplated with satisfaction. She seemed a part of that sweet, fragrant summer morning; at least, she found in it a very proper setting. Her complexion, now somewhat pale, was as delicate as a dog-rose; her eyes, which were very wide, were as blue as the flawless sky overhead; her hair was an aureole of sunbeams; and, to complete the lovely appeal of her, from parted lips came a cry for assistance. On her shoulder he observed, in his swift, comprehensive glance, a man's lean brown hand endeavouring to force her back into the chaise.

'Help!' she cried to him. 'Help! Oh, sir, deliver me!'

'Deliver you?' says the captain, taken aback. 'To be sure I will.' And then he added, 'I am the very angel of deliverance, so I am!' which was neat and quick of him, although the humour of it must of necessity escape her.

Another moment – time to pluck a barker from his holster – and he was roaring 'Stand!' in his grandest manner to the postboy.

The chaise rattled and creaked to a standstill, and the captain swung down from the saddle and threw open the door with an air. Here was romance, and it was for him to play his part in it. Out of the chaise came a fiery buck, in fine clothes and a mighty temper, using language that left no doubt that he must be either a great gentleman or a pickpocket. Considering a certain raffishness that hung about him and the deep-bitten lines in his face, which advertised an age beyond the first seeming, the captain placed him without hesitation outside the former class, and came promptly to the conclusion that he could have no business on so fine a morning in a chaise with that gracious little lady.

The froth of foulness being blown off, we come to the ale of his opening interjection.

'Who the devil are you, sir, and what the devil d'ye mean interfering between a gentleman and his wife?'

'I'm not his wife, sir!' cried the lady. 'Don't believe him.'

'I shouldn't dream of doing so, indeed,' says Captain Evans. 'Be good enough to honour me with your commands, ma'am, and depend upon their instant execution. I take it you want to be rid of this gentleman's company?'

'I do, sir – I do!' she cried, hands pressed fervently together in appeal to this potential rescuer, and fear in her glance.

'You hear the lady and you see,' said the captain. 'I hope you'll not stop to argue.'

The buck swore most unbecomingly through his teeth, threatened to do horrible things to this intruder, but kept his fierce eyes on the gleaming barrel of the captain's pistol.

'Sink me now!' he ended. 'D'ye make yourself this lady's champion?'

'It's a fine morning for knight-errantry, whatever.'

'Knight-errantry, d'ye say? Faugh! Look now! I don't know who the devil you may be, but since you come so cursedly interfering—' He broke off and glared at the captain. 'Now, why the devil should I be taking you into our confidence?' he wondered savagely.

'To save the lady the trouble,' suggested the captain.

'Knight-errantry!' sneered the buck again; and then a gleam of inspiration came into his bold eyes. 'You play knight-errant with a pistol! Faugh!'

'I'll play it with anything you please.'

The morning sun and the little lady had between them got into the captain's blood, so that business was quite forgotten.

'Will you? Will you take a turn with me as one gentleman with another, so that we may settle this matter of your unwarranted intrusion in my affairs?'

'You mistake,' said the captain. 'It's the lady's affairs I'm intruding in, and not unwarranted, but by her invitation, whatever.'

The gentleman sneered.

'You are splitting straws.'

'Shall I be splitting your windpipe?' says Evans, without heat.

'Let us to it, then,' says the gentleman.

'With all my heart.'

Thereupon the gentleman peeled off his laced coat and put it across the window, so that it hung half on one side, half on the other, of the open chaise door. The captain observed that it was a mighty fine coat, and wondered from force of professional habit what the pockets might contain.

Then the buck lugged out his small sword and stood waiting. The captain's preparations were less elaborate. He restored his pistol to its holster and came forward sword in hand. The little lady, standing now in the door of the chaise, with fluttering bosom and eyes in which fear was deepening into terror, cried out at this.

'Oh, sir, oh, sir, why do you consent?'

'I am wondering myself, ma'am.'

'Get your pistol again, sir. He will surely kill you. He is a dreadful – dreadful man.'

'The last one I killed was much dreadfuller – yes, indeed,' said the captain. He lied in this for the sheer humour of it, for in all his wild career he had never yet made himself guilty of taking life. With that he made a leg very prettily. 'Are you ready, sir? Then on guard, if you please.'

The buck flashed the lady a malicious glance – a glance which said as plainly as words, 'I'll deal with you presently, my girl, and you shall pay for having brought this upon me' – and so fell on guard.

In his readiness to fight, the captain found confirmation of his first judgement of the fellow as an adventurer embarking upon a shady enterprise. A gentleman sure of himself and his position would have taken any way but this to settle such a matter as the present one. Further, this same readiness to fight argued a confidence in himself based, no doubt, upon skill and experience. Now, the captain was no less confident of his own powers, being himself a considerable man of his hands; but he realized at once that, unless this affair were to have in one way or the other an issue more serious than he could desire, he must end it almost before it were begun.

It was a trick that had done him good service aforetime, and it did not fail him now. Scarcely had the blades touched each other in the first engagement than the captain dropped his point, whirled it under and round his opponent's hand, and then straightened his arm. It was all done in one movement with the speed of lightning, and at the end of it – almost before the fine gentleman realized that a disengage had taken place – there was a foot or so of the captain's blade well home in his sword-arm.

The fellow uttered a howl of pain and rage, and the sword dropped from his nerveless hand. Captain Evans wiped his steel with a dainty lace kerchief, then sheathed it, and tossed the handkerchief away with an air. Then he addressed his adversary, who was swearing and groaning and clamouring for help to staunch his wound, all in one.

'I think, sir, you're lusty enough to help yourself,' said he.

Thereupon our gallant, evidently in mortal terror lest he should bleed to death, pulls a handkerchief from the breast of his shirt, and, holding one corner of it in his teeth and the other in his left hand, sets about putting a bandage about his arm, going down on one knee by the side of the ditch for greater ease in doing so.

'Ma'am,' said the captain, 'there's a scoundrel disposed of, and you may continue your journey in peace. To ensure it I'll escort you some part of the way, if you'll suffer me.'

'Oh, sir!' said she consentingly, whereupon the captain slammed the door of the chaise, swung himself up into the saddle again, and ordered the postboy to proceed.

But at the first crack of the whip up jumped the wounded buck, suddenly realizing what was taking place. In expectation of this, the captain had pulled his mare squarely across the road to bar the other's way.

'My coat!' screams the other in a frenzy. 'My coat, sir, if you please!'

Now, it seemed to Captain Evans, as it must seem to you, more than ordinarily singular that a gentleman in the buck's position, a gentleman who apparently had lost so much that morning, should be so supremely concerned with the trifling loss of a coat. So impressed, indeed, was the captain that when miss would have thrown the gentleman his garment he interposed, and bade her retain it as a keepsake.

'You're a deal too hot,' he informed the buck. 'You'll be the better for a cooling.'

And with that rode off in the wake of the chaise, leaving our fine gentleman in shirt and breeches, the incarnation of dismay and rage.

88

A mile or so they may have ridden, miss ever and anon putting her head from the window to cast a remark at her escort, and her escort doing his best to answer her becomingly, when at last she gave the order to halt.

'Sir,' she said, 'could you not tether your horse behind and ride with me? I feel that I owe you explanations.'

'Madame,' quoth he, very gallantly, 'I could no more be guilty of forcing a lady's confidence than of refusing so charming an invitation.'

And he proceeded to do as she suggested.

'You'll think that I have behaved very oddly, sir, in claiming your assistance,' she began, as soon as he was settled at her side.

'Since dealing with the object of your trouble, ma'am, I think the behaviour very natural. What I don't understand is how you came to be running off with that fellow – for that, I suppose, was the situation.'

Round eyes looked at him in enquiry, and also in surprise at his penetration.

'He called himself your husband, ma'am,' the captain explained, 'which I took to be an anticipation of his hopes.'

'Oh, sir, I must tell you everything, and cast myself upon your mercy. Perhaps you will then direct me how to act.'

With that she told her story – told it with downcast eyes and troubled countenance, her hands listlessly folded in her lap. The gentleman's name was Lake – Mr Julian Lake he called himself – and, met by chance at Ranelagh in the first instance, he had followed her down into the country to Petersfield, where she dwelt with her guardian, Sir Henry Woodbridge. He had come into her life in a moment of crisis. A young gentleman – whose name she left out of her story – to whom she was promised in marriage, and to whom she was deeply attached, had run off with a lady whose identity she also refrained from disclosing. And then Mr Lake had swooped down upon her, an impetuous whirlwind of a lover, with an air of the great world about him to dazzle her, and, as women will in her case, she had snatched at this chance of showing her false lover how little she was troubled by his defection. With her consent, Mr Lake had written to her guardian; and her guardian, for reasons which he had omitted to disclose to her, had replied, refusing to receive the fellow or countenance his suit. Thereupon Mr Lake had proposed the elopement, and in despair she had consented.

They had set out from Petersfield soon after dawn that day. Mr Lake had made arrangements for their marriage at Guildford. But with every mile that they rode together the sense of what she was doing, and the fear of it, increased in the heart of Miss Helston, until in the end, being fully if tardily awake to the folly of entrusting her life to a man of whom, after all, she knew nothing, and for whom she felt no more than a simulated affection, having its roots in pique, she frankly told him so, and begged him to order the chaise to be put about, and either to conduct her or send her back to her guardian. It was then that Mr Lake revealed himself for the adventurer that he really was. Miss Helston was – or would be presently, on attaining full age, to which she was very near – a lady of very considerable wealth, and so you conceive the rage and chagrin begotten in the heart of our gentleman, who had been congratulating himself upon the snug acquisition of her fortune. His conduct had been abominable. He had allowed her to perceive that he would stop at no violence short of murder to compel her to carry out her undertaking to marry him, and but for the captain's very timely arrival on the scene, Miss Heston trembled to think what might have become of her.

It was a very moving tale, and Captain Evans, who was a little prone to sentiment, was deeply touched. Then he grew practical.

'And what's to be done now?' quoth he.

Miss looked at him with those melting, questioning eyes of hers. They had clattered through Godalming while her tale was a-telling, and were holding amain on the road to Guildford, the unreflecting postboy intent upon carrying out his original instructions, without regard to the change of passengers that had taken place.

'What – what do you advise?' she asked pathetically.

'Why, that you carry out your earlier intention of returning to Petersfield and your guardian. What else can you do, whatever? – unless you have friends with whom you would prefer to stay awhile until you can make your peace with Sir Henry.'

'No, no!' she said. 'I'll go back to him. I'll go back to Petersfield.'

Greatly relieved, the captain gave the necessary order. The chaise went about, and set out to return in its tracks. And then the captain bethought him of that important engagement of his for noon that day with the ostler of the Fox and Hounds at Petersfield – an engagement blown out of his mind by the events, and no longer to be kept with any degree of punctuality. It was striking one as they clattered for the second time over the cobbled streets of Godalming.

'I – I am very hungry' says miss pathetically. It was not a cry to which a man of heart could close his ears. 'I haven't tasted food today,' she added. And at that he called himself a brute, and awoke to the fact that his own appetite was keen enough.

They drew up, by his order, at the Swan – a house at which he was unknown – and in a private room which he commanded above-stairs they sat down a half-hour later to the best dinner the house could provide and a bottle of the landlord's best Burgundy. Having drunk a generous share of it, Captain Evans came to account the time well lost, and the business appointment at Petersfield a matter of small consequence compared with the sweet delight of protecting and ministering to this choice, helpless wisp of womanhood. That satisfaction with things as they were was soon to increase to thankfulness, and he was to see in all that had happened the hand of Providence befriending him. It was the chamberlain of the inn who came presently to enlighten him.

'I hear, sir,' he said, in the course of his ministrations, 'that the Portsmouth Road will be safer for travellers after today. That pest of the highway, Captain Evans, is likely to be laid by the heels before night.'

'And is that so?' says the captain, with sharp interest. 'Now, that's mighty good hearing – yes, indeed.'

'You're right, sir. A gentleman just arrived from Petersfield tells me that the sheriff and his men had spread a net for the rascal, in which he must have been taken before this.'

The captain poured himself the remainder of the wine with a steady hand.

'Yet what all the world knows Captain Evans himself may discover,' said he.

'Too late for that, sir. He'll be took by now,' said the chamberlain with confidence as he withdrew.

The captain raised his glass to pledge the lady who all unconsciously had been the means of saving him from what he now surmised to be a bait trapped for him by that scoundrel Tim. Aloud, he toasted her safe return, a toast to which she responded almost gaily.

Her spirits, too, had improved under the invigorating influence of meat and wine, and the dark cloud that had hung over her since morning began at last to lift. She took an optimistic view of the future, and envisaged a return to Sir Henry's house without any serious misgivings. When he knew all he would forgive the escapade. What troubled her far more at the moment, she confessed, was how adequately to return thanks to her preserver.

'You have been to me the best friend that ever I had,' she told him, 'for you came to me in the hour of my greatest need, and never hesitated to afford me your assistance.'

He looked into the dainty face, with its so delicate complexion and eyes of blue, over which the lids were shyly and alluringly fluttering, and heaved a sigh.

'I am thinking we have been good friends to each other,' said he. 'It will be something for me to remember afterwards.'

'Afterwards?' says Miss.

'To be sure, afterwards – when you and I have gone our separate ways again, having each of the other just the memory of this day.'

'It will be a very grateful memory to me,' said she; and he saw the faintest cloud gathering again about her eyes.

'And a sweet one to me,' said he, and sighed again.

Now, it may have been that sigh of his that touched her, or the Burgundy that had emboldened her, or both working conjointly.

'We shall meet again, of course,' says she. 'We – we should be friends after what has happened – after the way in which you have befriended me.' And she looked at him with such ravishing candour for a moment that he was put out of breath and out of countenance.

'You – you make too much of the little service I have done you,' said he, faltering.

She frowned, and as her eyes were lowered he observed a sudden deepening of the colour in her cheeks, and realized how ungracious his words must have sounded. She pushed back her chair and rose.

'Miss Helston,' he exclaimed, 'you must not misunderstand. I—'

'I do not, sir. Your honest sincerity is very charming to me after what I have suffered at the hands of your sex. I could not fail to appreciate it deeply.'

But the sarcasm in the words cut him sharply, the more sharply because he must suffer it in silence. What was there he could say?

She crossed to the window and looked out upon the sunlit inn-yard. A coach came clattering into it at that moment.

'Shall we be resuming our journey, sir?' said she. 'We have some way to ride – that is, if I may still count upon the honour of the escort.'

He got to his feet.

'Now, why do you say that to me?' he growled, half resentfully, 'Can't you see that I would—'

Her sharp outcry interrupted him. She swung to him, showing a white, scared face: her bosom raced.

'Sir Henry – my guardian!' she cried. 'He is here! He saw me! And there are people with him!'

Captain Evans received the news with positive relief. It would make an end to a situation that was beginning to occasion him some anxiety.

'In that case, ma'am, your troubles will be at an end.'

'Will they?' She looked at him, and then the door opened, and from the threshold a tall, lean, sardonic gentleman stood regarding them with a smile that was not quite pleasant.

Captain Evans blenched. But it was not the sardonic countenance of Sir Henry that occasioned his disorder; it was another face perceived over Sir Henry's shoulder, the round, jolly face of Sir Thomas Blount, the sheriff of the county; nor did he pause to think under the moment's shock that his own face could not be as well known to Sir Thomas as was Sir Thomas's to him. He saw that behind the sheriff there were several men, and he accounted himself lost. Somehow they had trapped him when he failed to walk into the trap at Petersfield. Perhaps they had come upon Mr Lake, and he had assisted them with information. With his glance he measured the distance to the window, mentally calculated its height from the ground, and strove to imagine what might await him in the inn-yard should he take the desperate decision to go that way. Meanwhile the drawling voice of Sir Henry Woodbridge – a voice that sorted excellently with the gentleman's sardonic countenance – was speaking.

'It would appear, then, that we arrive in time. I say it would appear so. And for your sake, Mr Lake, I sincerely trust that appearances do not deceive me, otherwise it will be for my friend Sir Thomas Blount to deal with you.'

He sauntered forward. The more corpulent sheriff rolled after him.

'Egad, yes, my buck,' gurgled the latter. 'Ye're caught red-handed in the hideous act of abduction. I've heard of you. I know something of your affairs, Mr Lake, and if you've had the services of a parson with this lady I promise you it shall go hard with you.'

Then forth trilled Miss Helston's laugh, and there was no mistaking its naturalness and freedom from anxiety.

'Why, Sir Henry,' she addressed her guardian, 'this is not Mr Lake—'

'Of course not,' sneered Sir Henry the sardonic, and from that Captain Evans, whose courage had revived upon discovering that he was not himself the object of the sheriff's pursuit, very promptly took his course.

'My dear,' he said, on a note of romantic sorrow, 'what purpose can it serve to deny my identity?'

'But—' she began, and there she checked. Something compelling in her preserver's glance interrupted her, and imposed – almost seemed to beg – silent acquiescence. And meanwhile there was Sir Henry sneering.

'No purpose at all, sir. You very foolishly left the gentleman's letter behind you, Mary. It only remains for you to tell me whether you are yet married, whether this' – and he waved a slender hand towards the table from which they had risen – 'was the wedding feast which we so inconsiderately interrupt?'

'We are not, sir,' said the captain, and, remembering what she had told him, added, 'We were to have been married at Guildford.'

'I remember that you mentioned it in your letter, Mr Lake. I am relieved by the tense you employ. It is very well for you, sir, that you can place it in the subjunctive and conditional perfect. My dear—' He crooked his arm, and proffered it to his ward, with something between mockery and command. Then, melting a little from his sarcastic haughtiness, 'Come, child,' he added, 'you shall yet come to thank me for saving you in time from this broken gamester.'

'Ay, ay; but are ye sure that you can take his word for't?' broke in the bustling little sheriff. 'I've been bubbled once today, when I should have been able to put my hand on that rascal Evans—'

'I am sure that I can take hers,' Sir Henry interrupted. He stood squarely before his errant ward, and looked into her pale face with its troubled eyes, that were now aswim with tears. 'Tell me, Mary – in a word, yes or no – are you married to him?'

'No,' she faltered. 'I am not.'

'That is enough, then. Let us be going.'

'Faith, it may be enough for you, Sir Henry,' quoth the officious Blount, 'but it is not enough for me. Abduction is a serious crime, Mr Lake, as you shall learn. Fetch him along, my lads,' he bade his men. 'We'll lodge him snugly in Guildford Gaol for tonight. He's a poor substitute for Captain Evans, but we'll take him along.'

At that she flung away from her guardian's arm, and came running to her preserver, fear, misery, and bewilderment all blending in the appealing eyes lifted to him.

'Oh, why—' she was beginning, when again he checked her.

'Believe me, my dear, Sir Thomas knows his business. Protests would never avail to turn him aside from it. He is, as you observe, a very conscientious and perspicacious gentleman. Pray let him have his way without waste of words. Good-bye!'

He bore her hand to his lips, and felt it tremble almost convulsively in his grasp. More than his actual words, his glance, so pregnant with a meaning that she could not read, commanded her silence, and – whatever else might baffle her – made her realize that this was the course which he desired that things should take.

And so they parted, she to return to Petersfield in her guardian's coach, he to be haled away a prisoner in a hired chaise to Guildford. Until they had left Godalming behind them, it had been his dread lest Sir Thomas should summon and question the postboy who had driven him that morning. Fortunately, the bustling sheriff neglected that detail as of no account, never conceiving that the postboy's story could do other than confirm the matter which the runaways themselves did not attempt to deny.

Captain Evans spent the night in Guildford Gaol, wondering where exactly his knight-errantry would land him. He was visited on the following morning by the sheriff. Sir Thomas was not in the best of humours.

'You are in luck, Mr Lake,' he said sourly.

'I've not yet perceived it,' said the captain.

'But you will. I cannot proceed against you unless Sir Henry Woodbridge prosecutes, and Sir Henry declines to do so.'

The captain sighed relief.

'That's vastly kind of him.'

'Kind! He doesn't do it to be kind to you, sir. He declines to prosecute because he realizes that to do so would be to blow upon the fair fame of his ward, Miss Helston. Out of consideration for the lady he must forgo demanding upon you the punishment you deserve. It was a fortunate thing for you, my lad, that he overtook you in time to prevent the marriage. If he had found her your wife, I believe she would have been your widow by now. Sir Henry can be mighty hot, for all his cool ways. Remember that, sir, and let it serve as a warning to you in the future. And now be off. I've work to do. I've to be on the heels of that damned tobyman Evans, who gave me the slip yesterday, and you're partly to blame for that.'

'Oh, Sir Thomas!' cried the captain, and his tone was pained. 'I swear you do me an injustice there. It's no fault of mine if you didn't gaol your highwayman.'

'It will be if you keep me talking here,' snapped Sir Thomas, and on that departed.

Captain Evans went off in a hired chaise to Godalming once more, and there sought his brother Will at the Black Boar. His arrival startled Will out of the deep dejection into which he had sunk, and he came to his feet with an oath at sight of his brother.

'How did you escape?' he cried.

'Escape?' echoed the captain. It was impossible that Will should have knowledge of his adventure. 'Escape what?'

'The trap that was laid for you at Petersfield.'

'Trap! Was it a trap?'

'Of course it was. That scoundrel Tim had sold you to the sheriff, and his men were waiting for you until night at the Fox and Hounds. Indeed, for all I know, they may be waiting for you still. Gadslife, Tom, I'd forsaken all hope of ever seeing you again. Where have you been?'

'With the sheriff,' says the captain.

'With the sheriff?'

'Ay – Sir Thomas Blount. I slept at Guildford Gaol, and parted from him there two hours ago. Let me explain.'

'I confess it's necessary.'

The captain told his story. 'So that, you see,' he ended, 'what time the sheriff and his men were waiting to take me, there was I safely hidden in the sheriff's own hands. Humorous, wasn't it?'

But Will was blind to the humour of it. He looked reproachfully at his brother.

'I suppose this ninny of a runaway girl beglamoured you, till you nearly lost your neck in the business.'

''Pon my soul, Will, that's ungracious, seeing that she saved me.'

'Saved you? Pshaw! If you hadn't allowed her to get you into danger there would have been no need for her to have saved you. You're an incorrigible sentimentalist.'

'I admit it. But it's been the salvation of me this time. And you're not to suppose that I neglected business completely. You'll remember that I came off with Mr Lake's coat.'

'Oh, Lake's coat!' sneered Will.

The captain dropped a bag of soft leather on the table. It squelched down with a melodious chink.

'There's fifty guineas in that; it was in one of his pockets. And here's a snuff-box – a pretty thing of gold and brilliants worth at least half as much. I thought I'd like it as a keepsake. Perhaps I am a sentimentalist.'

Will was mollified.

'But you've nothing of the girl's,' he complained.

'Nothing – tangible,' said the captain, and sighed. 'After all, you're no doubt right. I am an incorrigible sentimentalist. I must be.' And he sighed again.

DUROC

Duroc came down the Rue de la Harpe so stealthily that his steps scarcely made a sound. He moved like a shadow, and when at last he came to a halt before the house of the Citizen Representative Clairvaux it was as if he had totally effaced himself, as if he had become part of the general gloom.

There he paused considering, his chin in his hand; and perhaps because the ground-floor windows were equipped with bars, he moved on more stealthily than ever along the garden wall. Midway between two of the lanterns slung across the narrow street and shedding a feeble yellow light he paused again.

He stood now at a point where the shadows were deepest. He listened intently for a moment, peered this way and that into the night, and then went over the wall with the swift silent activity of an ape. He found the summit of that wall guarded by a row of iron spikes, and on one of these, for all his care, Duroc left a strip of his breeches.

The accident annoyed him. He cursed all *chevaux de frise*, pronouncing them a damnably aristocratic institution to which no true patriot could be guilty of having recourse. Indeed from the manner in which the Citizen Representative Clairvaux guarded his house it was plain to Duroc that the fellow was a bad republican. What with bars on its windows and spikes on its walls, the place might have been a prison rather than the house of a representative of the august people. Of course, as Duroc well knew, the Citizen Representative had something to guard. It was notorious that this modest dwelling of his in the Rue de la Harpe was something of a treasure-house, stored with the lootings of many a *ci-devant* nobleman's property, and it was being whispered that no true patriot – and a Citizen Representative into the bargain – could have suffered himself to amass such wealth in the hour of the nation's urgent need.

Duroc advanced furtively across the garden, scanning the silent, sleeping house. Emboldened by the fact that no light or faintest sign of vigilance showed anywhere, he proceeded so adroitly that within five minutes he had opened a window and entered a room that was used by the deputy as his study.

Within that room he stood quite still, and listened. Save for the muffled ticking of a clock no sound disturbed the silence. He turned and very softly drew the heavy curtains across the window. Then he sat down upon the floor, took a small lantern from his breast and a tinder-box from his waistcoat pocket. There was the sharp stroke of steel on flint, and presently his little lantern was shedding a yellow disc of light upon the parquetry floor.

He rose softly, placed the light on a console, and crossed the room to the door which stood half open. He listened again a moment then closed the door and came back, his feet making no sound upon the thick and costly rugs that were flung here and there.

In mid-chamber he paused, looking about him, and taking stock of his luxurious surroundings. He considered the painted panels, the inlaid woods, the gilded chairs and the ormolu-encrusted cabinets – all plundered from the hotels of *ci-devants* who were either guillotined or in flight, and he asked himself if it was in this sybaritic fashion that it became a true republican to equip his home.

He was a short, slender man, this Duroc, whose shabby brown garments looked the worse for the rent in his breeches. He wore a fur bonnet, and his lank black hair hung in wisps about his cheeks and neck. His face was white and wolfish, the jaw thrust forward and ending in a lean square chin; his vigilant quick-moving eyes were close-set and beady as a rat's; his thin lips were curled now in a sneer as he considered the luxury about him.

But that attitude of his was momentary. Duroc had not come there to make philosophy but to accomplish a purpose, and to this he addressed himself forthwith. He took up his lantern, and crossed to a tall secretaire that was a very gem of the court-finisher's art in the days of Louis XIV. Setting the lantern on top of it, he drew from his pocket a bunch of skeleton keys, gripping them firmly so that they should not rattle. He stooped to examine the lock, and then on the instant came upright again, stiff and tense in his sudden alarm.

A knock had fallen upon the street door, and the echo of it went reverberating through the silent house.

Duroc's lips writhed as he breathed an oath.

The knock was repeated, more insistent now. To the listening Duroc came the sound of a window being thrown up. He heard voices, one from above, the other replying from the street, and guessed that the awakened Clairvaux was challenging this midnight visitor before coming down to open.

Perhaps he would not come. Perhaps he would dismiss this inopportune intruder. But that hope was soon quenched. The window rasped down again, and a moment later the flip-flop of slippered feet came shuffling down the stairs and along the passage to the door. A key grated and a chain clanked – this Clairvaux made a Bastille of his dwelling – and then voices sounded in the passage. The door of the house closed with a soft thud. Steps and voices approached the room in which Duroc still stood immoveable, listening.

At last he stirred, realizing that he had not a moment to spare if he would escape detection. He turned, so that his back was to the door, snatched up his lantern and pressed it against his breast, so that while it might still light him forward, its rays should not strike backwards to betray him. Then in three strides he gained the shelter of the heavy velvet curtains that masked the window. Behind them, his back to the casement, he extinguished at last the light.

The door opened an instant later. Indeed had Clairvaux who entered, candle in hand, in nightcap and quilted dressing-gown, bestowed an attentive look upon the curtains he would have detected the quiver that still agitated them. After him came a tall young man in a long black riding-coat and a conical hat that was decorated by a round tricolour cockade to advertise his patriotic sentiments. Under his arm he carried a riding-whip, whose formidable quality as a weapon of offence was proclaimed by its round head in plaited leather with silver embellishments. He placed it upon a table beside his hat, and the thud with which it dropped to the wood further announced its quality.

The Citizen Representative, a short, stiffly built man whose aquiline face was not without some resemblance to that of his visitor, flung himself into a gilt armchair upholstered in blue silk near the secretaire that but a moment ago had been the object of Duroc's attention. He threw one knee over the other and drew his quilted dressing-gown about his legs.

'Well?' he demanded, his voice harsh. 'What is this important communication that brings you here at such an hour as this?'

The man in the riding-coat sauntered across to the fireplace. He set his back to the overmantle, and the ormolu clock with its cupids by Debureau, and faced the deputy with a smile that was almost a sneer.

'Confess now,' he said, 'that but for your uneasy conscience, my cousin, you would have hesitated to admit me. But you live in the dread of your own misdeeds, with the blade of the guillotine like a sword of Damocles suspended above you, and you dare refuse no man – however unwelcome in himself – who may be the possible bearer of a warning.' He laughed an irritating laugh of mockery.

'Name of a name,' growled the deputy, 'will you tell me what brings you, without preamble?'

'You do not like preambles? And a representative! Now that is odd! But there, Etienne, to put it shortly, I am thinking of emigrating.'

It was the deputy's turn to become mocking.

'It was worth while being aroused at midnight to hear such excellent news. Emigrate by all means, my dear Gustave. France will be well rid of you.'

'And you?' quoth Gustave.

'And I no less.' The deputy grinned sardonically.

'Ah!' said his cousin. 'That is excellent. In such a case, no doubt, you will be disposed to pay for the privilege. To carry out this plan of mine I need your assistance, Etienne. I am practically penniless.'

'Now that is a thousand pities.' The deputy's voice became almost sympathetic, yet slurred by a certain note of sarcasm. 'If you are penniless, so am I. What else did you expect in a member of the National Convention? Did you conceive that a representative of the sacred people – an apostle of Liberty, Equality, and Fraternity – could possibly have money at his disposal? Ah, my good cousin, I assure you that all that I possessed has been offered up on the sacred altar of the nation.'

Gustave looked at him, and pursed his lips. 'You had better reserve that for the National Assembly,' he said. 'It may sound convincing from the rostrum. Here—' he waved a hand about him at all the assembled splendours, 'it sounds uncommonly like a barefaced lie.'

The deputy rose with overwhelming dignity, his brows contracted.

'This to me?' he demanded.

'Why not?' wondered Gustave. 'Come, come, Etienne. I am not a child, nor yet a fool. You are a man of wealth – all the world knows it, as you may discover to your cost one fine morning. These are days of fraternity, and I am your cousin—'

'Out of my house,' the deputy broke in angrily. 'Out of my house this instant.'

Gustave looked at him with calm eyes. 'Shall I then go and tell the National Assembly what I know of you? Must I denounce you to the Committee of Public Safety as a danger to the nation? Must I tell them that in secret you are acting as an agent of the émigrés, that you plot the overthrow of the august republic?'

Clairvaux's face was livid, his eyes were bulging. He mastered himself by an effort. 'Denounce all you please,' he answered in a suffocating voice. 'You'll leave your own head in the basket. Sainte Guillotine! you fool, am I a man of straw to be overthrown by the denunciations of such a thing as you? Do you think to frighten me with threats of what you will do? Do you think that is the way to obtain assistance from me?'

'Seeing that no other way is possible,' flashed Gustave.

'Out of my house. Go, denounce me! Go to the devil! But out of here with you!'

'Take care, Etienne!' The other was breathing hard, and his eyes flamed with anger – the anger of the baffled man. 'I am desperate, I am face to face with ruin. I need but a thousand francs—'

'Not a thousand sous, not a single sou from me. Be off!' And Clairvaux advanced threateningly upon his cousin. 'Be off!' He caught him by the lapels of his riding-coat.

'Don't dare to touch me!' Gustave warned him, his voice shrilling suddenly.

But the deputy, thoroughly enraged by now, tightened his grip, and began to thrust the other towards the door. Gustave put out a hand to the table where his hat and whip were lying, and his fingers closed upon that ugly riding-crop of his. The rest had happened almost before he realized it; it was the blind action of suddenly overwhelming fury. He twisted out of his cousin's grasp, stepped back, holding that life-preserver by its slender extremity, swung it aloft and brought the loaded end whistling down upon the deputy's nightcapped head.

There was a horrible sound like the crunching of an egg-shell, and the Citizen Representative dropped, fulminated by the blow, and lay in a shuddering, twitching heap, whilst the colour of this nightcap changed slowly from white to crimson under the murderer's staring eyes.

Gustave stood there, bending over the fallen man, motionless while you might count ten. His face was leaden and his mouth foolishly open between surprise and horror of the thing he had done.

Not a sound disturbed the house; not a groan, not a movement from the fallen man. Nothing but the muffled ticking of the ormolu clock and the buzzing of a fly that had been disturbed. Still Gustave stood there in that half-crouching attitude, terror gaining upon him with every throb of his pulses. And then quite suddenly a voice cut sharply upon the stillness.

'Well?' it asked. 'And what do you propose to do now?'

Gustave came erect, stifling a scream, to confront the white face and beady eyes of Duroc, who stood considering him between the parted curtains.

In a long silence he stared, his wits working briskly the while.

'Who are you?' he asked at last, his voice a hoarse whisper. 'How come you here? What are you? Ah! A thief – a housebreaker!'

'At least,' said Duroc drily, 'I am not a murderer.'

'My God!' said Gustave, and his wild eyes turned again upon that tragically grotesque mass that lay at his feet. 'Is he – is he dead?'

'Unless his skull is made of iron,' said Duroc. He came forward in that swift, noiseless fashion of his, and dropped on one knee beside the deputy. He made a brief examination. 'The Citizen Representative represents a corpse,' he said. 'He is as dead as King Capet.' He rose. 'What are you going to do?' he asked again.

'To do?' said Gustave. 'Mon Dieu! What is there to do? If he is dead—' He checked. His knavish wits were racing now. He looked into the other's round black eyes. 'You'll not betray me,' he cried. 'You dare not. You are in no better case than I. And there is no one else in the house. He lived all alone. He was a miserly dog, and the old woman who serves him will not be here until morning.'

Duroc was watching him intently, almost without appearing to observe him. He saw the man's fingers suddenly tighten upon the life-preserver with which already he had launched one man across the tide of the Styx that night.

'Put that thing down,' he commanded sharply, 'put it down at once, or I'll send you after your cousin.' And Gustave found himself covered by a pistol.

Instantly he loosed the grip of his murderous weapon. It fell with a crash beside the body of the man it had slain.

'I meant you no harm,' panted Gustave. 'Do you know what wealth he hoards in these consoles, in that secretaire? You do, for that is what you came for. Well, take it, take it all. But let me go, let me get away from this. I – I—' He seemed to stifle in his terror.

Duroc's lipless mouth distended in a smile.

'Am I detaining you?' he asked. 'Faith, you didn't suppose I was going to drag you to the nearest *corps-de-garde*, did you? Go, man, if you want to go. In your place I should have gone already.'

Gustave stared at him almost incredulously, as if doubting his own good fortune. Then suddenly perceiving the motives that swayed the other, and asking nothing better for himself than to be gone, he turned and without another word fled from the room and the house, his one anxiety to put as great a distance between himself and his crime as possible.

Duroc watched that sudden scared flight, still smiling. Then he coolly crossed the room, took up the dead man's candle and placed it upon the secretaire. He pulled up a chair – there was no longer any need to proceed with caution – sat down, and producing his keys and a chisel-like instrument he went diligently to work to get at the contents of this secretaire.

Meanwhile Gustave had gone like a flash the length of the Rue de la Harpe, driven ever by his terror of the consequences of his deed. But as he neared the corner of the Cordeliers he was brought suddenly to a halt by the measured tread of approaching steps. He knew it at once for the march of a patrol, and his consciousness of what he had done made him fearful of meeting these servants of the law who might challenge him and demand to know whence he was and whither he went at such an hour – for the new reign of universal liberty had imposed stern limitations upon individual freedom.

He vanished into the darkness of a doorway, and crouched there to wait until those footsteps should have faded again into the distance. And it was in those moments as he leaned there panting that his fiendishly wicked notion first assailed him. He turned it over in his mind, and in the gloom you might have caught the gleam of his teeth as he smiled evilly to himself.

He was his cousin's heir. Could he but fasten the guilt of that murder upon the thief he had left so callously at work in the very room where the body lay, then never again need he know want. And the thief, being a thief, deserved no less. He had no doubt at all but that the fellow would never have hesitated to do the murder had it been forced upon him by circumstances. He reflected further, and realized how aptly set was the stage for such a comedy as he had in mind. Had not that fool compelled him to drop the very weapon with which the deputy's skull had been smashed?

No single link was missing in the chain of complete evidence against the thief. Gustave realized that here was a chance sent him by friendly fortune. Tomorrow it would be too late. In seeking his cousin's murderer the authorities would ascertain that he was the one man who stood to profit by the Citizen Representative's death, and having discovered that they would compel him to render an account of his movements that night. They would cross-question and confound him, seeing that he could give no such account as they would demand.

He was resolved. He must act at once. Not three minutes had sped since he had left that house, and it was impossible that in the meantime the thief could have done his work and taken his departure.

And so upon that fell resolve he flung out of his concealment, and ran on up the street towards the Cordeliers, to meet the advancing patrol, shouting as he went—

'Au voleur! Au voleur!'

He heard the patrol quickening their steps in response to his cry, and presently he found himself face to face with four men of the National Guard, who, as it chanced, were accompanied by an agent of the section in civilian dress and scarf of office.

'Down there,' he cried, pointing back down the street. 'A thief has broken into the house of my cousin – my cousin the Citizen Representative Clairvaux.' He gathered importance, he knew, from this proclamation of his relationship with one of the great ones of the Convention.

But the agent of the section paused to question him.

'Why did you not follow him, citizen?'

'I am without weapons, and I bethought me he would probably be armed. Besides I heard you approaching in the distance, and I thought it best to run to summon you, that thus we may make sure of taking him.'

The agent considered him, his white face – seen in the light of the lantern carried by the patrol – his shaking limbs and gasping speech, and concluded he had to deal with an arrant coward, nor troubled to dissemble his contempt.

'Name of a name!' he growled, 'and meanwhile the Citizen Representative may have been murdered in his bed.'

'I pray not! Oh, I pray not!' panted Gustave. 'Quickly, citizens, quickly! Terrible things may happen while we stand here.'

They went down the street at a run to the house of Clairvaux, whose door they found open as Gustave had left it when he departed.

'Where did he break in?' asked one of the guards.

'By the door,' said Gustave. 'He had keys, I think. Oh, quick!'

In the passage he perceived a faint gleam of light to assure him that the thief was still at work. He swung round to them, and raised a hand. 'Quietly!' he whispered. 'Quietly, so that we do not disturb him.'

The patrol thrust forward, and entered the house in his wake. He led them straight towards the half-open door of the study, from which the light was issuing as if to guide them. He flung wide the door, and entered, whilst the men crowding after him came to a sudden halt upon the threshold in sheer amazement at what they beheld.

At their feet lay the body of the Citizen Representative Clairvaux in a raiment that in itself seemed to proclaim how hastily he had risen from his bed to come and deal with this midnight intruder; and there at the secretaire, now open, its drawers broken and their contents scattered all about the floor, sat Duroc, white-faced, his beady rat's eyes considering them.

Gustave broke into lamentations at sight of his cousin's body.

'We are too late! Mon Dieu! We are too late! He is dead – dead. And look! Here is the weapon with which he was slain. And there sits the murderer – caught in the very act – caught in the very act. Seize him! Ah *scélérat*,' he raged, shaking his fist in the thief's white, startled face. 'You shall be made to pay for this!'

'Comedian!' said Duroc shortly.

'Seize him! Seize him!' cried Gustave in a frenzy.

The guards sprang across the room, and laid hands upon Duroc to prevent him having recourse to any weapons.

Duroc looked up at them, blinking. The his eyes shifted to Gustave, and suddenly he laughed.

'Now see what a fool a man is who will not seize the chances that are offered him,' he said. 'After that scoundrel had bludgeoned his cousin to death I bade him go. He might have made good his escape, and I should have said no word to betray him. Instead he thinks to make me his scapegoat.'

He shrugged, and rose under the hands of his captors. Then he pulled his coat open, and displayed a round leaden disc of the size of a five-franc piece bearing the arms of the republic.

At sight of it the hands that had been holding him instantly fell away.

The agent of the section stepped forward frowning.

'What does this mean?' he asked, but on a note that was almost of respect, realizing that he stood in the presence of an officer of the secret service of the republic, whom no man might detain save at his peril.

'I am Duroc of the Committee of Public Safety,' was the quiet answer. 'The Executive had cause to doubt that the Citizen Representative Clairvaux was in correspondence with the enemies of France. I came secretly to examine his papers and to discover who are his correspondents. Here is what I sought.' And he held up a little sheaf of documents which he had separated from the rest. 'I will wish you good-night, citizens. I must report at once to the Citizen-Deputy Marat. Since that fellow has come back take him to the Luxembourg. Let the committee of the section deal with him tomorrow. I shall forward my report.'

Gustave shook himself out of his sudden paralysis to make a dash for the door. But the guards closed with him, and held him fast, whilst Duroc of the Committee of Public Safety passed out, with dignity in spite of his torn breeches.

KYNASTON'S RECKONING

Under the date of the 18th August 1660, you will find the following entry in the diary of Mr Samuel Pepys: 'Captain Ferrers took me to the Cockpitt play, the first that I have had time to see since my coming from sea, "The Loyall Subject", where one Kynaston, a boy, acted the duke's sister, but made the loveliest lady that ever I saw in my life.'

Edward Kynaston was short of stature, and of a lithe and stripling grace, golden-headed, with a milk-and-rose complexion that any woman might have envied, and a countenance so delicately beautiful that it provoked from Mr Pepys the above ejaculation, and, further (on the 2nd of January following), this tribute: '...I and my wife to the theatre, and there saw "The Silent Woman". Among other things there Kinaston, the boy, had the good turn to appear ... in fine clothes, and in them was clearly the prettiest woman in the house.'

This Kynaston had been discovered by Sir William Davenant – the same who boasted himself to be the son of Master William Shakespeare – and such were his histrionic gifts and personal beauty that even when women were admitted at last to the English stage he continued for some time thereafter to be entrusted with the principal female roles, since no woman could be found to compare with him in the performance of them.

Some years later (on the 9th February, 1669) we find Mr Pepys writing as follows: 'To the King's Playhouse, and there saw "The Island Princesse", which I like mighty well as an excellent play; and here we find Kinaston to be well enough to act again; which he did very well after his beating by Sir Charles Sedley's appointment.'

It is with this beating and its consequences that my story is concerned. Ned Kynaston was by now in his twenty-second year, and whilst he was still engaged in the main for female parts, yet upon occasion he would play the youthful gallant – and have every woman in the house enamoured of him.

In what way Sedley offended him we do not know, nor does it greatly matter. We do know that Sedley was very prodigal of offence, and although at this time a man well advanced in the forties, yet age had not sobered him or given him dignity. He was still quite the most outrageous of all the rakes about the court of that prince of rakes, their sovereign. The audacity of his intrigues was second only to that of his royal master. It has been made the subject of a lampoon by his brother rake, my Lord Rochester. Once when, as a result of what Anthony Wood calls his 'indecent and blasphemous behaviour', he had raised a riot in the Cock Tavern in Covent Garden, and had been haled, together with my Lord Buckhurst and some others, before Sir Robert Hyde – Lord Chief Justice of the Common Pleas, sitting in Westminster Hall – Sir Robert caustically commended to him the perusal of a book entitled *The Compleat Gentleman* – a recommendation which galled him worse than the fine of Â£500 by which it was accompanied.

Pepys, too, tells us of a 'frolic and debauchery' of Sedley's and Buckhurst's, 'running up and down all the night, almost naked in the streets, and at last fighting and being beat by the watch and clapped up all night.'

It is not difficult to conceive that so turbulent a rake may have got foul of the players at the King's Theatre, and thus provoked Kynaston. Be that as it may, Kynaston chose to appear on the stage made up in so life-like a portrait of Sir Charles, and so naturally counterfeiting his accent and his posturings, that the whole house was convulsed with it when it had assured itself that it was not Sir Charles himself who strutted there upon the boards.

You imagine, I hope, the fine passion into which Sedley was flung when he knew of it. Those who overheard his threats to have the actor's life say that he foamed at the mouth in uttering them. But he did not take the direct way to achieve his purpose expected by those who were witnesses of his ravings. He did not send his friends and the length of his sword to Kynaston. How could he? Blackguard though he was by instinct and behaviour, it yet remained that by birth he was a gentleman; and it could not have become a gentleman to have so forgotten what was due to himself as to have condescended to cross swords with a rogue and a vagabond of an actor. Besides, Kynaston, for all his slight frame and almost womanish beauty, was of an extremely virile spirit, and of a singular address in all the exercises of his age. He played – as indeed you shall see – as pretty a rapier as any man in these islands.

So Sir Charles took another way – the way of the gentleman with the plebeian. He sent a couple of hired bullies to waylay Kynaston in the park one morning. They fell upon him, broke his sword with their cudgels, and so belaboured him that he was left almost for dead when they made off before the advent of those who ran belatedly to the poor actor's assistance.

Such was the resentment of town and Court – for Kynaston was a universal favourite – that for once the King frowned upon one of those who modelled their conduct upon his own august pattern. But beyond a transient coolness, his Majesty did not see fit to visit any other punishment upon Sedley, and Kynaston, seeing that there was none to avenge him, considered, so soon as he was restored to health, how best he might avenge himself.

The cowardly assault had raised in him such a thirst for vengeance as naught but Sedley's blood could assuage. He must take steps to make it impossible for the rake to do aught but set aside his gentleman's estate and measure swords with him; that much accomplished, at whatever cost or consequences, Kynaston was resolved to kill him without mercy.

He was about his murderous purpose on that sunny February morning on which Sir Lionel Faversham tells us that he met him outside the Dolphin in the Strand. He was dressed in a black camlet suit, very sober and simple, yet of an elegance that heighted his distinguished air. 'Actor though he was,' says Faversham, 'I'll swear that no courtlier figure might you see in Whitehall.'

Faversham found him pacing there like a sentry, with a heavy riding-whip tucked under his arm.

'Whither away, Ned?' he greeted him.

Kynaston tossed his golden curls, and with his whip he pointed across to the Dolphin.

'I am staying for Sir Charles Sedley,' he replied in that gentle and wonderfully musical voice of his. 'If you'll tarry here awhile, you'll see a reckoning paid, and a rakehell carried home to bed. 'Twill divert you, Sir Lionel.'

'Odds my life, lad! Are ye clean mad?' cried Faversham.

Having a very real affection for the young man, and foreseeing for him the worst possible consequences from such an affair, he set himself urgently to turn him from his purpose. They wrangled there awhile, and in the end, Sir Lionel's good sense prevailing, Kynaston suffered himself to be led away. Faversham carried him off to his own lodging in King Street, and kept him there out of mischief until the morrow. By then the actor's rage had so far cooled that he lent an ear to the reasonable counsel of his host.

'I'll be advised by you, Sir Lionel,' he said at parting, 'and I abandon all thought of repaying him in his own coin. 'Tis stupid currency when all is said. Yet, sink me, it shall be the worse for him! For you are not to suppose that I shall forgo the reckoning. I'll present it in another form, and, when I do, you shall see Sedley pilloried to the mock of the town.'

Faversham accounted all this to be no more than the vapourings of a histrionic temperament, the last flicker of the flame of the actor's resentment; and he deemed himself confirmed in this judgement when, as the weeks went by, the whole affair was permitted by Kynaston to fall into oblivion. Confidently he accounted the incident closed, which but shows that, despite his friendship for Kynaston, his knowledge of him did not go very deep.

It would be about a month after these events that town and Court were set agog by the advent of a new beauty at Whitehall in the person of Caroline Countess of Chesterham. Her coming had been heralded in advance in a letter from the septuagenarian Lord Chesterham to his old friend Faversham, who had been cornet of horse in a regiment commanded by his lordship at Naseby. He wrote from the remote wilds of Cornwall, whither he had retreated some years before, to announce that he had married a young wife.

What the town said of it is neither here nor there, and, in any case, is very readily imagined. Also, it is readily imagined with what curiosity the town looked forward to his announced visit, and to see this girl whose beauty he extolled at such length in another letter addressed to Lady Denham. His lordship wrote that, although he had never thought to forsake his hermitage again, yet having taken so young a bride he was sensible of the duty that he owed her, and that since it was her desire to see something of the great world, he could not find it in his heart to deny her.

A handsome house was made ready for them in Pall Mall by a steward, and a posse of servants sent ahead. And a few days later the news was put about that they had arrived.

Among the first to pay their devoirs were, of course, Sir Lionel Faversham and Sir John and Lady Denham. To receive them they found, however, none but the bride, installed in a nobly proportioned drawing-room whose windows looked out upon the park.

They had naturally assumed from his lordship's letters that she would be country-bred, but they found little to confirm the assumption in her appearance and her manners. She was of striking, of superb beauty – tall, straight, and slender, with a carriage of such grace and supple dignity that a queen might have been proud of it. If a fault there was in that glorious, gipsy-tinted face it was that it too closely matched her bearing. It was cold and proud, and it derived a something almost of boldness from the steady glance of her magnificent sombre eyes. Her gown was in the very latest mode of France, and her abundant, lustrous black hair, intertwined with a string of pearls, was dressed in the very noontide of fashion, whilst a round black patch – that very latest of fashion's mad conceits – sat roguishly upon her chin, and yet another on her cheek 'neath her left eye. Her voice was low and cultured and very rich, and none could have been more infinitely and nobly at ease than she when she explained the absence of her septuagenarian bridegroom.

She informed her visitors that within ten miles of town they had been overtaken by a courier, who brought them word that his lordship's brother had a seizure, and was not expected to live, whereupon his lordship had gone posting back at once, leaving his wife to end the journey alone and to await him in London, whither he would follow as soon as might be. She brought a little note from him to Lady Denham, in which he implored the latter's good offices of her – a charge which Lady Denham very amiably accepted, entirely ravished by the grace and dignity of Lady Chesterham.

Faversham tells us that he withdrew perturbed in spirit. He had conceived his old friend to have committed the regrettable imprudence of giving rein to an infatuation for some rustic Hebe, whereas instead he was driven to fear that he had fallen a prey to an adventuress of talent, who would not be long in covering him with that ridicule which so often falls to the lot of the old man who marries a young wife – the Pantaloon in the Comedy of Life.

The events most certainly nourished these fears of his, and did credit to his discernment. Presented at Whitehall by Lady Denham, Lady Chesterham created a greater sensation than in its day had been caused by the advent there of Barbara Palmer. Her triumph was to be read in the hostility with which the women received her. Metaphorically they recoiled before her. That cold assurance, amounting almost to boldness, which Faversham had detected in her bearing, proved repellant to the majority of her own sex. They discovered in her something almost approaching raffishness, which disconcerted their own more veiled immodesty. And then there was her astounding popularity with the men to quicken the venom of the ladies of the Court. The latter looked on with noses at a disdainful angle, whilst they stripped her character to its last rag, tore her reputation into tatters.

Yet she thrived amazingly in the assiduous court that was paid her by the brothers, fathers, and husbands of her instinctive enemies. The sultan Charles himself was vastly taken with her – which, after all, considering his temperament, was not wonderful. He went the length of visiting her in her splendid mansion in Pall Mall, a matter which caused Faversham to wring his hands in despair, and pray that her husband's brother might get his dying done with as much despatch as possible.

But there was worse to follow. All day, and often far into the night, a line of chairs and coaches stood before her doors, and in her ante-chambers, such was the press of courtiers that you might have deemed yourself at Whitehall.

In her social tastes she proved herself extremely catholic. Not merely were beaux and men of fashion welcomed; soon her rooms were thronged with wits and poets, painters, writers of plays, and even one or two actors haled thither in the train of Sir George Etheredge, who himself belonged to two worlds. To all she was alike gracious, until in the end, inevitably, she came to manifest to one a special favour. And this one, to Faversham's dismay, was none other than Sir

115

Charles Sedley, that devourer of hearts, that heartless blighter of reputations. And the worst of it was that the first advances came undoubtedly from her. She it was who ogled the rake and lured him on to pay his assiduous court.

Soon her name, coupled with Sedley's, was on the gay town's lips. Faversham – immensely daring – breathed a warning to her. She measured him with her bold black eyes, 'twixt raillery and scorn.

'I protest I find him vastly amusing,' said she.

'I pray Heaven, madam, you may always say so,' said Faversham impressively.

'You are more devout than witty, sir, which is to say, you are a dullard,' was the fleeting answer with which she quitted him.

Some days later, in the Rhenish Wine House, which was full of company at the time, Sir Lionel came face to face with Ned Kynaston. The actor had a flushed, excited air, and his eyes were bright.

'What's this I hear of Sedley, Sir Lionel?' he cried out, in a voice that drew attention. 'They are coupling his name with Lady Chesterham's. But an hour ago I all but had a duel on my hands through it.'

Faversham's lips tightened. He froze. Were matters indeed gone so far that her name was thus flung about a wineshop? Yet because of his affection for Kynaston he tempered the rebuke that had arisen to his lips.

'Lady Chesterham's affairs,' he replied gravely, 'are her own and Lord Chesterham's, who, no doubt, will demand an account of any who presumes to lend her name to scandal-mongers.'

'Faith, then, he'll need to be returning soon, or he'll find his work done for him by another. Curse me, Sir Lionel, I tell you no man shall say a word against her ladyship in my hearing but I'll ram his lies down his dirty throat with the point of my cane!'

Faversham took him by the arm.

'Be silent, Ned!'

'Silent?' roared Kynaston. 'Shall I be silent what time that foul fellow Sedley's verses upon her are being sung up and down the town? I'll do more than write verses in her honour to prove myself her slave!' And he declaimed, adapting:

I'll sing my praise of thee in trumpet sounds, And write my homage down in blood and wounds.

Faversham's grip upon his arm tightened. He dragged him out of the tavern into the pale February sunshine.

'Art mad, Ned?' he growled. 'Another word in that strain in public, and I shall quarrel with you. If you respect the lady as you pretend, afford by silence some testimony of that respect.'

But the mischief was done. Kynaston had been abundantly overheard. His words were, of course, repeated. The women got hold of the story, and it suffered nothing in their fierce retelling of it. This bold wanton was so lost to decency, so greedy of admirers, that even players were admitted to sun themselves in her smiles. As for Kynaston, there were no limits to what was said of him. It was most plausibly suggested that, availing himself of the opportunity her lack of circumspection was affording him, he meant to oust Sedley from her favour, and thus take vengeance upon Sedley for the beating he had received by his appointment. Since her tastes were admittedly base, it was deemed not impossible that he might prove victorious in this contest, though, to be sure, it would be a victory that could bring him but little glory. Thus the ladies.

That pretty tale overran the town like wildfire. It came to Sedley's ears, and set him in a seething passion. In this he went off to Lady Chesterham's.

'Madam, what is't I hear?' he burst out at sight of her.

From the couch where she reclined she eyed him languidly.

'I see that you are come to set me riddles,' she drawled. 'But I warn you that they weary me.'

'Riddles?' quoth he. 'Ay, a riddle in sooth. 'Tis said that you favour that low fellow Kynaston; that you receive him here; that he has the temerity to proclaim himself the champion of your good name!'

'Does he so?' she cooed. 'I vow 'tis vastly sweet in him.'

'Vastly sweet?' he roared. 'Fan me, ye winds! Do you realize what it means? Would you have him blast your fair repute, madam?'

She considered him with half-closed eyes, smiling insolently over the edge of her gently moving fan.

'Do you desire to be alone and absolute in the enjoyment of that privilege?' quoth she.

He looked at her blankly a moment, speechless. Then he stamped his foot.

''Tis not to be borne!' he cried.

'Who bids you bear it, sir, whatever it may be?' she countered scornfully. 'Did I bid you to come pestering me with your sheep's eyes and your sighs and your silly speeches? If the dear lad please me, what is't to you, pray? Who gave you rights upon me? La, now! I protest you weary me.'

'Caroline!' he began unsteadily. He advanced and stood over her, glowering down into that mocking, gipsy-tinted face. He swallowed, and began again. 'You are to understand, madam, that it is not safe to play fast-and-loose with me.'

The jewelled fingers of her fine long hand moved her fan gently to and fro again. Her lip curled.

'You are a mirror of the politenesses, sir.'

'Curse me, madam, I do not aim at politeness!'

'In that case you will be the less put about.'

'Ha! You rally me! You make a mock of me!' he raved, beside himself with anger. 'You have brought me to this – to this! And now—'

He flung his arms wide and let them fall again, his face very pale.

She sat bolt upright.

'Sir Charles,' said she, 'I was warned of your presumption and your ill-repute.'

'If that dog Kynaston has dared malign me—'

'Believe me, 'twere impossible – beyond the compass of his invention. It is time, Sir Charles, you understood that you have no right or claim upon me beyond such as it may be my pleasure to confer. Such rights belong only to my husband.'

'Damn your husband, madam!' he snapped in his rage.

She rose, frowning.

'Sir Charles, you forget the respect due to me,' she rebuked him, with a great dignity, her face forbiddingly cold. 'You have my leave to go.'

He gaped foolishly, stricken by her sudden iciness.

'Forgive me!' he pleaded. 'I – I am a little disordered. I—'

'Faugh!' she broke in. 'I could forgive your being disordered, but I cannot forgive you for being maudlin and tiresome. Heaven be my witness I never could endure a tiresome man. I give you good-day.'

He flung out in a rage, not trusting himself to say another word. In his heart he cursed her for a wanton who had but lured him on that she might subject him to this humiliation. But anon, as he cooled, he came to consider that perhaps he had been precipitate. His vanity argued that her self-respect must have compelled her to resent the too-masterful tone he had taken with her. He had been foolish; he had displayed no more tact or judgement than an oaf.

Hence it happened that he came contritely to her house upon the following morning, intent to make his peace with her, confident of his power to do so. He reflected that no cloud would ever have troubled their relations but for that rascal Kynaston. The very thought of the fellow was enough to fling Sir Charles into a fresh passion. But he curbed his mood, bethinking him that to give way to it was to suffer defeat in the end. After all, Kynaston was most rarely handsome, and he had gifts – Sir Charles deemed it prudent to admit his enemy's strength – which might entrap the heart of a wilful, headstrong woman such as Caroline Chesterham. Women were such fools in these matters, he considered. They never could distinguish between a rogue and a gentleman.

He entered the spacious hall at the foot of the main staircase – a hall which served the purpose of the mansion's principle ante-chamber. Here he found the usual company assembled, but, if anything, more numerous than usual, which put him out of temper. Yet perhaps she would do him the honour of granting him immediate and private audience?

He approached one of her splendid servants, and slipped a guinea into the fellow's hand and a message into his ear. The lackey pocketed the coin, and vanished. He returned almost at once.

'Her ladyship's compliments, Sir Charles, and she desires to be private until she announces herself disposed to receive.'

Vexed, Sir Charles turned aside, and fell into absent-minded talk with Buckhurst. Ten minutes passed, and then there was a sudden stir in the courtly groups about the hall.

Down the stairs, serene and graceful, came a young man in a suit of heliotrope satin edged with silver, a wealth of lace at wrist and throat, his plumed hat under his right arm, and an ebony cane dangling from his left wrist. His hair fell in a shower of golden ringlets, a bunch of them caught in a heliotrope ribbon on a level with his left ear.

It was Ned Kynaston. As Sir Charles stared incredulously he could scarcely believe his eyes. A red mist rose at last before them; he felt a tightening at the throat. He and some twenty of the first gentlemen of the town were left there to cool their heels like lackeys whilst she was private with this low-born fellow, who descended now as self-assured and supercilious as though the house belonged to him.

Men nudged one another, and Sir Charles felt every eye turned upon him. He told himself that he was become their laughing stock.

Then, on the fourth step from the foot of the stairs, Kynaston paused.

'Her ladyship's compliments, gentlemen, to you all,' he announced – ladies there were none present at this levee – 'and she bids me beg you to hold her excused, as she desires to rest herself this morning.'

This was too much for Sedley. Rudely he shouldered his way through the throng to the foot of the stairs, and every eye was upon him, every face betrayed its gleeful expectancy of a scene.

'So,' he growled, hoarse with passion, 'you play the lackey, do you, Kynaston? Faith, I never saw you better fitted with a part to suit you.'

The actor, still on that fourth step – a position which gave a certain advantage over his enemy – paused to take snuff daintily before replying.

'Ha, Sir Charles!' he said, in his clear, bell-like voice, and never had an audience hung more intently upon his words. 'I have a word for you in addition to what I have announced already.' He shut his snuffbox with a snap, and dusted fragments of the Burgamot from his ruffles. 'If her ladyship does not receive this morning the fault, Sir Charles, is yours. I see no reason to spare you the humiliation you seek when you thrust yourself in here despite her ladyship's definite dismissal of you yesterday. Yet her ladyship would have spared it you, and 'twas to that end – that she might not be forced to single you out – that she determined today, being informed of your presence, to deny herself to all.'

Mad with anger and mortification, intent only upon insult, Sir Charles flung forward with the retort:

'You lie, you dog of a play-actor!'

That was Kynaston's great opportunity. In a flash he took it; took it like one who has been waiting in leash for it. His right hand swung up, and he caught Sir Charles a buffet full upon the cheek, that knocked him into the arms of Sir John Ogle.

There was a pause until Sedley recovered from his astonishment. Then, bellowing blasphemy, he lugged at his sword. Instantly a dozen hands fastened upon him.

'Not here, Charles!' cried Buckhurst. 'We'll not suffer it in her ladyship's house. You shall not make her name the talk o' th' town. Elsewhere, Charles! Elsewhere! Not here!'

Thus they – his own friends – committed him to it. He glared at Kynaston, who, leaning now upon his cane, looked down upon him with a crooked smile.

'You dog!' he roared. He was foaming at the mouth, his handsome, dissipated face aflame with passion. 'I'll kill you for this! My friends shall wait upon you!'

'You sent your friends to me once before. Faith, they were the friends I should expect in you,' drawled the actor.

Through Sedley's furious mind there flashed then a suspicion that all this was an elaborate trap in which he was caught. But still he did not realize its details.

'It shall be cold steel this time!' he bellowed. 'Get measured for your coffin.'

The meeting took place at eight o'clock next morning in Leicester Fields, and it presented some unusual features. In the first place, Ned Kynaston did not come to the ground with his friends, as is prescribed by all sound authorities on the formalities of the duello. And when Faversham and Etheredge, who had consented to act for him, made their joint appearance at five minutes to eight, their principal was not yet come.

Sedley, stripped to shirt and breeches, was already there with Buckhurst and Ogle. Also there was such a throng of spectators that every rank of life was represented. This was a matter that increased Sedley's fury. If he must disgrace himself and soil his sword in the blood of an actor, he would, at least, have desired to have been private. However, being thrust into so unworthy a position, he must perforce bear himself as best he could. He turned to Faversham with a sneering laugh.

'Odds death, Sir Lionel!' quoth he. 'Is your friend like to keep us waiting longer? I've gotten an appetite from this early rising, and I'm in haste to get to breakfast.'

That taunt was followed by others that became more and more barbed as time passed and still there was no sign of Kynaston. Faversham tells us that, mortified, he was on the point of offering to take his principal's place when at last a chair was espied advancing from St Martin's Lane.

It must be Kynaston at last! But when the bearers had set it down and raised the roof, out stepped, not Kynaston, but Lady Chesterham, to the dumbfoundering of every man present. Instantly she ran to Sedley.

'Sir Charles!' she cried, a note of appeal in her voice, and tears in her lovely eyes. 'Forgive me for what I have done. There will be no fighting this morning.'

Sir Charles looked down at her. He was very white, and his lips were twitching.

'Madam,' he muttered at last, 'let me beg you to take some thought for your name, and withdraw.'

'My name!' she cried. 'What care I for my name? I can take thought for nothing but his life, Sir Charles.' (A spasm rippled over Sedley's face.) ''Tis my fault. 'Twas I bade him bear that message to you. I'll not have him murdered for what was of my doing.'

'Did he send you hither?' snapped Sedley.

'Send me? Not he, poor lad. He's safe enough, and no harm can come to him. But you shall not fight him.'

'By Heaven, madam, shall I take a blow? And from such a dog as that?' quoth he. 'The quarrel was of his seeking.'

'Nay, 'twas of yours; 'twas you gave him the lie. What could he do, poor boy?' She looked up at him in distress and appeal; but he remained unmoved before it, mindful only of his wrongs.

'Madam, let me entreat you to withdraw.'

'Not until I have your promise that you will spare him. Why are you so set on killing him? What is his life to you?'

'What is it to you, madam?' countered Sedley fiercely, himself forgetful now of spectators.

But if he was lost to shame she was a thousand times more so.

'He is everything to me,' she answered; 'and I care not who hears me! If he dies, I shall die. If you wish to kill me, kill him. Ah, bethink you, he is so young, so gentle, and so lovely—'

Perhaps that plea was ill-considered. Sir Charles stepped back, his face set and scowling.

'This is idle, madam. Worse than idle. You humiliate yourself in vain.' And he waved a hand to the assembled throng, all greedily watching this extraordinary scene.

123

'You are resolved to fight, in spite of all that I have said?' she demanded tragically.

'Madam, I am!'

'Be it so, then!' she answered, in a sudden fury. 'In that case you shall fight me!' And before Faversham knew what she was about she had snatched the sword from his side. Flourishing it, she advanced upon Sedley. 'On guard, sir!' she challenged him.

'Madam, you are mad,' he answered; and he believed it. 'I implore you to be more circumspect. There are those who hear you—'

'I desire them to hear me,' she answered, and her voice seemed to take on a deeper note. 'And they shall see me, too,' she added.

And then the amazing thing took place. She tore off her plumed hat, and with it tore away her lofty mass of lustrous black hair, leaving in its place a ripple of golden locks about her neck. She flung off the long black cloak in which she had been wrapped; her furbelow fell away about her feet; and forth from that burst chrysalis, under the eye of the gaping company, stepped Ned Kynaston himself.

Kynaston indeed it was, and yet even now the face was hardly his own: it was still in part transformed by the darkened eyebrows, the olive-tinted cheeks, the patches under lip and eye, and other cunning touches which the theatre had taught that masterly player of feminine roles, and which had gone to make him in real life what so often he had been upon the stage – the loveliest lady that ever Mr Pepys saw in all his life.

Like a ripple over water ran the truth through the assembled crowd, and after its first gasp under the shock of that revelation a great peal of laughter broke upon the morning air.

Sedley looked on, white to the lips, cut and wounded to the very soul of him. He had no delusions on the score of the laughter. It was himself was the object of it; he it was who had been fooled to the very top of his bent; he who must die under the ridicule that would convulse the town. Had he not made love to Caroline Chesterham? Had he not written verses in her honour? Had he not languished and sighed and fondled her hand by the hour? Had he not come to fight this very duel out of jealousy aroused by her?

124

With a snarling cry he hurled himself upon the actor. But meanwhile Kynaston had kicked aside the discarded furbelow and cloak, and stood free to receive this onslaught – graceful, alert, and poised like a fencing-master.

Faversham would have interposed. But the actor waved him away.

'In Heaven's name,' he laughed, 'let him have what he came for.'

The blades met and jarred, then Sedley's was deflected; there was a twinkling disengage, and Kynaston's point flew straight and unhampered at the region of his opponent's heart. Within an inch of the body it paused, and Kynaston drew back his arm. As all saw, he had spared his enemy. Sedley came on again, and for the second time the actor got within his opponent's guard, yet again he checked his point at the very moment of touching the other's body. If aught had been wanting to complete Sedley's humiliation it was afforded in that fine display of fence, and the almost contemptuous mercy with which it was accompanied.

The end came soon. Kynaston, supremely the master, made a fresh opening, went in for the third and last time, and transfixed his adversary's sword-arm.

Perforce that was the end, and Kynaston went off to breakfast with his seconds; whilst the crowd dispersed to put this amazing story about the town.

'I shall look to you, Sir Lionel,' said the actor, when they had got to table, 'to make my peace with my Lord Chesterham should this affair ever come to his ears. You'll have guessed by this that 'twas I, myself, who wrote the letters of introduction which I brought to you and to Lady Denham. No doubt 'twas a gross libel on his lordship, who, belike, has no thought whatever of marrying again.' Then he sighed and laughed in one. 'Odds life! That house in Pall Mall and the rest of it will cost me a year's earnings. But Sedley's is the heavier reckoning. I promised you it should be heavy.'

Heavy it was, indeed. Sedley left town immediately, unable to face the ridicule in store for him, and for a year thereafter he abode quietly in the country, no man knowing where. Nor does it transpire that he ever attempted to pit himself against Ned Kynaston again.

JACK O'LANTERN

Jack o'Lantern was the name bestowed upon him by the Bow Street runners whom his elusiveness was exasperating. His real identity was as unknown to them as his countenance, which he covered with a black visor, whenever operating. The speed of his movements was such that he seemed to multiply himself. No sooner was the hue-and-cry raised in Kent for the robbery of a nobleman on Gad's Hill at noon, than they heard of him holding up the Oxford coach beyond Watford in the evening. They identified him by a general description: his genteel methods; his good shape and his military exterior; a laced hat cocked over the right eye, an elegant, full-skirted coat, a steinkirk and so on. He rode a bay mare, presenting, however, no peculiar characteristics.

On that afternoon in May when just beyond Kentish Town he relieved Squire Kendrick of a purse of fifty guineas, a gold snuffbox, a diamond ring of price and a handsome small-sword that took his fancy, he was led by his ill-starred meeting with Mr Richard Lessingham to depart from his usual practice of setting out at once to put a score of miles between himself and the scene of the outrage.

He could not have chosen a worse moment for the encounter. At the best of times Mr Richard Lessingham would have proved an awkward customer, for, like most men endowed with a strong dash of rascality, he was a considerable fellow of his hands. Today he happened to ride in a furious temper, feeling that life had declared war upon him, and all but looking for an opportunity to deliver battle.

He was the nephew and heir presumptive of that wealthy nawab Sir John Lessingham, who, following a fashion and a taste for the district, common in his day with so many of his kind, had built himself out of the plunder of the Indies a handsome house in a handsome park on the north side of Highgate Hill. For any inheritance beyond the baronetcy and the little estate that went to adorn it, Richard Lessingham must depend upon the relations between his uncle and himself. Sir John had been more than generous with him. He desired that his nephew and heir presumptive could cut a prominent figure in the world of fashion wherein, himself, he had failed. For English Society looked askance on these nawabs and their suspiciously acquired wealth. To this end he made the lad a princely allowance. But it had not proved liberal enough to meet the extravagances of a vain, ostentatious, and fundamentally worthless nature. Horses and cards and other extravagances had run Mr Richard heavily into debt.

On the first occasion the nawab had relieved the obligations with a laugh. The name of Lessingham would gather lustre from being well gilded. Later he had relieved obligations again, but he had not laughed. Later still he had stormed whilst paying, and warned his nephew that he would pay no more excesses of the allowance. The warning, however, was powerless to curb extravagances that by this time had become settled habits. All that had resulted was that when next Richard found his debts submerging him, instead of seeking his uncle, he had sought – on the advice of a fellow-member of White's to whom he had lost a deal of money at ombre – a certain Mr Nicholas Magdalen, who in a back office in Essex Street was amassing an incalculable fortune by the benevolent assistance of young gentlemen of quality in financial distress.

Mr Magdalen, an elderly little man with a moist, red face and greasy black hair that straggled untidily about a skull-cap, had displayed a solicitude of the friendliest. He could not have been more distressed over his new client's plight if Richard had been his own child. He invited him to dismiss all concern. There was neither sense nor right in that a fine young gentleman of his quality and a future baronet should be plagued over a matter of a mere couple of thousand pounds. His little short-sighted eyes beamed through his horn-rimmed spectacles as he thanked his gods that it was in his power to play the fairy godfather. The money should be paid to Mr Lessingham's bankers without fail in the morning. He would, of course, make a charge for the accommodation. One had to live. But – again thanking his gods – Mr Magdalen was no usurer, like some that he could name. Thirty per centum was the uttermost interest he would consent to take, considering how good must be the security that Mr Lessingham would supply.

It became necessary to explain to the ignorant but immensely relieved Mr Lessingham the exact meaning of the term 'security'. His relief was diminished by the explanation. Dismay finally replaced it.

'But I have no property. No property whatsoever.'

Mr Magdalen's smile was reassured. 'Not *in esse*, as we say. No. But *in posse*, my dear sir, there is Lessingham Park, which your uncle has entailed to go with the title.'

'But that's not mine yet.'

The benign smile of Mr Magdalen became broader. 'The prospect is enough, my dear sir. It would not be enough for everybody. Nor would I do this for everybody; for, of course, the risk is considerable. If you should predecease your uncle, the post-obit will be so much waste paper. But we can provide for that risk in the rate of interest. I am afraid I must make it sixty per centum. But, then, you'll not account that unreasonable, considering...'

'What is a post... What d'ye call it?'

Mr Magdalen gently explained the nature and effect of the post-obit.

'Ecod!' said Mr Lessingham to this wealth of instruction into mysterious and unsuspected ways of finance.

He departed with the assurance that the cash would be at his disposal on the morrow, and he came back again in six months' time not only gloomily to confess that he could not find a matter of twelve hundred pounds due for interest, but that he had pressing debts for another thousand and didn't know where the devil to seek it.

Mr Magdalen's undiminished benignity at once dispelled his apprehensions.

'No cause to distress yourself, my dear young friend. We add the interest to the principal, and that's the end of the matter. Forget it. Amuse yourself. As for your present debts, I will provide the thousand pounds at once.'

Six months later, Mr Lessingham found himself owing something over two thousand pounds for interest, whilst one or two creditors were pressing him for debts which in all amounted to about eight hundred pounds. It began to be borne in upon the dull wits of the nawab's nephew that a morass awaited him at the bottom of the easy slope to which he had set his feet. The benignity of Mr Magdalen on this occasion did not suffice to allay his very real anxieties, especially when he discovered that whilst Mr Magdalen would again be content to add interest to principal, he was by no means prepared to advance the further moneys so immediately necessary. The little estate, he pointed out, was not worth above twenty thousand pounds, and the risks attached to post-obit made it impossible to increase the capital liability already incurred.

Mr Lessingham was appalled. He made a mental calculation and presented the results to Mr Magdalen. That he was capable of it shows the extent to which his education in financial matters had lately improved.

'Ecod, sir! At this rate in a couple of years' time Lessingham Park will be your property, and all that I'll have had will have been a matter of three thousand pounds. Blister me!'

'Sir John may die before then,' said Mr Magdalen hopefully.

'Damme! Sir John won't die in the next ten years. God knows he's hale enough for another twenty.' Mr Lessingham sucked his breath in sudden terror. 'What'll be owing you in twenty years at this thieving rate?'

With pursed lips Mr Magdalen opined that it might be rather more than the whole fortune of the nawab. But he begged Mr Lessingham to dismiss such gloomy conjectures. Mr Lessingham, however, could not dismiss them.

'Sold myself for a mess of pottage, ecod!' said he, and black, vicious despair looked out of his livid face at the benevolent little usurer. A snarl crept into his voice. 'I've a mind to…'

'Now wait a moment. Wait a moment,' Mr Magdalen begged him. 'Between friends there are always ways of arranging matters, and I hope, Mr Lessingham, sir, that you will consider me your friend. There's a proposal I might make to you that I give you my word I wouldn't make to another man living. 'Pon honour I wouldn't. Have you… hem… have you ever thought of marriage, Mr Lessingham, sir.'

'Marriage!' sneered the young gentleman. He became cynical. 'I've never met a lady well enough dowered.'

'That', said Mr Magdalen, 'is where I might help you.'

'Faith, ye're a marriage-broker, then, as well as a moneylender? If your rate of interest is as unconscionable…'

'There's no rate of interest at all. The lady is perhaps the wealthiest heiress in England, and her dowry will be … ah … princely.'

Mr Lessingham's handsome face was darkened in a scowl.

'Let me know more of this. Be plain with me.'

Mr Magdalen was plain. And forth came a proposal which had already been made to a half-dozen other young gentlemen of title, actual or prospective, in straitened circumstances. Mr Magdalen possessed a daughter who would one day inherit the ill-gotten millions in which his only joy had been that of accumulating them. It would, however, he felt, be vain to leave her the wealthiest woman in England unless at the same time he could assure for her a place in those exalted social circles where wealth enabled life to be lived at its fullest and most brilliant.

It had become an obsession with the little usurer. The fact that in the past five years the proposal had been declined by the needy noblemen to whom it had been made, had merely served to sharpen Mr Magdalen's desire to a desperate keenness.

On the understanding that he made the offer subject to the lady's own consent – a consent which he opined, with an appreciative eye for Mr Lessingham's attractive exterior, was not likely to be refused – he invited Mr Lessingham to consider how happy an issue from all his troubles lay for him in marriage with so well-dowered a lady. He did so with confidence, gloating secretly over the fact that Mr Lessingham was in a vice far tighter than that in which he had held any of the gentlemen who had declined him. Nevertheless Mr Lessingham was prompt, outraged and virulent in damning the moneylender for his impudence. As foul-mouthed as a drayman, he practised no decency in his comments upon Mr Magdalen's probable ancestry. But when he came to express assumptions concerned with Mr Magdalen's only descendant, the moneylender checked him suddenly.

'Say nothing that will make it impossible for you to change your mind,' he warned him, in a thin, hard voice from which all benignity had departed. And at once he turned the screw of the vice in which he held his debtor. 'There's a matter of two thousand five hundred pounds for interest that was due from you yesterday. I don't wish to be hard, Mr Lessingham, sir, but unless I have the money by four o'clock this afternoon, I shall wait upon Sir John with the post-obit in the morning, and ask him if he would wish to redeem it.'

To Mr Lessingham this was a blow between the eyes. For a moment it almost stunned him. Recovering, he was first violent, then plaintive, then violent again. But Mr Magdalen, now tight of lip and hard of eye, remained unmoved, and the end of the matter was that Mr Lessingham went off to Highgate and Sir John with ruin staring him in the face. For he knew his uncle too well to doubt that the disclosure of how he had raised money on the prospect of the nawab's death would put an end to all his hopes of inheriting a shilling beyond the wretched little estate that went with the title.

At all costs that knowledge must be kept from Sir John.

In sheer despair, rather than consent to marry the daughter of that greasy little thief in Essex Street he chose the lesser evil of an appeal to the already exasperated nawab.

He may or may not have been mistaken in making his prayer more or less in the form of an accusation. It was Sir John's hardness towards him, he urged, that had driven him into the clutches of a rascally moneylender. To extricate himself completely he needed at once a matter of six or seven thousand pounds. The nawab's reply amounted to a sketch of his nephew's character as succinct as it was accurate and blistering, at the end of which he bade him go to the devil.

Mr Lessingham accounted that to marry Magdalen's daughter would be tantamount to obeying this injunction. But if he was to avoid the ruin of his hopes and the immediate possibility of debtor's gaol, there was no choice but to consent to make this probably greasy wench the future Lady Lessingham. It would be necessary to humble himself to the dust so as to obtain from Mr Magdalen a renewal of the offer he had so insolently rejected; and he must lose no time. It must be done at once if he would prevent Mr Magdalen's journey to Lessingham Park tomorrow with the post-obit.

He came raging to the summit of Highgate Hill. Without eyes for the fine prospect, with London under a haze at his feet, and the broad ribbon of the Thames visible for a dozen miles with its burden of shipping, he spurred his big black horse down the slope towards Holloway.

It was at the foot of the hill that Jack o'Lantern met him, and, to his undoing, was tempted to arrest his headlong course.

At the sight of the black-visored horseman and the levelled pistol, Mr Lessingham stood, as he was bidden. But as for delivering, it came to him as a climax of irony to swell his already excessive rage that such an invitation should be issued to a man in his desperate case.

Jack o'Lantern was, of course, not to know this. Nor had he any means of perceiving that the horseman he had brought to a standstill was a reckless, dangerous fellow at the best of times, and in particularly savage mood this afternoon. By the time he might have suspected it, he was beyond suspecting anything. For, with sudden, lightning speed, Mr Lessingham's heavy riding-crop had crashed into his temple and knocked him senseless from the saddle.

When the highwayman recovered consciousness, he was lying on the turf of a meadow beyond a belt of trees by which the horses were tethered, with his assailant sitting cross-legged and watchful beside him.

Mr Lessingham had taken the natural precaution of depriving him of his weapons. He had drawn a second pistol from its holster, and he had removed the sword the highwayman was wearing, a pretty piece of workmanship with a mother of pearl handle and for pommel a milky crystal the size of a pigeon's egg, that might have been a moonstone. It was attached to a baldrick of red Spanish leather adorned with a pattern of oak-leaves in gold bullion, and by this it was now slung from Mr Lessingham's own shoulder. To make sure that the rascal had no other weapon about him, Mr Lessingham had gone through his pockets. Amongst some lesser effects, he had found a gold snuff-box, and a heavy purse of red silk mesh that was stuffed with guineas and contained in addition a diamond ring of price. Perceiving no sin in robbing a thief, Mr Lessingham's easy conscience regarded these valuables as a windfall, and he transferred them to his own pocket. After that he sat down to await the man's recovery, and he smiled as he waited, for it seemed to him that nothing could have been more opportune. The encounter which had so infuriated him had ended by bringing inspiration. It prompted an easier way to deliverance from his difficulties than that to which he had been so dejectedly riding.

Jack o'Lantern sat up, straightened his wig on an aching head and in doing so became aware of the lump on his brow. He looked about him with eyes that were still dazed, met the derisive smile of Mr Lessingham and awakened a little further.

'What the devil...' he began, and checked there.

'Give yourself no concern, my friend,' said his captor. 'The worst has happened to you, unless you show no more sense than a woodcock.'

The highwayman's eyes alighted on the baldrick with the oak-leaves pattern. He felt in his pockets. Then his lip curled.

'So that's what you are,' said he. 'A dog that eats dog.'

Mr Lessingham laughed joyously, as a man will whose soul has suddenly been delivered of a burden of care. 'A mastiff that dines on poodles, if you will. But a tobyman by proxy, and that for one occasion only, provided you show sense. In that case you may go your ways to the devil when you've served my turn. In any other you'll ride with me to the Bridewell.'

Jack o'Lantern gathered up his legs and embraced his knees. Out of a lean, keen young face, wide of mouth and tip-tilted of nose, a pair of astute eyes calmly took the measure of Mr Lessingham. Whatever the rascal's emotions, he kept a mask upon them, and fear was certainly not amongst them.

'Could you be plainer?' he asked.

'As plain as you please. Early tomorrow we take the road together, hereabouts. That belt of trees will supply the screen we'll need, and we'll wait for a certain hackney coach that'll be coming from London on its way over the hill there. There'll not be many hackneys come as far as this, so we're not likely to be mistook, besides ye'll not stir until I've seen who rides in it. When I give you the word, you'll halt it. You'll require the traveller to strip himself and hand you his clothes besides anything else in the way of baggage that he may have with him. When you've delivered these to me, you may go your ways. Is it clear?'

'Clear enough, codso! I'm to pull chestnuts from the fire for you, so as if any fingers is burnt it'll be mine. But what do I get for doing it?'

'It's what'll you get for not doing it. The gallows. That's what you'll get.'

'Spoke like a gentleman,' said Jack. Then he passed a hand over an aching brow. 'Ye've got a pistol at my head. I must stand and deliver, I suppose. Do the dirty work ye're too fine to do for yourself.'

'I'm glad ye're sensible. And speaking of pistols, an empty one will serve your turn tomorrow. Our subject is an old man, and the hackney driver's only thought will be to keep a whole skin. So don't be building any false hopes.'

'Ye take no chances,' said Jack with the suspicion of a sneer.

'None, as you'll find. Remember it. For tonight you'll be my guest for bed and supper.'

'I had a notion that it was you might be mine, being as ye've filched my purse,' said Jack.

Mr Lessingham got up. 'I'll trouble you to keep a civil tongue, my lad. Get that into your brain-pan, and let it simmer there. Come on now. Up with you.'

Jack o'Lantern came slowly to his feet. He stood swaying a little, a hand to his head again.

'Odsbud! I'm giddy. Lend me your arm, sir.'

A smile twisted Mr Lessingham's full, cruel lips. 'I'll lend you nothing. Step out ahead, and no tricks, you rogue, or you'll forfeit your only chance of postponing acquaintance with the gallows. You'll not slip through my fingers; not if you were as slippery as Jack o'Lantern himself.'

Jack's only answer to that was a wistful smile. He went forward staggering a little, Mr Lessingham following closely, his riding-crop in readiness. Thus they reached the horses, untethered them, mounted, and picked their way through the trees to the road.

With the highwayman leading by half a length, so that the eye of this captor who took no chances was upon his every movement, they came, as dusk was closing in, to the Bull at Islington, where Mr Lessingham had resolved that they should lie the night, in readiness for the morrow's business of waylaying Mr Magdalen.

They left their horses with the ostler in the yard, and strode forward towards an open side-door from which the light was shining, the highwayman leading ever, with Mr Lessingham close upon his heels. Voices met them, coming from a room at the far end of the passage by which they were advancing, and what Jack o'Lantern heard made him check in his stride. The movement was instinctive, but so momentary that he seemed merely to have stumbled.

'And a bay mare, ye say, sir? I'll wager my bones that'd be Jack o'Lantern, as sure as my name be Tom Bowles.'

Impelled by his follower, Jack perforce went on, and as he reached the open door, the answer came delivered in a voice that was shrill with rage.

'Jack o'Lantern or another. What's the odds? A crying scandal to you all that such things should be done in daylight. In broad daylight. On the King's highway. It shows the worth of your vigilance. It shows the worth of all these measures of which Sir Henry Fielding makes a boast. Measures that were to clear the country of this vermin. Why, things were no worse a hundred years ago.'

The speaker was still inveighing when Jack came to the doorway. And Jack was not encouraged when in this speaker, a portly gentleman in high leather gaiters and a short skirted frock under the tails of which his hands were now thrust, he recognized the victim of his robbery that afternoon.

Squire Kendrick's face was inflamed with the anger into which he had lashed himself whilst denouncing the outrage suffered. For audience he had a couple of rustics, the landlord in shirt sleeves and apron, a man who held a constable's staff and a couple of tough-looking fellows who at a glance might be recognized for Bow Street runners.

It was not the sort of company into which Jack o'Lantern would normally have cared to thrust himself. Yet now he swaggered in, a smile on his lips, a jauntiness in his step, fully approved by Mr

Lessingham who followed more closely than ever upon the parlour's sanded floor. Heads were turned to see who came, and the landlord was detaching himself from the group to give welcome to these new guests, when Jack's hearty hail momentarily arrested them.

He had taken a swift step aside, away from his companion, and tossed up his head with a laugh of satisfaction.

'Well met, my hearties,' he greeted the Bow Street men, 'and in the very nick of time. If it's Jack o'Lantern ye're hunting, I'll be claiming the reward. For here you have him, led by the nose into your very arms for you.' And he flung out a hand to indicate Mr Lessingham.

There was a moment's silent, round-eyed amazement. Then it was Squire Kendrick who moved. His head craned forward on his stout neck, and his eyes bulging, he advanced on Mr Lessingham. Mr Lessingham, more taken aback than any of them by what he accounted a futile impudence, was uttering a fleeting laugh when Squire Kendrick flung out an accusing arm.

'Seize him,' he roared. 'I recognize him.' And at the word the Bow Street runners were upon Mr Lessingham like hounds upon a stag.

He struggled, panting and snarling in their arms, turning a face of fury upon the squire.

'What do you mean, you pot-bellied dotard? You recognize me?'

The Squire was upon him, whilst the runners held him.

'I mean this, you impudent rogue. This!' He seized the sword-belt of Spanish leather with the pretty oak-leaf pattern, upon which the ready-witted Jack o'Lantern had counted when he so boldly made his staggering announcement. 'I may not recognize your face, for that was masked; but, ecod! I recognize my own baldrick, ay, and the sword of which you robbed me this very afternoon, you damned hedge-creeper.'

The constable rolled forward importantly. 'Here. Give way whiles I search him.'

Lessingham abandoned the struggle, commanding himself now that he began to recognize that violence would not get him out of this trap. Forth from his pockets they brought a gold snuff-box on the lid of which was the squire's crest, a hand holding aloft an oak-leaf, and a heavy purse in which, in addition to the guineas, there was a diamond ring of price which had left the squire's finger three hours ago.

Mr Lessingham strove desperately to be calm. 'It looks like evidence, but it isn't. I can explain it all.'

'Ecod! so you shall,' chortled the squire. 'At Bow Street tomorrow morning. Keep your lies for the magistrate. Away with him.'

'Tomorrow morning will be too late, you fools,' Lessingham was suddenly beside himself, thinking of what would happen in the morning. 'I have an engagement to keep tonight. An important engagement. You shall hear me now, sir.'

They drove him to frenzy with their mockery until the squire, wearying of the sport, bade them away with the rascal.

The constable was looking round. 'But where's the gentleman that took him?' he asked.

He was answered by a clatter of departing hoofs on the kidney stones outside. Jack o'Lantern was proving true to his fame. And it was on the big black horse that he rode away, leaving the bay mare as further evidence against Mr Lessingham.

THE DEVOURER OF HEARTS

She came upon me unexpectedly as I was walking in my garden at Choisy, bewailing the Autumn that swooped down apace like a bird of prey to devour my cherished blossoms. The rumble of a coach heralded her coming, and as in my curiosity I craned my neck to see who my visitor might be, out stepped Léonie herself, as beautiful a thing, I'll swear, as any of God's making. She came to me all smiles and archness; and in that sisterly manner which she was wont to assume toward me, but which of a certainty she had refrained from adopting had she guessed how deeply it hurt, she announced that she had need of my assistance. I swore myself her humblest slave as ever, and she proceeded:

'I have been to the King, Guy,' she cried, 'and my intercessions have won Lawrence's pardon. See,' and she drew from some mysterious corner of her gown a portentous parchment. 'Here is the Royal warrant. His Majesty's sole condition is that the Vicomte shall absent himself from France for three years, until Castelnaudary and this rebellion be forgotten.'

'His Majesty is very clement,' said I. 'But then – you interceded.'

She laughed coyly, and her blue eyes flashed me a well-pleased glance – for, *bon Dieu!* she was the vainest beauty in all Paris.

'I shall carry him this pardon myself,' she continued. 'The poor boy is hiding somewhere in Languédoc, and we must find him, Guy.'

'We?' quoth I. 'What companions have you chosen?'

At that she felt confused, but only for a moment. Presently her eyes were raised to mine again, and she was smiling in allurement.

'I came to ask you to go with me, Guy. You see I am all alone, with the exception of Madame la Comtesse, who is much too enfeebled to undertake the journey. Then, too, on such an errand a male escort is of necessity, and my brother is with his regiment.'

'But, Léonie,' I cried aghast, 'bethink you what you are proposing. What will the world say? Mademoiselle de Montivry has left Paris under the escort of Guy de Chatellerault. A fine story that, on my life!'

'What shall it signify what the world says? I go to my affianced husband, and when I return it shall be as his wife, and so sheltered from evil tongues.'

I vow I turned pale at that. That some day she would wed the Vicomte I knew, just as I knew that some day I must die. The thing had been arranged while she was in her swaddling clothes, and she had been educated to the idea ever since she had begun to grow into the lovely creature that she had become. She did not love the Vicomte – indeed, she scarcely knew him, for she had not seen him half-a-dozen times all her life. But her marriage to him she looked upon as an inevitable something that must come to her with womanhood. It I seem to suggest that she did not love him because she did not know him, let me hasten to disabuse your mind. Because she did not know him she did not hate him.

No worse, perhaps, than most courtiers of the days of Louis XIII, yet I vow he was as bad as any, and the scandals that attached to his name defied all reckoning. Since his father's death his indiscretions had grown more flagrant, until in the end His Majesty had banished him for a spell from Court. Smarting under the indignity, he had offered his sword to the Duke of Orleans and had fought at Castelnaudary among the Spanish riff-raff that Gaston had brought into that field of scurvy memory. Proscribed and hunted as were his fellow-rebels, from Montmorency downward, his fate – so richly deserved – had been a source of unrest to that angel, Léonie, until in the end she had interceded and won his pardon from Louis.

That her wedding should be accelerated by the very facts that should have retarded it, shocked me inexpressibly. I was filled with a dull anger against Villebon, against her, against myself; and that anger, to my shame I write it, found expression. I had known her from childhood; we had been as brother and sister, until it had come to me to alter the relationship. That was two years ago, and since then I had made love to her desperately, ardently, passionately – but, alack, fruitlessly! Ever had she chid me for my gentle ways, my slender frame, my dainty hands. I was a man of songs, she had said, of pretty utterances; whilst her lover – but that she was already affianced – must have been a man of action; a hero of great deeds; the victor of a hundred combats. This I cast back at her now in my reply.

'What shall a writer of verses do upon such an enterprise?' I asked her bitterly. 'You will require a paladin for your escort.'

'But no,' said she, ignoring the ungenerous quality of my words, 'there will be no fighting.'

At that my manner grew yet worse. I was brusque as any clown. I bade her – the precise words I have mercifully forgotten – seek elsewhere for a protector. But when I had done she nestled up to me; her eyes raised to mine, and her hand was laid caressingly upon my arm, so that all my harshness fell from me on the instant.

'That is unlike you, Guy,' said she. 'Are my troubles of so little account to you – you who call yourself my friend?' I humbly craved forgiveness, and swore my readiness to do whatever she might command me.

'Now you are the Guy I know. The dear, kind, gentle Guy who is my friend.' She moved a step or two away from me. 'When you are so I have a kindness for you,' she said.

'Yes,' I rejoined, my bitterness returning, 'such a kindness as have I for my roses when they bloom.' And I waved an angry hand over a faded bush.

'And were I not affianced to M. de Villebon – ' She stopped short, and over her shoulder she threw me a glance from eyes that laughed at once in mockery and affection.

'Léonie!' I cried, and in an instant I was beside her. I caught her in my arms and held her there with a force that must have hurt, whilst into her ear I poured once more the story of my love for her. I reminded her that this Villebon was nothing to her; that she did not love him; that she would never love him – yet was I gentleman enough even in my madness to say nothing of those ugly tales that all Paris was reciting touching the Vicomte's disreputable adventures.

At last she broke from me, and confronted me panting, an angry spot of red on either cheek. Then she smiled wistfully.

'You have told me all, Guy, have you not?' she asked softly. 'And we will speak of it no more – is it not so, my friend? You have confessed. I absolve you, and here make you your act of contrition and sin no more, for if you do I may not even count you my friend. And so I value your friendship, Guy. But love' – she sighed – 'it is something that I think will never come to me; which, after all, is very well, for I am to marry M. de Villebon. You'll not desert me, Guy?'

What could I answer? What could any man answer who truly loved with a devotion that amounted almost to awe – as true love should do. I promised that I would allow my folly to transpire no more. I would curb and suppress it, and she might count upon me to help her find the worthless Vicomte to whom she was betrothed.

On the morrow we started for the South – she in her coach, attended by her maid; I on horseback, with my servant Charlot riding at my heels. Yesterday's scene seemed all forgotten by her, and when she saw me booted and spurred for the journey, encased in a jerkin of leather and with a great sword girt to me, she laughed and made a mock of my warlike trappings and the martial air which she swore I had put on with this grim raiment. I suffered her jests in silence; I even smiled when she called me Duguesclin: for all that the gibe cut me sorely.

Some slight adventures had we when we came into Languédoc, and during the diligent search I instituted for M. de Villebon, owing to the suspicions of the peasantry, who were one and all for the Duke Gaston, and who doubted the intentions of our quest for one of his adherents. At last, however, success attended my efforts, and I gleaned the information that at Les Martyrs – a little village on the spurs of the Cevennes – I should probably find him we sought.

Thither we rode, therefore, and we gained the place one evening at dusk. We repaired to the Auberge Béarnaise – the only hostelry of any consequence in the only street of that hill-side village. We proceeded with caution, and it was not until we had seated ourselves to sup in the common-room – there was no other – that I thought it well to broach the matter which had brought us. Such knowledge as they might have they were inclined to deal with as a snail with its horns.

There were four men in the room, sitting over by the chimney with the landlord, and by way of introduction I called upon the host to lay a couple of his best bottles at their disposal. It was done with alacrity, and, having thus gained their good favour, I engaged those burly, evil-looking mountain men in conversation. I touched in passing upon the state of France and the late disturbances, and I spoke of the Cardinal with a grimace, of the King with a sneer, and of Gaston with a sigh and an adjective of praise. My manner gradually thawed them, and when presently I grew bolder in my allusions, to the point, I'll swear, of being guilty of high treason, an air of utter good-fellowship settled over us.

Mademoiselle supped in silence, but her glance of approval was encouraging. She had been kinder to me of late; for perhaps she had come to see that when the occasion demanded it I could become, to some extent at least, the man of action that she chid me for not being.

Deeming them ripe at last, I touched more closely upon the business that had brought us, informing them that we were in quest of a gentleman who had followed the fortunes of Gaston into the disastrous field of Castelnaudary, and whom we desired to equip with the means of taking himself into safety beyond Pyrenees.

'If you were to tell us his name, Monsieur,' said Dangeau, the landlord, 'we might assist you.' He was a superior fellow, this Dangeau, a man of speech and manners somewhat above his station, and no doubt a man of much consequence upon that countryside, holding himself in high esteem.

'It is Monsieur le Vicomte Laurence de Villebon whom we are seeking,' said I, and had I cast a bomb into their midst it could not have surprised them more. Seeing them start, and noting the significant glances that passed between them – 'Clearly, my masters,' I added, 'the name is not unknown to you.'

'It is not indeed, Monsieur,' returned Dangeau, with a greater cordiality than he had yet shown us, 'and if your friend be the Vicomte, you are very welcome.'

A girl who had entered the common-room at that moment, hearing the words, stood still to survey us. She was a handsome wench, strongly resembling Dangeau. She was tall, with a shapely length of limb and an admirably poised head, richly crowned with soft, lustrous black hair. Black, too, and remarkable were her eyes, and as I now returned her glance it crossed my mind that one might travel far before chancing upon her equal in looks and grace. That air of superiority to the surroundings that I had remarked in Dangeau was carried in her to the point almost of aloofness.

'These *voyageurs*,' said the landlord to the girl, 'are friends of M. le Vicomte.' The girl continued to stare at us in a fashion that showed me plainly her manners were far below the level of her grand air.

'I am charmed, M. l'Hote,' said I, 'to discover that we have fallen among people who appear no less friendly disposed to him. Where, sir, can I find the Vicomte?'

He seemed on point of answering, when suddenly the girl set her hand on his arm.

'Are you satisfied that we can trust them?' she inquired.

'Ah,' quoth Dangeau, taking a deep breath. Then to me – 'Monsieur will forgive me, for you must appreciate the dangers. Can you give me any proof of your attachment to M. le Vicomte? What is your precise relationship with him?'

'This lady, Master Dangeau,' I announced, 'is the Vicomte's betrothed, and she has journeyed into Languédoc to wed him and to go with him into exile.'

Now if awhile ago the mention of Villebon's name had sown surprise amongst them, the effect it had produced was as nothing compared with the disorder into which this fresh announcement appeared to throw them. Again there were gasps and glances exchanged, whilst the girl's great eyes seemed to dilate, though otherwise she remained erect and cold. Then Dangeau exploded.

'It is a lie!' he shouted, bringing down his fist upon the table so violently that a jug of wine was overset into my lap. That said, he eyed me a moment with deepening suspicion, and as I essayed to rise he thrust me back into my chair. 'Look to the door, Pierre,' he called to one of the four ruffians. 'We have spies amongst us, it seems, but, by God, we shall know how to deal with them.'

'When you have recovered the use of your wits,' said I, coolly mopping the wine from my *haut-de-chausses*, 'perhaps you will explain how I have provoked this thunderstorm?'

'You need explanations, do you?' he sneered. 'You have told, me plainly enough that it is for no friendly purpose that you seek the Vicomte. Bah! I know you well enough. The province is infested by spies of your kidney, lending themselves to the work of trapping these poor fugitives. You played your *rôle* finely, and had you not overshot the mark, you had duped us. But when you present your companion as the Vicomte's betrothed, you go too far; for the Vicomte's future wife, my master, stands there.'

And he pointed to his daughter. There was a sudden catch in Mademoiselle's breath as she rose to her feet, but the swiftness with which she grasped the situation and the calm with which she spoke amazed me.

'Since that is so, Monsieur, our journey has indeed been wasted, and nothing remains for us but to withdraw, regretting the intrusion.'

The words were ill-timed, and they added fuel to the host's suspicions.

'Withdraw?' he roared. 'By the Mass, you shall not stir foot from here until it please me, and it is more than likely you'll never stir at all. We have a short way with spies. Here, my lads, lay hands on these friends of my Lord Cardinal.'

Mademoiselle grew pale at that for all her spirit, and her eyes that were turned toward me said, as plainly as if she had spoken: 'If only you were a man of action, my poor Guy!' And be it that that glance spurred me to it, or be it that the latest militant instincts of my blood welled up to meet the occasion – a man of action I became. I had risen now, and picking up a three-legged stool – for my sword I realised would avail me little in the rough-and-tumble that was like to follow – I waved it lustily.

'Let but a finger be laid on Mademoiselle, and I'll brain the man that dares it,' I threatened.

There was a short laugh from one of them, and he sprang toward me. I have a notion that I closed my eyes – for I was new to skull-cracking, and haply a trifle squeamish. But I brought my stool down with a sickening crash upon his stupid head, and felled him. Again I raised that improvised battle-axe, and this time, with eyes wide open that I might not err, I caught another ruffian, who had set hands upon Léonie, so well gauged a blow that he staggered backwards, and throwing up his arms dropped full length, whilst the blood, streaming from a gash in his forehead, seemed to cover his face in an instant.

With a moan of horror Mademoiselle shrank back against the wall and put her hands to her eyes. I – suddenly transformed into a very *Jupiter tonans* – stood my ground defiantly, ready to launch that thunderbolt of a stool upon the next who should try conclusions with me. Then suddenly old Dangeau seized a musketoon that had stood in a corner, and it would have fared ill with me but that before he could raise it to his shoulder a cry from his daughter arrested him. The door had been pushed open, and on the threshold stood the Vicomte de Villebon himself. A pause fell upon all present, as with a look of the profoundest amazement the Vicomte advanced into the room, his eyes devouring Léonie. It was he who broke at last the silence that now reigned.

'You here, Mademoiselle!' he exclaimed.

'As you perceive, Monsieur,' said she very quietly, her face giving no sign of concern beyond its extreme pallor. 'If you have any influence with these good people, perhaps you will give yourself the trouble of prevailing upon them not to cut our throats.'

'But what has happened?' he inquired, and in the place of the easy, graceful dignity that was usually his, his bearing was now a mixture of bewilderment and sheepishness.

'These people,' Dangeau explained in truculent accents, 'came here to seek you, but they introduced themselves with the falsehood that this lady is your affianced wife.'

'It is a falsehood, is it not, Laurence?' cried the girl, stepping close up to him, and putting the question in beseeching accents.

'Oh *ça*, my dear Sophie,' he laughed brazenly, as who would say: 'How could it be other than false?' Then to Dangeau – 'Let me have a word in private with these good friends of mine,' said he, his attempt at jauntiness failing miserably. 'They were well-intentioned in the statement that they made; for that they may have transcended accuracy in their zeal to discover me.'

Scarcely believing my ears, I looked at Léonie. She was smiling curiously.

'If you are playing fast and loose with us,' began Dangeau, his brow black with menace. But the Vicomte, drawing himself up with an assumption of his usual arrogance, cut him short—

'Monsieur,' said he, 'what I have pledged my word to do I do.'

But when presently we three – the Vicomte, Mademoiselle and I – were in an inner room, Villebon's words were less high-sounding.

'Mademoiselle,' he said, 'to you it will be clear that this undignified position in which you find me has been forced upon me by necessity. My marrying this girl is a matter too preposterous for consideration.'

'Ah,' said she coldly, 'and the breaking of that child's heart no doubt a matter too insignificant to need consideration either.'

At that his manner became suddenly offensive.

'Why are you come to Languédoc, Mademoiselle?' he demanded insolently – so insolently that I had visions of resuming my performances with the three-legged stool.

'To drive a bargain with you, M. le Vicomte,' she answered, a note of anger ringing in her voice as well. 'Tell me – how came you into such relations with that girl?'

Villebon, the devourer of hearts, answered her with easy flippancy and an expressive shrug.

'*Faut s'amuser*,' he declared. 'It was so dull and *ennuyant* hiding from the King's gentlemen.'

Léonie demanded details, and he afforded them. It was just such a story as I had expected to hear. Dalliance was to the Vicomte as the breath of his nostrils – a necessity of life. The trouble that in Paris it had visited upon him had not taught him any salutary lesson; in the provinces he had resumed the pastime, and heaven alone knows how many banal affairs he had not scattered in his passage through Languédoc. But here at this inn at Les Martyrs he had entered upon one that was to bring him more serious consequences. Whilst in hiding there, protected by this staunch Orléaniste, Dangeau, he had amused himself by making love to Sophie. To him it could be no more than amusement; but it was an amusement of which the poor girl – not being a fine lady of Court – knew nothing. To her it was a serious matter, and she accepted each well-worn phrase of gallantry in its literal sense, as a true expression of sentiment. Realising at last the indiscretion of his behaviour, Villebon had sought to beat a retreat. But at the first sign of this, old Dangeau had stepped forward. He had observed, and in his simplicity taken as earnest the Vicomte's wooing of his daughter – for those *montagnards* of Languédoc have a curious ignorance of the distinctions of rank that prevail in other provinces – and he was not minded that this debonair young rebel should break his daughter's heart. He had protested against the Vicomte's departure; he had reasoned with him touching Sophie, and I am satisfied that the musketoon was advanced as a weighty piece of logic. Moreover, Villebon realised that Dangeau might even avenge himself by delivering him up to the King, and he had no appetite for being broken on the wheel, so that out of fear he had temporised by a promise to marry Sophie so soon as he might conveniently do so.

'But,' the Vicomte concluded, with a deprecatory smile, 'you will agree, Mademoiselle, that it were a heavy price to pay for the amusement of expressing a few pretty sentiments.'

'I own it heavy, but you must pay it, Monsieur,' she said, whereat I stared at her in my amazement.

''Tis a good jest, that,' he laughed, displaying his fine teeth.

'It is no jest at all, Monsieur.'

His jaw dropped, and he eyed her in bewilderment, sobered by her sternness.

'But, Mademoiselle, I am betrothed to you!'

'We will not speak of that again, if you please,' she answered coldly. And, ashamed, he hung his head, realising that indeed for one who had promised marriage to Dangeau's daughter to speak of being betrothed to Mademoiselle de Montivry was an insolence too gross.

They wrangled awhile after that: she telling him that he must wed the girl, he laughing the notion to scorn.

'You pledged your word,' she cried at last, burning with indignation – for she was beginning to know this very choice Vicomte. 'In my hearing you renewed the pledge. Will you be dishonoured?'

At that he abandoned mockery, and grew solemn as a father-confessor. He expostulated with her, whereupon she turned to threats and to the bargain which she had come to drive with him.

'Monsieur de Villebon,' said she, 'at Jarnages, this afternoon, we passed a company of the King's dragoons. They are closing round this part of the Cevennes, and at this hour your escape will already be impossible. By morning you will be a prisoner. Your fate you can guess, Monsieur.'

He turned pale at that. On the battlefield he may have been brave as a lion; but the thought of the wheel gave his stomach an unpleasant turn.

'Now, Monsieur, attend to this. I have it in my power to save your life. I can open a way for you into Spain, and within three years I can promise your return to France, where you shall find your estates unsequestrated. But before I do this for you I will see you wedded to Sophie Dangeau.'

'How will you fulfil all these fine promises?' he asked, amazed.

'I do not lie, Monsieur. I have said that I can do it. Be that sufficient. Will you accept my conditions, or will you be taken to Toulouse and the scaffold? Resolve yourself.'

For all that his heart was numb with fear, he still sought to temporise. But Mademoiselle was obdurate. When he advanced that Sophie was not a wife he could take to Paris, she answered him that there was no need for it. Indeed, Paris would be unhealthy for him for years to come. There was his estate in Picardy. Let him take her there when he returned from Spain, and let him spend the first year of their wedded life in preparing her to become a creditable Vicomtesse. In the end the gallant Villebon was beaten and forced to yield.

He was barely in time, for scarcely had he accepted Léonie's terms when the door opened to admit Dangeau, with a scared face.

'Les Martyrs is surrounded by dragoons, Vicomte,' he announced.

'Trust to me,' said Léonie. Then turning to Dangeau – 'The Vicomte,' she informed him, 'is safe, but he will be compelled to start at sunrise for Spain. Your daughter, he will tell you, goes with him as his wife. There is no time to lose, and you had best send for Monsieur le Curé at once.'

While the priest was being sought the dragoons arrived, and the officer in command entered the inn and formally arrested Villebon. But Mademoiselle took the Captain aside, with the result that five minutes later he desired the mystified Vicomte to be in readiness to start for Spain at daybreak under his escort.

We saw the nuptials solemnised that night, and when as day was breaking the troop was ready to conduct the Vicomte across the border, Léonie took him aside.

'So far I have done what I promised,' she said, 'and you may rest assured that I shall keep my word till the end. When the three years of your exile are at an end you shall receive a pardon warranting your return to France. But this I promise you only on condition that you are good to that child, and that you make her a worthy husband. Fail me in that, and you are not likely to see France again as long as you live.'

Solemnly he swore to resign himself to what he now accounted his destiny. With that oath he took his leave of Léonie and accompanied by his wife he set out in the charge of the dragoons.

When at last he was gone –

'An eventful night, Guy, was it not?' quoth Léonie. 'And I think that we both acquitted ourselves well. I have wronged you in the past, my friend, for you fought like a lion.'

'The greatest fight was yours – on that girl's behalf,' I answered.

'Nay, Guy, not on her behalf; on my own. It was my liberty from Villebon which I was fighting for.'

'You are wonderful, Léonie,' I cried, adding with a sigh – 'I wish with all my heart that I had not promised you a week ago, in my garden at Choisy, n ever to speak of love again.'

She looked at me for a moment with a smile so tender and kind that a doubt surged wildly through my mind. Then holding out both hands to me she turned my doubts to certainty.

'We will go back to your garden at Choisy, Guy; and if you should elect to break your promise, I'll think you none the less a very gallant gentleman.'

THE CAPTAIN OF THE GUARD

Sleek, black-haired Bernouin, with his bright, observant eyes and his thin-lipped, circumspect mouth, stood at his window, gazing idly across the courtyard of the Palais Cardinal.

The afternoon sun, falling athwart the quadrangle, whilst leaving his window in the shade, illumined the interior of Captain d'Attignac's room opposite, and revealed to the eyes of Bernouin that worthy gentleman writing busily. Now, for all that the Cardinal's valet was no spy, yet it had long been his habit – and who am I that I should cast a stone at it? – to observe all things that were to be observed. And so, since chance and the afternoon sun revealed to him the Captain of the Guard at a time when the Captain did not dream himself observed, Bernouin concluded that to neglect the opportunity would be unworthy of a man of sense. That Captain d'Attignac should write at all was in itself a fact to be remarked, but that when he had written he should take up his hat, and carefully conceal the letter he had penned in the lining, was a matter that struck Bernouin as curious. Then d'Attignac went to the door, opened it, and appeared to call; which done, he went back to his table and sat down again. A few seconds later his door was opened, and into his room stepped a soldier of the Guard, who saluted and stood hat in hand, awaiting. In this new-comer, Bernouin recognised a dull-witted clod from Béarn named Barseau.

And now the Captain's behaviour grew singular to a degree. He was not famed for affability, yet he waved the Guardsman to a chair; and when the fellow was seated he pointed with his pen to the table, saying something as he did so; and Barseau placed his hat there. Beside it stood a little bowl of goldfish. For some moments Attignac wrote assiduously, and Bernouin asked himself what little comedy he might be about. At last he stopped, and, without looking up, put out his hand for the sandbox; and so clumsy was he that in taking it up his elbow caught the glass bowl, and shot its contents into Barseau's hat. In the hat, on the table, and on the floor itself Bernouin could see the flashing of the leaping, wriggling fish. Barseau was on his feet grabbing at and catching them, only to find himself empty-handed, again and again to grab and catch. In this manner one by one they were got back into the bowl, which Attignac had righted, and in which there was still some water left.

The Captain appeared to be uttering endless regrets. Barseau was ruefully shaking his sodden castor, its beautiful red feather turned limp. Then Attignac rose to the occasion, and, snatching the dripping thing from the fellow's hand, he pressed upon him his own hat, which lay close by, and which Bernouin remembered had a letter in the lining. Barseau protested, but the Captain was inexorable in his generosity; and so, with Attignac's hat on his head, and Attignac's second letter in his pocket, Barseau presently quitted the Captain's room.

'Odd!' muttered Bernouin. 'I wonder now – I wonder – ' He paused, turned abruptly from the window, and as abruptly left his room; for Bernouin had a passion for unravelling mysteries; and here was one that gave fair promise of being interesting.

He overtook Barseau almost at the Palace gates.

'Hi, Barseau! Monsieur Barseau! A word with you.'

The Guardsman turned, a sharp answer that he was in haste trembling on his lips. But when he saw who it was that called, he left the words unspoken, for in common with many another stout fellow he stood in awe of this lean, quiet man with the pale face and the keen eyes.

'I was on my way to the Guardroom to inquire for you,' said the valet, who had learnt, in the Cardinal's service, to lie with easy dignity. 'Will you step into my room? I have something to say to you.'

The tone, though free from menace, was of a vagueness that filled the poor Béarnais soldier with uneasiness. He muttered something touching his errand for Captain d'Attignac, but Bernouin peremptorily swept the objection aside; the message could wait a few moments. Indeed, he hinted that it might be necessary to find another messenger, whereat with tremblings of spirit, but never another word of protest, Barseau went with him. As they moved down the long, gloomy gallery, Bernouin made a sign to a couple of idling Guardsmen, who at once started to follow them. This Barseau observed, and his uneasiness grew apace. The valet ushered him into his room, and, closing the door, he left the two attendant Guardsmen without. Barseau uncovered his head, for Bernouin was not a person to be lightly treated, and stood waiting in an attitude of exceeding humility.

'I am desolated to say, Monsieur Barseau,' the valet began, 'that there is a very grave charge proffered against one of His Eminence's Guards, whilst the evidence we have gathered points strongly to you.' The Guardsman started. 'It is so grave a matter that I hardly dare disclose it to you yet; since, should I find you not to be the culprit, it will be as well that you should remain in ignorance of the affair.'

'But, Monsieur Bernouin, unless I know with what I am charged, how can I defend myself? My conscience, I assure you, is clear, and makes me no reproaches.'

'I am glad, sir. His Eminence has left me to sift the matter; and there is one simple method by which I can deal with you, and ascertain your innocence. Will you do me the favour to tell me where you were to be found at ten o'clock last night?'

'At ten o'clock? I was at the Green Pillar Inn in the Rue St. Honoré.'

'Ah!' And Bernouin's face took on a smile of encouragement. 'Come, monsieur, that is good news! There were, no doubt, others with you who can prove this?'

'But certainly, Monsieur Bernouin.'

'Do me the favour to sit down at that table and write out the statement you have just made to me, and the names of those who were present – the names of, say, four or five of them.'

Deeply puzzled, Barseau put his hat on a chair, and sat down to do Bernouin's bidding. Whilst he wrote, the valet opened the door and bade the two Guardsmen enter. When Barseau had written, and before he had time to rise, 'Messieurs,' said Bernouin to the two soldiers, 'take Monsieur Barseau into that alcove, and wait there until I call you.' Then, turning to Barseau, 'I shall lay this before His Eminence, and I hope within a few moments to inform you that you are cleared of all suspicion. Take him away, messieurs.'

When the door of the alcove had closed upon them, Bernouin took up the hat from the chair, where it had been left, and, pulling down the lining, he set himself to seek the letter he had seen concealed there. He had need to look closely, for the paper which he ultimately found was so thin and small that it would certainly have escaped the notice of any man not acquainted with its existence.

On this scrap of paper, which bore no superscription, Bernouin read:

'Mazarin has been warned that at the masque at the Hôtel de Liancourt to-night the plotters will meet. He knows the password that will gain admittance to the chamber set aside for them, and it is his intention to attend. He will wear a green domino and a black mask. The occasion should be propitious.'

Bernouin took a deep breath and sat still a moment. Mazarin had suspected that the Frondeur supporters of the Duke of Beaufort were meditating something to gain their champion's enlargement from Vincennes; and it had not surprised him when he learned that the conspirators had arranged a meeting. In resolving to himself attend it, he had for object to ascertain who were the ringleaders, that he might draw their fangs. He had been far, however, from suspecting that his being made acquainted with that meeting was but the part of a deep-laid scheme for his own undoing, as this letter now made clear to Bernouin.

The valet wondered for whom this letter might be intended, but, remembering the other missive which he knew Barseau to be the bearer of, he saw that this would not be difficult to ascertain. Deep in thought, the valet sat a while, pondering what course he should take.

His first impulse was to go straight to Mazarin, and lay the letter and the facts before him. But, upon second thoughts, he resolved to act on his own initiative.

He thought, too, of d'Attignac, this upstart who owed his position to the Cardinal's favour; and he cursed him for a foul, ungrateful traitor to have so projected selling his master. And then, in a flash, a measure of poetic justice suggested itself.

Acting upon this, he replaced the letter in the lining of Barseau's hat, and put the hat on the chair where the Guardsman had left it. That done, he strode over to the door of the alcove, and threw it open.

'Monsieur Barseau, you may come out,' said he pleasantly. 'I rejoice to inform you that His Eminence is satisfied that you are not the man we are seeking.'

Barseau, who had spent a very uncomfortable quarter of an hour, allowed the joy occasioned by this prompt release to shine on his honest, stupid countenance as he took his leave of Bernouin.

'You said something of an errand,' murmured the valet. 'I trust we have not unconscionably detained you. To whom are you bound?'

'To Monsieur le Marquis de St. Marcel with a letter from Captain d'Attignac.'

Again expressing the hope that the delay would give rise to no inconvenience, and promising forthwith to explain matters to Attignac, Bernouin dismissed him, and repaired, as he had said, to the Captain's quarters.

D'Attignac received him cavalierly. He accounted himself a very exalted personage, whose dignity it would ill become to sort with lackeys, even where it was a question of His Eminence's body-servant. Bernouin was distant yet respectful as he delivered the Captain a fictitious order from the Cardinal. This message enjoined Attignac to set out at once for Choisy, and there receive at the Hôtel de Connétable certain documents that would be handed him by a gentleman from Béarn. The name Bernouin could not disclose; but the matter, he urged, was of the greatest moment, and His Eminence required a trusted messenger. Attignac's brows went up in dignified astonishment.

'Why,' he inquired, 'did not His Eminence send for me and give me his commands in person?'

'Is it for me to explain His Eminence's motives?' Bernouin reproved him. 'The matter is pressing, and Monseigneur expects you to start without losing an instant. Should you be the first to reach Choisy, His Eminence wishes you to await the arrival of the gentleman in question.'

With that he left Attignac and repaired to the Cardinal's ante-chamber, so that, should the Captain seek His Eminence before setting out, Bernouin might intercept him. But from the windows which overlooked the courtyard the valet had the satisfaction of watching Attignac's departure some ten minutes after their interview.

Satisfied that he was gone, Bernouin quitted the ante-room, and presently he rode out himself, armed, cloaked, and booted. He trotted briskly up the Rue St. Honoré, and then down a side-street towards the river, which he crossed by the Pont Neuf, making his way to the Rue Serpente – a dismal, narrow lane off the Rue de la Harpe. Before a dingy hostelry, choicely named the Devil's Tavern, he drew rein and entered. Crossing the common-room with the assured step that bespeaks acquaintance with the surroundings, he opened a door and descended a short flight of steps into an unclean hole of a room where two men were blaspheming over three dirty dice.

They sorted well with their surroundings, did these two; and it was a matter for some marvelling that a man of so fastidious and scrupulous an exterior as Bernouin should smile so affably upon beholding them.

'Ah, you are there, Pistache,' he exclaimed; and at the sound of his voice one of the men – the taller, fiercer, and more unkempt – sprang up and removed his dirty hat. 'I was afraid you might be absent. I need you and a friend you can trust.'

Pistache bowed and pointed with his thumb to his companion. 'There is Grégoire here. He will follow me to the death,' he said grandiloquently.

Grégoire bowed as he pocketed the dice, and Bernouin acknowledged the bow by a brief nod.

'Buckle on your swords,' said the valet sharply. 'I am in haste. At the corner of the Rue de la Harpe you will find a groom with two horses. The word is 'Choisy.' Utter it, and he will surrender you the reins. Mount and ride back in this direction; then follow me – but at a distance. Come, bestir yourselves.'

'I thirst,' growled Pistache. 'A stirrup of Red Anjou ere we – '

'Ouside!' thundered Bernouin. 'Have I not said that I am in haste? To-night you shall have the wherewithal to drink yourselves as full as a Spanish wine-skin. There are ten pistoles for each of you when the business is over; and no risk to speak of. Now be off.'

The mention of the gold showed the advisability of swift obedience, and out they went with a fine swagger and a majestic flutter of their tattered cloaks.

About an hour later Bernouin pulled up before the sign of the Connétable at Choisy, and waited for them to come up with him ere he dismounted. He sat with hat thrust forward, and his cloak well across his face, concealing it.

'Pistache,' said he shortly, 'you will enter the common-room with Grégoire, and you will sit drinking a stoup until I call you or until you hear a smash in the inner room. Thereupon you will come to me immediately. You understand?'

Pistache protested with many a tavern oath that he was all comprehension, and Bernouin got down and entered the inn. He called for a jug of wine for his attendants, and requested the host to lead him to the gentleman lately arrived from Paris, whereupon he was ushered into the presence of the waiting Attignac, in the chamber beyond the common-room. The unsuspecting Captain bowed,

'I understand that you have letters for His Eminence,' said he.

'That may be,' replied Bernouin, thickening his voice. 'But you will forgive me if I hesitate to deliver them to a traitor, to the man who conspires with the Marquis de St. Marcel against the hand that pays him.'

'Par le mort Dieu!' swore Attignac, setting hand to his sword; ' you are over well informed to live.'

A burst of laughter answered him from the folds of the masking cloak.

'I am right, then, in my surmise,' said the valet, 'and you are clearly the very man I want. Put up your sword, sir; I did but seek to ascertain that you were indeed he of whom St. Marcel had spoken to me.'

His mouth agape, and his sword half drawn, d'Attignac stood, looking very foolish.

'The blow,' said Bernouin, 'is, I have just been informed, to be struck to-night at the Hôtel de Liancourt, whither His Eminence is being lured. Monsieur, I have no letters for Mazarin. That was my pretext to gain this interview; for if the conspirators have resolved to go to extremes I would humbly offer myself as the instrument of vengeance. I have my reasons.'

Before proceeding to deal with Attignac it was Bernouin's object to gain comfirmation of his suspicion that it was the Cardinal's life that was threatened. From what he had said – although much he could not understand – Attignac could not doubt that this man was one of them. Else how came he so well informed?

'You are singularly correct in your surmise, monsieur,' said he. 'Mazarin is doomed. But for the rest, another hand is to have the honour of despatching him. It is the task Monsieur de St. Marcel reserves for himself. My God! *You!*'

The cloak had fallen from Bernouin's face. He had hitched it from his shoulders; and as it fell about his feet he kicked it clear of him, and drew his sword to defend himself against the Captain's furious onslaught.

'Fool!' sneered the valet; 'you lack even the discretion of a plotter. Fie, Monsieur d'Attignac! To blab so weighty a matter in a roadside tavern to a stranger who does not show his face! I blush for you!'

'As God lives you shall bleed for it! I'll kill you!' bellowed the Captain of the Guard. But scarcely was the boast uttered than he realised how fraught with difficulties was its fulfilment. For by a smart turn of the wrist Bernouin had counter-parried his deadliest *botte*, and got inside his guard in a disconcerting manner. Why he had not pushed the advantage to the end, Attignac could not understand; but he did understand that this fellow. whom he had regarded as a mere man of costumes and pomades, was a fencer of an awe-inspiring calibre. A feinte and a lunge drove him back until he was shouldering the wall, and Bernouin, as he advanced, took up with his left hand a large earthenware jug that stood upon the table.

'*Voyons,*' he sneered, 'I could cut you into ribbons, you boaster, were I so minded. But I have a better purpose for you. I mean to employ you in the saving of His Eminence's life to-night.' With that he flung the jug into the fireplace, where it fell with a crash.

As promptly as though they had stood waiting for the signal – as indeed they had, alarmed by the ring of steel – the door was flung open. and Bernouin's tatterdemalions rushed in, their rapiers drawn, to his assistance.

'Do not hurt him,' cried the valet sharply. 'Beat the sword from his hand. Pshaw! Stand aside, fools,' he commanded, noting the rough manner in which they went about it. He made a thrust, which the Captain parried; then, instead of disengaging, he continued the stroke, as if no parry had been offered, until his hilt struck his opponent's and forced his sword so that it pointed upwards. Suddenly putting forward his left hand, he seized Attignac's rapier by the quillons, and before the Captain could tighten his hold he had wrenched the weapon from his grasp.

'Now take him and truss him up,' said Bernouin quietly, and they obeyed, the Captain too demoralised to offer them resistance.

♦   ♦   ♦   ♦   ♦

At the Hôtel de Liancourt that night the twelve conspirators who had the slaying of Mazarin for scope were on the very tiptoe of expectation. Some anxiety, too, was theirs. Would he come? they asked one another, fearful lest some contretemps should yet thwart so excellently contrived an opportunity. Meanwhile the fiddlers fiddled blithely, the maskers stepped the coranto with verve and sprightliness, the air was heavy with the scent of ambergris, and little was there to indicate that that merry scene was but as the fine linen that hides a cancer.

At nine o'clock, during a pause in the dancing, a stir ran through the assemblage, and the eyes of those present were drawn to a couple of fresh arrivals. They were both men of tall, imposing figures, to which the long, flowing garments added height. One of these wore a green domino and a black mask; the other a black domino edged with white, and a black velvet visor.

Their arrival seemed as a signal for the twelve plotters to pass one by one from the ballroom and repair to the chamber which was to be the scene of the projected drama. The last to enter was St. Marcel himself.

159

'Messieurs,' he said softly, 'they are coming.'

'You are sure there is no mistake, Marquis?' inquired a cautious one.

'Perfectly. I stood close beside them a moment ago, and I heard Bernouin whisper 'This way, Eminence,' to his companion, In five minutes, gentlemen, France will be rid of this foreign adventurer. God give me strength and accuracy!'

The twelve stood grouped in the middle of the room as the door opened, and they were quietly joined by the victim and his companion. One of the conspirators detached himself from the group, and went to secure the door.

'Messieurs,' came St. Marcel's harsh voice, 'but twelve of us were bidden to attend here, and I count fourteen. There are spies among us, it would seem.' He was close to the green domino by now. 'I need not trouble you to unmask, for there are two men present who do not wear the badge.'

Bernouin, looking about him, observed that on each man's shoulder a ribbon of crimson silk was shown.

'Tuez!' cried a voice. 'Kill the interlopers!'

'That is well said,' St. Marcel made answer, 'and may France be as easily rid of all interlopers!'

His arm was suddenly raised, and in his hand glittered a steel which a moment later was buried in the breast of the green domino. The tall figure swayed a second; then, as the murderer withdrew his dagger and plunged it in a second time, that tall, imposing figure suddenly collapsed, and sank in a heap on to the floor without so much as a cry.

But a cry there was from Bernouin, who, shouting that murder was being done, sprang to the door of the chamber to escape. After him, in swift strides, came St. Marcel, his reeking poniard upraised again. And into the middle of Bernouin's back that blade descended, there to be snapped by the shirt of mail the valet had seen fit to don ere he entered that murderous company.

'Tenez!' exclaimed the Marquis; 'this dog is armed, The door, Flamand!'

160

But Bernouin caught Flamand in his strong, nervous grip. He took him by the throat with both hands, and, dragging him from the door, he flung him in the middle of the room.

St. Marcel now had the valet by the shoulders, but he lacked the strength to hold him. He had wrenched the door open, and his voice sounded to alarm.

'To me!' he shouted. 'To the rescue. *À moi*, Brulin!'

Now, Brulin was the sergeant of His Eminence's Guard, and that Bernouin should call him thus told the company that soldiers were at hand. With quaking hearts they stood, to hear the regular tramp of the Guards approaching by the gallery, and knew themselves trapped. St. Marcel made an attempt to rouse their drooping spirits. Ignoring Bernouin – for of what account was the life of a lackey? – he turned to them and removed his mask.

'What does it signify, gentlemen, that we be taken? Our task is done. They cannot restore life to that carrion; and if they hang us for this night's work, we shall be but martyrs in a noble cause, and we shall have for consolation and reward the knowledge that we have rid France of that plague.'

And he pointed to the weltering body on the floor.

Then Brulin, the sergeant, appeared on the threshold; and, at his heels, a company in blue and silver, numbering a full score.

'What is afoot, Monsieur Bernouin?' he inquired.

'Murder has been done!' cried the valet.

'Not murder, sir – justice,' St. Marcel amended. 'There, Brulin, lies he who was your master; and I, Eustace de St. Marcel, have killed him!'

'Arrest him!' said Brulin shortly; and two of his followers – the whole company was now ranged inside the chamber – advanced to seize the Marquis.

The door had been closed, but now it was flung open suddenly; and a stalwart Swiss stepped forward, to electrify the company with the announcement:

'His Eminence, my Lord Cardinal!'

St. Marcel caught his breath. His face turned grey, and it seemed to him that his pulses had stopped, frozen by the sight of Mazarin himself, towering upon the threshold with questioning eyes. His fine, majestic figure was arrayed in his scarlet robes, and on his lofty Italian countenance sat a grim look of scorn and mockery.

'Who is that you have murdered, St. Marcel?' he demanded coldly. Then more sharply he added: 'Remove his visor, one of you. Let us look at his face.'

A Guardsman stooped to do his bidding; and every man present, forgetting almost his own desperate condition in the excitement of that moment, craned forward to behold the face of the dead.

And at the sight disclosed by the removal of the mask and the uncovering of the head, a shudder ran through their ranks and then a cry of astonishment. For the countenance, distorted, in part by a hideous death grin, in part by the cruel choke-pear with which he had been gagged, was that of Attignac, the Captain of the Guard, their fellow-conspirator and the Judas who had sold his master.

Mazarin looked on unmoved, his face an expressionless mask, whilst in the lines of Bernouin's thin mouth lurked the faintest smile of contempt.

The Cardinal understood the fate that had been prepared for him as he noticed on the body the domino he was to have worn, as he saw the gag which had kept d'Attignac silent, and the fellow's arms strapped to his sides, whilst dummies filled the sleeves of his domino. It had been a cunningly contrived justice.

'I know not, St. Marcel, what motives actuated you to slay poor Attignac,' said Mazarin. 'But this I know; that you are very like to hang for it. As for you others, if any one of you sees the outside of the Bastille within these next ten years he will be singularly fortunate. Come, Bernouin, attend me!'

And, turning on his heel, he passed out, calm and stately, leaving them to ruminate upon the fact that no fame of a great conspiracy would attach to them, no glamour of martyrdom be shed upon their punishment. France would account them no more than the perpetrators of a vulgar murder.

And as Bernouin, reflecting upon this, followed His Eminence down the steps of the Hôtel de Liancourt, it occurred to him that in the matter of administering poetic justice he might yet learn something from my Lord Cardinal.

The Abduction

Mr. Granby ca me away from the Manor and his interview with his old friend, Squire Clifford, in anything but the most satisfied frame of mind. He was face to face with a very knotty problem – for a lover. However much the squire might favour his suit, the fact remained that sweet Jenny Egerton – the squire's ward – whilst very friendly disposed towards Granby, was obviously careful to be nothing more.

Mr. Granby strode through the dusk kicking the snow before him and making for the lights of the town at the foot of Manor Hill, and as he went his thoughts were very busy with what Squire Clifford had said. Jenny's nature was romantic, and if Mr. Granby would win her heart as well as her hand the squire opined that he might be well-advised to present himself romantically to her consideration. But Granby, for all that he was a stolid, unimaginative man, realised that, rising forty as he was and being a shade wider at the waist than at the shoulders, in aiming at the romantic he might achieve no more than the ridiculous.

Still brooding, with hands deep in the pockets of his riding-coat, whip under his arm, and three-cornered hat pulled down over his brows, he strode on through the town, where the snow was becoming slush under the traffic that was toward. He made his way up the High Street with ears deaf to the shouts of the busy shopkeepers and busier vendors at the booths of the Christmas fair, and, still deep at his thoughts, he turned into the King's Arms. He nodded carelessly to the drawer in the tap-room, and his ill-fortune guided his steps to the bar parlour and into the company of three graceless young neighbours of his, who sat with wigs awry and coats unlaced in a cloud of smoke over a bowl of punch.

He stood in the blaze of candle-light, the fine powder of snow that had gathered on the shoulders of his scarlet coat being rapidly transmuted by the warmth of the room into glittering diamonds of water, whilst those merry bloods hailed him noisily. Mr. Granby had long been a choice butt for the practical jokers of the country-side, though he had never yet perceived it.

They hailed him to the fire; they gave him punch to drink – a hot, delicious beverage of brandy, muscadine, lemon, and spices – which so warmed his heart and choked discretion that, when presently they toasted Jenny Egerton, and drank to her speedy union with Mr. Granby, he must needs pour out the whole story of his unprospering love affair and the quandary in which he now found himself, winding up with an appeal to those merry jesters for advice and guidance in the pursuit of the romantic.

Their response was prompt and hilarious. As with one breath, they urged him to carry his tale to Ned Pepper, who, they swore, was the very man to help him.

'You couldn't find a better man for your business in the whole country,' one of them assured him. 'Ned Pepper's the most romantic young dog in England.'

'And he's upstairs now,' added another, 'drinking himself out of his senses in solitude.' And so they urged him noisily to go up at once.

'But if I should intrude,' he faltered. 'Mr. Pepper and I are but slightly acquainted.'

'Ned Pepper will give you a warm welcome,' they assured him amid fresh laughter; and so, persuading and pushing, they got him above-stairs to the room where Ned Pepper sat wondering what might be the source of the bursts of merriment that floated up to him through the floor.

Granby found Mr. Pepper – a comely young gentleman, with a good chin and a roguish eye – very much at his ease before a blazing fire. He was comfortably ensconced in a spacious oak chair, and rested the shapeliest silk-cased legs in Surrey upon a second one. There was a bowl of steaming punch at Mr. Pepper's elbow, a pipe between his fingers. His head was rested against one of the wings of his chair, his peruke – which he had doffed for greater comfort – was perched upon the other, his broidered vest was open, and he had undone the silver buckles of his lacquered shoes. As I have said, Mr. Pepper was very much at his ease.

At the foot of the stairs the young bloods stood grouped expectantly, with smirks and nudges and smothered guffaws. They knew Ned Pepper to be as peppery as his name implied, and they had reason to believe that he would presently be kicking Mr. Granby downstairs. Therefore they waited.

But they were disappointed. At sight of Mr. Granby hesitating in the doorway a flicker of interest had for a moment lighted Mr. Pepper's dark eyes; then he smiled lazily, and as lazily invited him to come inside.

'A cold night, Mr. Pepper,' said Granby civilly.

'Ring for another glass,' said Mr. Pepper, like a man taking a hint, and with the stem of his long pipe he pointed to the brew, thus clearing up any obscurity in his meaning.

The glass was brought, and, having helped himself, Granby drew up to the fire and took a pipe.

'I hope,' said he, 'I'm not intruding, though I must confess that I am taking a great liberty. I have come to you for advice. I have been advised to do so.'

Mr. Pepper took the pipe from between his teeth, and gave his guest every encouragement to proceed. They were alone in that cosy parlour. The punch warmed and expanded Granby's simple nature, and he remembered the assurances he had received that Mr. Pepper was the very man to help him in his quandary. So out came the whole story, all but the names, which, with a remnant of discretion, Granby thought better to omit.

'And do you tell me you were sent to me for advice in this matter?' quoth Mr. Pepper, whose eyes had now lost all sign of drowsiness. 'By whom?'

Granby told him, and Pepper nodded with a slow smile.

'I am sore perplexed,' added the luckless lover earnestly. 'I don't know whether you have ever been in the like position.'

'I have, indeed,' answered Mr. Pepper, 'with this difference that with me the maid was willing, but the father, who accounted me a

166

hairbrain, wouldn't hear of it. I carried her off; we were overtaken, and I was laid by the heels for a time. Her father was too friendly with the sheriff.'

'You carried her off,' mused Granby. 'Now that was a romantic enough thing to do!'

Mr. Pepper stared at him. 'If it's romance you want, you may do the same. As for me, I prefer to wait until the lady is of age. The county gaol cured me of any leanings towards romance.'

'But our cases are hardly parallel,' Mr. Granby reminded him. 'I have no pursuit to fear since her guardian is my friend.'

'True,' said Pepper with a roguish smile, 'but, then, you say the lady isn't, and you'll hardly make her so by a display of violence.'

'Ah!' sighed the unimaginative Granby, and his honest, rugged face grew clouded. Pepper puffed in silence for a moment or two; then spoke.

'To abduct her forcibly, and against her will, were to do a monstrous ill thing. Your suit thereafter must be hopeless and deservedly. But—' And be paused solemnly, raising a delicate white hand that sprouted from a cloud of lace, and poising it in line with Granby's suddenly uplifted eyes – 'but if someone else were to do the thing, and you were to prove the heroic rescuer— '

'Gad!' cried Granby, and the pipe slipped from his fingers, and was shivered on the floor.

'You would reap the heroic rescuer's reward,' concluded Pepper. 'By your promptness of action you would inspire gratitude; by your ready courage – there might be a little sword-play in the comedy – admiration; and by your restraint and courtesy to the lady in her plight, you should awaken confidence and trust. These, my friend, are the compounds that go to make up that poison men call love.'

'Yes, yes,' gasped Granby, in some amazement at the other's fertility of imagination. 'But how would you go about it, Mr. Pepper?'

Mr. Pepper pondered awhile, puffing vigorously. Then, setting down his pipe, he leaned forward, and propounded the result of his cogitations. On the morrow there was a Christmas dance to be held at Sir John Tyler's, two miles away, to which, no doubt, Squire Clifford and his ward would be going.

'Clifford?' gasped the startled Granby, leaping to his feet. 'How guessed you I spoke of them? I never mentioned— '

'The whole country-side knows all about it,' said Pepper shortly, and Granby sat down again. Pepper proceeded with his expounding. At Kerry's Corner Mr. Granby was to post some obliging rogue who would play the highwayman for him; he would hold up Mr. Clifford's coach, but at sight of the lady be so taken with the jewels that were her eyes, as to have no thought for other riches. The highwayman should request her to alight, and then make off with her on his crupper, the Squire being forewarned to offer no resistance.

'Away goes the amorous highwayman,' Pepper proceeded, 'whereupon the lady lets out a cry or two, which attracts the attention of a very staid and sober gentleman riding in the opposite direction. That gentleman is yourself. You call upon the ruffian to stand; he rides on, and you give pursuit. A pistol shot or two – in the air, of course – will add effect, and show the general earnestness of the affair. And now you are racing through the night, and the highwayman is racing ahead of you; the race must be protracted. To overtake him too soon would be injudicious. You must wait until the lady's feelings of terror have been wrought to their highest pitch. She knows a rescuer is behind, and when, towards dawn, that rescuer comes up, and compels the highwayman to mend his manners and deliver up the lady, lo! she discovers that it is the man to whose gallantry, courage, and resource she has so long and so foolishly been blind. If she does not promise to marry you there and then, you are the most hopeless bungler that ever tired of being a bachelor.'

In a burst of enthusiasm Granby tore at the bell-rope; then he crossed the room, and grasped one of Mr. Pepper's slender hands in his own massive fist.

'You're a man of heart and brain, Mr. Pepper,' said he; 'a man I'm proud to call my friend.' Then, to the drawer who entered, 'Another bowl of punch,' he ordered. And with that the enthusiasm went out of him as suddenly as it had flared up.

'But, rat me!' he cried, 'where am I to find a man who will play the highwayman for me?'

'Surely,' said Pepper, 'that should not be difficult. You'll have some friend— '

'But the task asks more than friendship. It asks tact, it asks resource, it asks – I scarce know what.' And then he grew inspired. 'Now, if you, Mr. Pepper— '

'Alas!' sighed Pepper. 'It is just such a frolic as would sort well with my rascally instincts, such a night ride as I should relish. But, unfortunately, I am bidden, myself, to Lady Tyler's ball.'

'If that be all, surely the difficulty might be overcome. But perhaps I make too bold, sir. I presume, maybe, when I consider that you might stand my friend. Our acquaintance is, after all, but slight.'

'A misfortune which the years may mend,' said Pepper pleasantly.

'You mean that?' quoth the simple Granby.

'If you need proof of it – why, I am your man in this affair.'

♦   ♦   ♦   ♦   ♦

Thus was it planned, and on the following night – or, rather, towards two o'clock of a sharp and frosty Christmas morning – was the plan put into execution.

Half a mile from Kerry's corner – which was a mile, or so, from Tyler Park – Mr. Granby walked his horse up and down in the moonlight, waiting.

A coach rolled past him, followed soon after by another, whereat, realizing that these were homeward bound guests from Lady Tyler's, Mr. Granby waxed impatient for the arrival of Mr. Pepper. Presently hoofs rattled in the distance, growing rapidly louder and nearer, and ringing sharp and clear on the still, frosty air. A horseman riding madly down the road loomed black in the moonlight, and Mr. Granby rode to meet him.

Affairs had sped well with Mr. Pepper. He had held up Squire Clifford's coach, and carried off Squire Clifford's ward, what time the Squire instructed in his role, bellowed and trumpeted, but took care to do nothing that might hinder the make believe highwayman in his task. The girl had not gone without a struggle, it is true. But in the end, masterful Mr. Pepper had swung her to the

169

withers of his horse, and dashed off, his left arm embracing and supporting her, and her head – for she seemed to have lapsed into a half-stupor – fallen back against his breast. Thus they rode until they came upon Mr. Granby ambling in the opposite direction. The girl struggled, and let out a cry or two for help as she was swept past that bulky figure, and Mr. Granby, taking his cue from that, wheeled about, and called upon the abductor to stand. Mr. Pepper laughed for answer, and rattled on. Shots went off in the night, with no hurt to anyone, and Mr. Granby flung himself into hot and gallant pursuit.

He gained on them too quickly at first, so he slackened his pace, mindful of Pepper's instructions that the chase should be a long one. Suddenly something stirred by the roadside; a third horseman loomed on that lonely road, barring Mr. Granby's path; a pistol barrel gleamed before him, and –

'Stand!' thundered a gruff voice.

Mr. Granby stood. He was not by nature foolhardy, and his common sense told him that a man with a levelled pistol was a man to be obeyed. He slipped a hand towards one of his holsters, furtively, to withdraw it again as he remembered that he had discharged both pistols at the commencement of his chase of Mr. Pepper.

'If it's my purse you want— ' he began, in haste to push on.

'I want more than that,' came the answer, interrupting him. And then, in the politer manner affected by gentlemen of the road, 'Sir, it grieves me vastly to put you to discomfort. But the messengers are after me, and my horse is spent. I'll trouble you to dismount.'

'But— ' began Granby in dismay.

'Dismount!' bellowed the highway man, dropping all courteous affectations. 'Dismount this instant, or I'll blow your brains out.'

Mr. Granby came quickly to the ground. In an instant the tobyman was beside him. Another moment, and he had swung himself into Granby's empty saddle, and was off at a gallop into the night.

There stood Granby – Granby, the heroic rescuer of distressed dames – on the white, sparkling snow, in sore perplexity, anger, and chagrin. Then, in a spirit of philosophy determining to make the best of matters, he mounted the spent horse that had been left him, the sorriest nag that ever wore a saddle, and gave it a touch of the spur. After all, his loss amounted to no more than a horse, and Mr. Granby was wealthy enough to envisage that loss without great concern. But what of Pepper and the lady he was to rescue? Surely Pepper would lag behind, and wait for him. But soon – being unable to get more than a walk out of the animal he bestrode – he realized that unless Pepper came to a standstill, there was no chance of his being overtaken; and if he were so foolish as to come to a standstill to wait for Granby to come up with him, then the whole scheme would be betrayed, and must miscarry. The horse staggered a quarter of a mile or so under the stimulus of Granby's frantic spurring; then it foundered altogether, and Granby was forced to dismount.

He pondered the matter as best his rage would let him. To take the horse farther was out of the question. There was no choice but to leave the beast and push on afoot, trusting to Mr. Pepper's ingenuity to afford him an early opportunity of coming to that pretty sword-play they had agreed upon. Mr. Granby set off at a run, taking the road that led to Guildford, for Guildford was the goal arranged. But Guildford was twenty miles away, and it was not until after eight o'clock of that Christmas morning that Mr. Granby dragged his weary body over the bridge that spans the Wey, and up the precipitous High Street of that ancient town.

He was a man utterly disillusioned, a man in whom the thought of his own physical discomforts had quenched all amorous aspirations, a man whose only remaining ambition was to dry his sodden boots in some comfortable inn parlour and mend his physical discomforts with an ample breakfast. If a thought he gave to any other matter, it was to curse the idiotic Pepper for having ridden on, as he appeared to have done, heedless of whether Mr. Granby was in pursuit or not.

He stamped wearily into the yard of the 'Black Bull,' swung into the inn, and making his way down a passage, opened the first door he came upon. A lady and a gentleman were at table there, and Mr. Granby, realizing that he intruded, was for withdrawing hastily, when a cheery voice hailed him.

'Mr. Granby! Gad! You're come at last!' Mr. Pepper had risen from the table, and was advancing towards him with a smile upon his pleasant young face. Granby gasped, and looked at the lady. It was Jenny.

'At least,' cried slow-witted Granby, thinking that matters were to be righted after all, 'it seems I am not come too late.' And he put his hand to the hilt of his small-sword. But Pepper only laughed.

'If it's the pretty show of sword-play you're thinking of, you're too late altogether. Come in, man, and break your fast with us. I make no doubt you'll be nigh dead of hunger.' And he drew Granby, despite himself almost, into the room.

'What – what do you mean?' he demanded, scowling, for he noticed now that Jenny's air was not such as her position should inspire; her cheeks were red, and she seemed a prey to laughter.

'Why,' said Mr. Pepper airily, advancing a chair for his guest, 'when you never came, what was I to do with this lady on my hands? I ask you, what would you have done in my place?'

The question quenched all Mr. Granby's vexation. Engrossed as he had been in his own calamities, he had given no thought to Mr. Pepper's quandary.

'You'll agree,' continued Mr. Pepper, 'that I could scarce ride on with her after daylight. We should have been stopped. Besides, there are limits to a horse's endurance, and to a man's. We must stop somewhere. At the first inn would be Miss Egerton's opportunity. She has but to call for help, and in what case should I find myself? I have been in gaol once, as I have already had occasion to inform you, and I have little fancy for repeating the experience. I hope, sir, that you realize my delicate position.'

'Indeed, sir,' murmured the confused and bewildered Granby, 'I own it must have been trying!'

'You see, then,' Mr. Pepper cut in, 'that it was necessary to do something that should put me in shelter from the law.'

'And he did,' Jenny explained, laughter sparkling in her eyes and dimpling her smooth, fresh cheek, 'what you will agree was the only thing to do. He told me the truth. Oh, shame, Mr. Granby! Shame on you for setting such a scheme on foot and subjecting a poor girl to so much misery and discomfort.'

'But, madam— ,' groaned Mr. Granby unable to say more.

'Mr. Pepper was wise to tell me the truth, and cast himself, as he did, upon my mercy,' she concluded.

Mr. Granby said nothing. He sat nursing his hat, his gaze averted, abashed like a child caught in a naughty act. How different was all this from the brave plan they had made!

'Miss Egerton very charitably forgave us,' said Pepper, 'and we determined to break our fast here whilst awaiting you.'

Granby screwed up his courage to ask: 'And now?' in a very sheepish voice.

'You see,' Pepper explained confidentially, 'even having made my peace with Miss Egerton, I felt myself far from secure. You'll remember why I was in gaol two years ago. I told you the reason.' Granby nodded.

'Therefore,' put in Jenny, 'it became necessary for Mr. Pepper further to protect himself.'

'In her mercy,' Pepper resumed, 'she realized how unpleasant it might be for me if I were discovered here – by her guardian, say – alone with a child upon whom I had no claim of kinship. Besides, the lady has a reputation, and I could not in honesty have called myself your friend if I had allowed the reputation of a lady whom you had thought of making your wife to be placed in jeopardy. So while breakfast was cooking we stepped across the street, and were quietly married by the most civil parson in the world.'

'Odso!' roared Granby. 'You are fooling me, then?' And he got heavily to his feet, his face purple with indignation.

'Fooling you?' cried Pepper. 'Not I. I am telling you the truth. I ask you what else was I to do? You yourself forced the situation upon me. What other way out of it had I? And, rat me, sir, where have you tarried all night that you never overtook me as we had arranged?'

'Bah!' said Granby, who was now beginning to understand things. 'I have been walking a matter of twenty miles since the knave you hired deprived me of my horse.'

He paused, summoning invective to his aid, his wits now penetrating to the very heart of this situation. It flickered in that moment through his mind that Squire Clifford had made some allusion to a spark for whom his ward was suspected of a fancy. This, then, was the sparking question, and Granby had been fooled by him. And it was into the keeping of this hair-brained young scapegrace – who had been gaoled already for running off with some girl or other – that Jenny had given her sweet young life! Granby felt naturally vindictive. He planted himself squarely on his feet, and dully eyed the couple at the table.

'Will you tell me,' he asked with grim unction, 'the name of the lady for whose abduction you were gaoled two years ago, Mr. Pepper?'

Mr. Pepper looked disconcerted, Granby thought with relish.

'It's something of an ordeal, sir, to be forced to confess to such follies in the presence of my wife, and – and on my bridal morning. Still, if you insist— '

'I do,' said Granby firmly. 'She shall know what manner of man she had wed.'

'It's two years ago, and that's a long time in a young man's life,' said Pepper. 'My memory may be at fault, but I believe it was a Miss Egerton, of whom you may have heard, sir.' And from the ripple of laughter that broke from Jenny's lips, Granby knew that he was being mocked with the truth.

It was more than he could bear. He swung out of the room, and out of the inn, and tired, damp and hungry though he was, he determined to get a horse and ride back to Clifford Manor to tell the squire what had befallen. He realized with angry shame how those merry young gentlemen at the 'King's Arms' had fooled him the night before when they sent him to Pepper for guidance in this delicate matter.

While he waited in the yard for a horse, he could not resist a peep through the window of the room where the bridal couple were at table. A bright firelight played upon walls and ceiling, and relieved the lingering gloom of that Christmas morning. Jenny, he noticed, sat with a kerchief to her eyes, and Mr. Pepper with an arm round her neck strove to console her. The sight affected Granby oddly. Maybe she was

174

weeping out of pity for the treatment he had received; maybe she was thinking of her guardian and the trouble he would make for them. Mr. Granby was honestly fond of the child, and he felt a lump in his throat as he pondered the matter of her tears. Tears on her wedding-day!

He noticed now how well-matched they were in youth and looks, and he realized how ill-matched would she have been had she wedded him as was intended. He remembered, too, now that his mood was softening, that, after all, Pepper was little to blame for what had happened. It was those rascally wags at the 'King's Arms' who had fooled him rather than Pepper. In Pepper's place he might himself have done just what Pepper had done.

And then a peal of joybells crashed suddenly upon the morning air to remind Granby of what day it was, and what the message of that day was.

He straightened himself. He may have been dull, podgy and unimaginative, but he was a good fellow at heart. Back into the inn and into their parlour he strode, and so full of purpose was his step that Jenny looked up in alarm as he thrust wide the door. He advanced, his face rather red, his eyes more sheepish than ever.

'I forgot,' said he, 'to wish you a merry Christmas, and I've come back to do it. If you'll ride to Clifford Manor with me, I think I can persuade the squire to let us all spend this bridal Christmas happily together.' And he held out a hand to each of them.

THE MALEDICTION

I stood erect and defiant, the point of my sword – to which the rash fool's blood still clung – resting upon my boot, and with cold contempt in my glance, I let my eyes wander over the score of idle dogs that encircled me – dogs that barked, yet dared not bite.

Two of them had raised my vanquished and unconscious opponent from the ground, and were endeavouring to staunch the blood which spurted freely from the wound I had given him. The others stood around us in a circle, growling and snarling like the curs they were, but taking care to keep beyond my reach.

'It is a nasty wound, Mein Herr,' said one of those who tended the fallen man.

'The quarrel was of his own seeking,' I exclaimed, angrily, 'and he received his wound in fair fight. If there be one here who says that it is not so, to him I'll answer that he lies, and prove it upon his body if he dare to come forth and play the man.'

Their snarling was arrested by the fierceness of my tone and gesture, and albeit their looks were black and sullen enough, their tongues were silent.

I vented my contempt in a harsh laugh of derision.

'So, my masters,' I said, sheathing my sword and moving towards a point where the rabble was thinnest, 'since none disputes my word, I pray you let me hence.'

A way was opened at my approach. Not for me – as I had thought at first – but for another.

A tall, spare man, in the habit of a Capuchin monk, and with the cowl drawn over his head, elbowed his way through to where I stood.

His deep-set eyes met mine, and for a moment he held my gaze with a look of mingled sorrow and anger.

'So! You have been at your foul work again, Master von Huldenstein,' he said in even, solemn tones that brought the blood to my face.

'You presume upon the safety of your sack-cloth,' I answered hotly.

'And you, you presume upon the death of the Duke of Retzbach,' he retorted with a show of righteous indignation. 'When the Duke lived the edict was enforced, and men of your kidney were appalled from the ways of murder by the grim shadow of the Schwarzenbaum gibbet. But take heed, sir,' he continued, raising his voice, 'you shall not pursue your accursed trade with impunity. I will appeal to the King if need be, and you shall learn that there is still justice and retribution in Schwerlingen.'

White with passion I stepped up to him, but he brushed me aside with a gesture almost of scorn, and my tongue – usually so nimble – clove to my teeth.

He bent over the unconscious man, whilst I looked on quivering with rage, and vainly racking my brain for a fitting answer.

Presently he turned to me again with flashing eyes.

'This man may die, sir,' he cried. 'Do you hear me? He may die!'

'Then do your shaveling's trade, and shrive him,' I answered with callous cynicism.

Wonder and indignation seemed to choke his utterance for a moment. Then—

'Oh, God will punish you, you son of Cain,' he exclaimed. 'Your own murderous sword shall work your undoing, and if ever in your wasted life there should open out a way for better things' – he raised his right hand aloft, and his gaunt frame seemed to dilate and grow before my fascinated eyes – 'may your accursed sword prove an insuperable barrier. In such an hour, if ever it should come to you, may God's curse strike you, and may His vengeance lay you low!'

A shudder ran through the crowd, as much at the words as at the frightful tone in which they were delivered, and many crossed themselves as if that monk had been the Devil.

'Silence, priest,' I muttered, stepping close up to him, with my eyes on his. 'Do not drive me to do that which I might regret hereafter.'

'Hence, hence!' he retorted boldly enough. 'There is more already on your soul than—'

He stopped abruptly. Almost unconsciously I had half drawn my dagger, and his eyes caught the glitter of steel. The colour left his cheeks, and he fell back mumbling some Latin fragments.

I laughed at his sudden fears, and pushing back my poniard I turned to depart. The crowd made a way for me in silence, and thus I passed out of his presence. I retraced my way to the city which half-an-hour earlier I had left in the company of him who now lay between life and death, tended by a vulgar rabble and a Capuchin monk.

The sun was setting as I passed beneath the arch of the Heinrichsthor, and little did I dream of all that would come to pass before it rose again, or of how the dawn would find me.

I stalked moodily along towards the inn of the Sword and Crown, where, methought, I was likely to find an evening's entertainment.

In my heart I carried many an evil thought against the priest who had dared to beard me in public, and launch upon my head his puerile malediction, but scarcely one for the poor wretch I had transfixed, and who – for aught I knew or cared – might die before morning.

From the scene of my encounter to the Sword and Crown inn I had come direct, and at a fair pace, yet the news of what had taken place was there before me. Even as I set my foot upon the lintel, old Armstadt came hurrying forward, his wonted suave and obsequious manner laid aside and replaced by a rude and offensive bearing that was new to me.

'Not into my house, Master von Huldenstein,' he cried harshly, barring my way with his burly frame. 'You shall find no fresh victims beneath my roof.'

This was plain speaking – and from a scullion to whose house I had brought endless custom! Herrgott! had I lived to be refused admittance to a tavern, and insulted by a gutter-bred wine-seller?'

'Sacrament! You do not mince your words, you knave. Stand aside!' I thundered advancing a step.

But he did not budge.

'This house is mine,' he answered insolently, 'and mine it is to guard its reputation. Shall I have it said that the Sword and Crown is a harbour for assassins and deriders of priests? Away with you!'

For a moment I looked about me in doubt, anger bidding me punish the insolent hound as he deserved, prudence telling me to begone.

Three or four passers-by had already stopped, curious to see the outcome of this unusual altercation. To own myself beaten and withdraw beneath their eyes was hurtful to my pride. And yet, to linger and persist in a desperate endeavour might provoke a scene from which withdrawal would be still more humiliating.

With a dull feeling of baffled rage, I realised that I must go; and so I went with the best show of dignity I could muster, and watching to see if any of the onlookers dared to comment upon my going. By my soul, if one of them had so much as smiled I would have picked a quarrel with him. But knowing me, they were wise, and let me go in peace.

Clearly I realised as I quitted the threshold of the Sword and Crown, how the wine-shop was from that hour symbolical to me of the attitude of all Schwerlingen. The town was closed to me. Go where I might the same reception would await me. To remain in the capital of Sachsenberg I must starve, and starving is an unpleasant occupation.

I realised to the full how much the Capuchin's malediction was accountable for this, and in my heart I repaid that meddling monk with curse for curse.

A pretty situation, truly! And yet not unexpected. Long ago I had foreseen that such would be the end of the vile life I had led, ever since my father had thrust me from his house in just and righteous anger.

Aye, I had seen it coming. Step by step I had come down the steep incline of knavery and dishonour, clearly beholding that which lay below, yet never striving by a single effort to stay my infamous descent. Possibly the devil had courted a greater blackguard, probably he had not.

Was there any degradation left through the mire of which I might still drag the proud old name of Huldenstein and my besmirched escutcheon? Methought not. I was like a man who had sunk into a morass – too deep to ever extricate himself, too firmly gripped to be able to push on, and for whom there is no choice but to await the end in the foul spot he has floundered upon.

But if I must wait, I would not wait in Schwerlingen where I was known, and where every glance bestowed upon me would henceforth be an insult. I must go at once! Go where?

This was indeed an unanswerable question.

Then a sudden longing seized me. A longing to behold again the castle of my father in the province of Hattau, the home that had once been mine, and that belonged to all who bore my name, saving myself – the outcast. I grew suddenly eager to see those from whom I had been separated twelve years ago.

There was my old father. Who could tell? – perchance old age had softened his heart, and the approach of death would cast a forgiving mood upon him. There were my sisters; Esther, the eldest – she would be grey by now – and little Stephanie, who cried the night I left the castle. Then there was Fritz. Would he still remember the big brother who had been the first to teach him to sit a horse and hold a sword? I shook my head in doubt. Twelve years had slipped away since then, and Fritz was a boy of ten in those far-off days. He would be a grown man ere now!

As I brooded over all these things the resolve grew strong within me. I would go, I would set out at once! Then suddenly I came to a standstill, and a groan escaped me.

How was I to go? I had no horse – I had sold my last one a fortnight before; I had no money; I might almost say that I had no raiment. The very doublet on my back was threadbare and worn to its extremity; my breeches were in no better plight, and my boots were such as any groom might blush to own.

And yet go I must, and, by the Mass, go I would – aye even if – . Horror-stricken I checked the ugly thought. A while ago I thought there was no quality of dishonour that I had not tasted. I was mistaken; there was still one. I might still become a thief, and demand money at the sword point. But I could not do it! I was still something of a Huldenstein!

Then I laughed – or was it through my lips, perchance, that the very devil mocked my better self? I know not. Suffice it that I derided my own scruples. I had grown over-nice in my conscience of a sudden, that I shrank from wresting an over-loaded purse from some rich fool who would not miss it. I had done deeds as foul if in a different way. Why should I stop at this? To a man whose honour was clean, it would be indeed, impossible; but to me – Bah! 'Twas the only course, and it would lead me – home.

I had wandered aimlessly through the streets during my ill-starred musings, and meanwhile night had fallen and it had grown late. The air I clearly recollect was sharp and frosty, although we were in April.

I came to a halt before the Church of St. Oswald, and stood for a moment with bent head, whilst the Tempter wrestled with my Guardian Angel. For the nonce the Spirit of Evil was overcome, and I turned at length, and wended my way towards the dismal house in the Mondstrasse, wherein I occupied a room on the ground floor. My way lay through the Northern quarter of the town, in which no lamps were hung until Wallenheim became minister in 1645 – two years later than the events I now set down. There was a fair moon, however, and the sky being clear, the light was tolerably good – would that it had been otherwise!

I turned the corner of the Mondstrasse with a brisk step, and was already within fifty paces of my own door, when my attention was drawn to a tall cavalier approaching from the opposite end of the narrow street. His cloak fluttered behind him in the breeze, and the silver lace on his doublet glinted in the moonlight. That it was that, coupled with his stately bearing, made me suppose him a bird worth plucking, and – again fostering the vile intention which awhile ago I had stifled – drove me back into the shadow of a doorway.

I glanced up and down the street. Not another being was in sight. Absolute silence reigned, saving only the ring of his spurred heel on the uneven pavement. Of a truth the devil was in the business to deliver him thus into my hands!

I felt the hot blood surging to my head – driven there by shame for myself and the vile act which circumstances seemed impelling me to perform. The air was full of mocking sounds, even the faint rustling of the wind seemed to hum the word 'thief' about my ears.

I loosened my sword in its scabbard and stood waiting. How slowly he came! I put my hand to my brow, and withdrew it moist with perspiration – the cold perspiration of horror. Pshaw! I was a fool, a sickly coward! Life is a game and the dice had fallen against me.

He was abreast of me, walking with bent head, and humming softly as he went.

Deaf to the last appealing cry of honour and conscience, I sprang out from the shadow, and drawing my sword I set the point against his breast, and barred his way.

He looked up, throwing back his head like a horse that has been suddenly reined in, and showed me a thin, aquiline countenance and pointed beard.

His lips parted, but before he could speak—

'If you utter a cry, as God lives, I'll drive this home!' I said fiercely.

'You are a bold knave,' he murmured in tones that were light with easy banter, 'but you are presumptuous. Holy Virgin, do I look like a woman, that you fear I shall cry for help at the sight of a single scare-crow?'

'Bravely and most wisely spoken, O fool!' I answered, stung not a little by his attitude and words. 'Maintain that reasonable frame of mind, and our business will soon be settled.'

He smiled serenely, the condescending, tolerant smile that a great lord might bestow upon a horseboy.

'You speak of business, may I inquire its nature?'

'Your purse and jewels. Quick!'

182

'If that be all,' he said, composedly, drawing a couple of rings from his fingers, 'we need waste no time.'

He held out the trinkets, and I put forth my hand to receive them, keeping my eyes on his the while. One of the rings dropped into my palm, the other brushed against the edge of my hand, and fell to the ground. Instinctively I attempted to follow it with my eyes. That was my undoing. Quick as lightning, he availed himself of my momentary inattention, and knocking up my sword, he sprang back with a laugh.

Before I quite realised what had taken place, and the trick that had been played upon me, he had whipped out his rapier and thrown himself into a defensive attitude.

'Now, my master,' he jeered, 'I am in a better position to discuss with you the question of right to my purse – if, indeed,' he added with fine scorn, 'you still be minded to pursue the argument.'

I was loath to do it, but there was no help. Courage, or rather the contempt of death, which only those who own a worthless life can know – was the last semblance of a virtue left me. To be held a coward, even in the estimation of one who knew me not, I would not suffer.

My sword clattered against his, and there we stood, engaged, with every nerve alert, and every muscle ready. Then of a sudden the priest's malediction recurred to me, and struck a chill through me. Was that glittering point that danced before me in the moonlight, destined to carry out the Capuchin's curse?

I shook the grim thought from me. Indeed, he forced me to it. It would need all my wit and strength if I would keep my life, for if ever Caspar von Huldenstein met his match 'twas then.

Up and down that silent street we went in our fierce combat, with set teeth and stertorous breathing. Trick after trick I essayed to circumvent his guard, and yet, for all he had a parry and a counter. Moreover the light was bad and the ground uncertain. But in the end I coaxed him to attempt a lengthy lunge; I swerved aside; he over-reached himself, and before he could recover I had run him through from breast to back.

He sank down at my feet with a stifled groan, and there lay still.

I glanced about me with a feeling that was near akin to dread. There was no one in sight.

Then I knelt down beside him, and scarce knowing what I did, I completed my vile task, and stripped him of his jewels and a heavy purse. I arose staggering to my feet, and looked again fearfully about me. For a moment it occurred to me to attempt to dress his wound; but I dismissed the notion. I knew the nature of the hurt from the course my sword had taken. Why prolong his agony?

Next a wild panic seized me, and I fled madly down the street to my miserable lodging, which was but a dozen paces from the spot where he lay.

The door was locked, and I had not the courage to knock, lest whoever came to open should see the figure on the ground. I struck my hand against the window. It proved to be unfastened, and opened to my touch. A moment later I stood in my room, shivering with the full consciousness of the foul deed. I flung away the purse as if it burnt me. My God, what had I done? Would I ever dare to go home now, and clasp my father's honourable hand in mine – mine that was now soiled with this double crime? How long I stood there thinking over what I had done, and sorrowing that it was not I who lay out yonder, I cannot tell.

Ah! Shall I ever forget those terrible moments? Shall I ever forget how the sudden realisation of the long career of sin and debauchery that lay behind me – the career that had culminated in the vile act just committed – how it overcame me and shook me with a strange, unknown terror – a feeling that the monk's malediction had in truth been the malediction of God? No; all this I am certain to remember until my dying day. Nor shall I ever forget how those dreadful fears for a moment passed away to give place to old memories that were as beautiful as they were sad. I lived fleetingly through the years which had preceded my downfall; and it was just those placid, trivial hours, when we neither enjoy deeply nor are deeply pained, that came back to me with such poignant force. For are they not the happiest hours of life – those hours of mere peace and content? All this swept through my brain in a few moments, and once again the present, with its peril and crime, returned, and, rousing

184

myself with an effort, I crossed the room and groped for the tinder box. With trembling hands I struck the flint perhaps a dozen times before I succeeded in lighting the taper that stood upon the table. I flung myself down on the nearest chair, and burying my face in my hands, I sat there until a light tap at the door made my heart stand still. I sprang up to listen. Perchance I had been seen, and the guard had been summoned. If it were so – who knew? – perchance the monk would make his appeal to the king, and the edict would be enforced. I should die the felon's death at the hangman's hands, and then truly would his malediction fall upon me.

Then I laughed at my fears. Pshaw! The law came not with so timid a knock. Again I heard it, and unable to endure the suspense, I seized the taper, and went to the door. As I opened it a body fell across the lintel. It was my whilom opponent, and at the sight of him I shuddered, beset by a thousand fears.

He must indeed be a man of strong vitality to have dragged himself thus far. Was it mere chance that brought him to my door? It must be so.

Quick, before he could raise his eyes, I had let the taper fall and extinguished it with my foot. Then I knelt beside him and raised his head.

'Thanks, friend,' he murmured faintly. 'The light from your window guided me hither. I am dying. I was set upon by a robber in the street. He has given me my death wound in exchange for what money I possessed.'

'Let me see to it,' I answered, dissembling my voice.

'Tis useless; you will but waste time, and I have not many moments left. Listen, I have something to say.'

He paused for a moment, then—

'Do you know in this Schwerlingen a man named Huldenstein – Caspar von Huldenstein?'

'I have heard of him,' I answered, with a vague tightening at the heart.

'Then seek him out. Tell him – tell him that he is now the Lord of Huldenstein. Tell him that his father died a week ago, and,

185

dying, forgave him all. With his last breath he charged me with this message, and I came hither rejoicing that I might convey to one who, I believe, is destitute the news of his altered fortunes. As you see, he will never hear the message from my lips, but promise me that you will deliver it to him tomorrow. Promise me!'

'In God's name, who are you?' I cried.

'I am Fritz von Huldenstein, his brother,' he gasped. He added something which I did not catch, then his head fell forward, and he lay still in my arms. I dimly recollect how – almost bereft of reason – I relighted the taper, and closely scanned the face of my dead brother, seeking to find some traces of the features of the boy I had known and loved. Then I flung away the light, and with a wild, mad shriek I fled from the house leaving the door wide open.

And that is how it came to pass that at sunrise I fell fainting on the threshold of the convent of the Capuchins at Loebli, and that today Caspar von Huldenstein is no more.

In his place there is Caspar, the lay brother, who in sack-cloth, with vigils and scourge, with fasting and prayer, seeks to make some atonement for the past; whilst waiting for the hour of his deliverance from the mental anguish for which there is only one cure.

THE SIEGE OF SAVIGNY

Heigh-ho! A man of twenty in love is a sad fool. Yet who would not be a sad fool that he might be twenty and in love?

I sat idling in the guard-room of the Castle of Nogent one July morning, my twenty-year-old mind running upon a lady who dwelt at Juvisy, whose very name was unknown to me, but whose eyes – the bluest that I ever looked into – had nonetheless made a fool of me. That pair of eyes had drawn me oft of late to ride across the league and a half that lay 'twixt Nogent and Juvisy, so that I might pass beneath her window, and earn for all reward perchance a glance, perchance not that. So, thinking of her, as had become my constant wont, sat I that July morning when one of M. de Crecqui's men came to bid me wait upon the Governor.

I was genially received by my kind patron with the intimation that a hazardous enterprise awaited me if I were minded to undertake it: the business being his own rather than the King's. The Château de Savigny, which lay some ten leagues distant from Nogent, and thirty leagues this side of Paris, and which was the property of M. de Crecqui, had been forcibly seized by his brother-in-law, M. de Monravel, upon the plea – inaccurate, my patron said – that the demesne formed part of his wife's marriage-portion.

M. de Crecqui had garrisoned the place pending the legal settlement of the business, confident in his influence with the King to bring it to the issue he desired; but the audacious Monravel, knowing how weighty an argument at law is the possession of the disputed ground, had duped my patron's men, and seizing the château, had set a slender garrison of his own – six men, as I afterwards learnt – to hold it against M. de Crecqui. Monravel relied as much upon his influence with the Parliament to establish the justice of his pretensions as did

Crecqui build upon his influence with our good King Henry the Fourth.

In such a pass stood matters now; and, piqued by the affront that had been put upon him, it was M. de Crecqui's desire that I should start forthwith for Savigny, taking half-a-dozen men-at-arms with me, and there by force or strategy oust Monravel's knaves, and at any cost regain possession of his castle, holding it as a *place de guerre*.

I liked the business much; yet I was not blind to the risk that I ran did the Parliament prove the place M. de Monravel's. But my patron promised me in all solemnity that he would sustain me against all risks, and himself answer to the King for all that I did as being done in his name and by his express commands.

Thus reassured, I picked my men, and with the six of them in back and breast plates and pots of burnished steel, I rode out for Savigny without more ado, and preserving the utmost secrecy as to our destination.

I went by way of Juvisy, and had for my reward a glimpse of my lady coming out of the Church of St. Jacques as we rode by. She was attended by an elderly waiting-woman, who came behind her at a respectful distance, and she walked with eyes demurely downcast and folded hands, as becomes a maiden fresh from her devotions; but the clatter my fellows made in passing caused her to lift her eyes. They met my impassioned gaze, and for a moment they were not withdrawn. Mayhap the ardour of my glance it was, mayhap the brave figure I cut in my glinting corslet and plumed hat: I know not which of these, but this I know – that into her eyes, which hitherto had never bestowed upon me but an indifferent, almost contemptuous look, if they had looked at all, there seemed to leap a light of interest. Her lips – surely it was not my enamoured fancy – assumed the faintest of smiles; a smile of kindliness methought it. The blood rushed to my head, and so far drowned my usual timidity that, bending low upon the withers, I doffed my hat in the courtliest fashion I was master of. Thus far did impulse bear me, but no farther. Draw rein I dared not, but passed on; and, growing presently conscious that my troopers' faces were all agrin, I swore softly to myself, and harshly bade them travel faster.

It is not my purpose to set down in detail how we took possession that very night of the Château de Savigny. The thing was accomplished with a simplicity rendered possible by the carelessness of the garrison and the unexpectedness of our attack. I turned all Monravel's creatures from the place, with the exception of an elderly dame who had charge of the kitchen, and whom we thought it convenient to keep with us. Four of our six troopers I sent back to Nogent, retaining but Barnave and Grégoire, for the place was of such strength that three men alert might hold it against an army.

Four days later an *huissier* sent from Paris by the Parliament presented himself at Savigny to demand of me that I should let down the drawbridge and deliver up the castle. I answered that I did not know him, and that I would obey nought but a written order from M. de Crecqui, who had entrusted his castle to my keeping. That black-coated rascal answered me with threats of the hangman; whereupon I bade Barnave open the postern beside the portcullis and throw a plank across the moat. This done, I invited the bailiff to enter. He came gingerly enough, for he was unaccustomed to such narrow bridges. Had he known what awaited him he had not come at all; for when he was midway across, the plank was suddenly tilted over, and he was flung headlong into the slimy water. With a rope we rescued him, and sent him, wet and sorrowful, back to Paris and his Parliament.

This outrage must have made a fine stir, for three days later Savigny was visited by no less a person than a councillor, who came with all the pomp of office and a guard of honour of six archers. He was prodigal in threats – so prodigal that, grown weary of them, I bade the plank to be thrust out to him; but, knowing what had befallen the bailiff, and deeming that I intended him a like affront, he grew purple with rage, and with a parting volley of threats, he rode off in high dudgeon. Had I been older it might have afforded me uneasiness to think that I had derided the Parliament, flouted its commands, and insulted its ambassadors.

It was on the morning of the second day after the councillor's visit that Grégoire brought me word that a lady was at the gates demanding speech of the master of the place. Now, if that information caused me some slight astonishment, it was as nothing to my amazement when, upon looking out from the postern, I beheld the very lady that was mistress of my thoughts: the lady of Juvisy. The horse she rode was bathed in sweat, flecked with foam, and breathing hard.

'Are you the master of this castle, monsieur?' was her panted greeting.

' I am in command here, madam,' I answered timidly.

'Then, monsieur, of your courtesy, of your chivalry, I crave shelter. I am being pursued.'

'Pursued, madam?' I cried, touched already by the distress in her voice. 'By whom?'

'Oh, what does it signify?' she cried, glancing fearfully behind her. 'By M. de Bervaux, my guardian. For Heaven's sake, monsieur, protect me!'

What answer could I make any woman who thus appealed to me? What answer could I make to her of all women?

'*Holá* there!' I shouted. 'Barnave! Grégoire! Quick, let down the portcullis.'

Breathing a prayer of gratitude to the god of lovers for this signal favour, I went hat in hand to assist her to alight in the courtyard, the while a very torrent of thanks rained down upon me from her lips in a voice so rich and musical that I listened as one enthralled; and when presently she paused abruptly, I looked up to find her eyes riveted upon my face, and her brows knit, as though she looked on something that was puzzling her.

'Surely, surely, monsieur,' she said at last, 'we have met before?'

I went red from chin to hair. 'Indeed – indeed, madam, I have seen you often,' I stammered.

'At Juvisy, was it not?'

'Yes, madam, at Juvisy.'

'Ah!' And with the utterance of that monosyllable, so kindly and so witching a smile lighted her face that I know not what folly I had wrought but that shouts sounded without at that moment.

Grégoire came up with the news that a party of mounted men stood before the castle.

'Monsieur!' cried the lady in high distress, 'you will not give me up? Pity me, monsieur! I am a poor defenceless maid, and there are those without who would force me into a hateful marriage for the sake of what little wealth I am possessed of.'

190

'Say no more, Mademoiselle.'

'Ah! but, monsieur,' she broke in tearfully, 'you must tell them that I am not here. In your mother's name, monsieur, I beg you, pity and help me!'

'I swear they shall go hence without you,' I answered firmly; whereupon she caught my hand and kissed it, blessing me for a brave and noble gentleman – my lips envying my hand the while.

At length I bade one of my knaves call Catharine, the woman that had been left behind by Monravel's men, and to her care I consigned mademoiselle. That done, I approached the window and looked out. I beheld a very magnificent gentleman, bravely arrayed and well mounted, and with him two fellows whom at a glance I took to be serving-men.

'*Holá*, my master!' I shouted, 'what seek you?'

'I am in search of a lady,' he replied, with princely hauteur.

'*Ohé*! A lady? Has she fallen into the moat?'

'You are pleased to jest, Master Jackanapes,' quoth he with a scowl. 'I am in search of the lady who has sought shelter in this castle.'

'Jackanapes in your teeth, you dog!' I answered. 'Were I not—'

'Answer me, sir,' he thundered, interrupting me. 'Are you harbouring a lady? I demand it.'

'*Oui-da*! You *demand* it? Monsieur, I would have you know that my name is Armand de Pontis, and that.' –

'I *am* answered,' he broke in angrily, 'And you shall smart for it, you knave. I am the lady's legal guardian, and deliver her to me you shall.'

'If you stay there another minute,' I answered, losing all patience, 'I'll deliver you a handful of carbine-shot.'

'I shall appeal to the Provost,' he threatened.

'Appeal to the devil, sir!' I retorted; and, slamming the window, I left him to his own devices.

191

As I turned I found mademoiselle standing behind me, her eyes alight with excitement.

'We have gained a respite, mademoiselle; but I fear that he will return, and the Provost with him.'

'What then, monsieur?' she cried in alarm. 'You will not abandon me to them?'

'Never, mademoiselle,' I answered resolutely. 'We shall fight this battle out together.'

To seal the bargain – and deeming that I had earned a right to this – I gallantly raised her hand to my lips.

'And I warrant you we will prove good comrades,' quoth she with an arch coyness that made me dizzy with hope.

Now, albeit M. de Bervaux was gone, he had left behind him his two servants on guard in the clearance before Savigny. It occurred to me to make a sortie and scatter them, and I mentioned this to Grégoire in mademoiselle's presence.

''Twere easily done,' said he; 'but it would avail us little unless' – His glance at mademoiselle completed the sentence.

'Mademoiselle remains here,' I answered, interpreting his glance.

That evening a letter reached me from M. de Crecqui.

He lauded in it my treatment of those whom the Parliament had sent to me, and urged me to stand firm and give way to no threats, since he would be answerable for all. He was on the point of setting out for Paris to lay the matter before His Majesty. He ended with some touching professions of friendship, and promises of future advancement did I continue in this matter to show myself as staunch and trustworthy as hitherto. That promise of his was a pretty thing to dwell upon, and with his letter for a foundation I built myself as glorious a 'castle in Spain' as ever sprang from the hopeful soul of an ambitious boy; and in that castle of fancy dwelt I and Henriette de Chandora – for such, she had told me, was her name. I pictured myself a knight of romance, and her the lady I had rescued in her hour of need; and as the days sped by this pleasant fancy grew and absorbed my every thought.

M. de Bervaux returned that night with the Provost and twenty men-at-arms – half of whom appeared to have been enlisted from the peasantry of the neighbourhood; and I was now called upon to give up the lady I had kidnapped. 'Kidnapped' was the word the Provost used, and 'tis small wonder I was out of temper at it. I was discreet, however, and did no more than swear by my honour that I had kidnapped no lady. He persisted that I held her a prisoner in Savigny; and, since I would not grant him leave to enter and search the place, he despatched a messenger to Paris to inform the King and the Parliament of what was passing. That done, and with wild threats of using cannon against me, he encamped his men in the clearance before the castle, and sat down to besiege me.

Four days went by ere the Provost's messenger returned, and were I minded to set down in detail all that had passed in those four days 'twixt mademoiselle and me, the thousand things we said, the million thoughts I kept for later utterance, I should fill a volume as copious as the Bible.

On the night before the messenger's return we were walking on the ramparts – she wrapped in a man's cloak, and trusting to this and to the darkness to screen her from any prying eyes of our besiegers. I stalked along, talking as only a man of twenty will talk when the stars are overhead, the air is warm, and the woman of his heart doth bear him company. She listened and answered, and was kind, and so the thing came about; and before I quite knew what had chanced I was on my knees holding her hand in mine, offering her myself and all that I owned, and bewailing that my offering was so poor a thing – in which, in all truth, I did myself no more than justice. She said me neither yea nor nay, yet from her kindly tone and the touch of her sweet hand upon my head I gathered hope, and promised to wait, as she besought me, another day. She cried out that I bewildered her; that she must think at least until the morrow. And so we parted.

The morrow brought a more imperious summons from the Provost and M. de Bervaux. The Provost had word from the Parliament that I and those with me were to be held outlaws and taken dead or alive unless I could prove that Mademoiselle de Chandora was not in the château. The news staggered me. What was M. de Crecqui about that such a decree as this was passed? And then I bethought me that this matter of mademoiselle was a thing apart from the mere holding of Savigny against M. de Monravel, and beyond the pale of M. de Crecqui's influence. The fear of disaster loomed suddenly before me.

'What proof will satisfy you, Master Provost?' I demanded.

'None but a search of the château,' he answered firmly.

'I have already told you, sir, that M. de Crecqui, my master, has forbidden me to open the gates to any one.'

'Have a care how you trifle, M. de Pontis,' he cried. 'I am empowered by the Parliament to proceed to extremities if you withstand me. M. de Crecqui's affairs are nought to me. Unless you admit me before sunset I'll send to Juvisy for cannon, and talk to you with them.'

Here was a pretty situation! And what would M. de Crecqui say if Savigny were demolished by cannon? I went over to the northern wing of the château, where mademoiselle had her apartments, and having found her, I told her what had passed.

'There is but one remedy,' said she, with a sigh.

'That is?'

'To hand me over to my guardian.'

'Were I minded to do so vile a thing, 'twould be too late; for if the Provost can prove that I have detained you I shall certainly be arrested.'

'Oh monsieur,' she cried, wringing her hands, 'is it for such a reward that you have befriended me? What can I do – what sacrifice can I make to save you from the consequences of your generosity?'

'So that you love me' – I began, when some one knocked. With an oath I strode to the door.

Barnave was there with a letter. It had been flung on to the ramparts with a stone attached to it from the eastern side, which was unguarded by our besiegers. Taking the package, I dismissed him, then eagerly tore it open. As I had already guessed, it was from M. de Crecqui, and dwelt at some length upon the charge which had been preferred against me.

'I more than half suspect,' he wrote, that this is a trumped up lie of Monravel's, a pretext to gain admittance to the château and to overcome you. But the accusation is a serious one, and you must admit the Provost and one or two men – not more – to make their search. Keep close watch over them whilst they are in the place, and see that, as they enter and depart, your gates are not rushed. If by any chance the story be true – which I cannot bring myself to credit – and you have a woman in the castle, we are all undone. I shall of a certainty lose Savigny, and as for you – may God have mercy on your soul!'

My heart sank at the last words, and in silence I handed the letter to Henriette. She took it, read, and fell to pondering with knitted brows. At length she looked up.

'If you were to get me secretly out of the château,' she said slowly, 'and then let the Provost make his search, would not the difficulty be overcome?'

'Ay, *ma mie*,' I answered, 'it would indeed. But how is it to be accomplished? The château is besieged.'

'On one side only,' she returned quickly. 'The eastern side is unguarded.'

'There are no gates,'

'But there are windows.'

'The lowest is thirty feet above the moat.'

'I might climb down a ladder.'

'Into the moat?' I asked. 'Child, the wall sinks sheer into the water.'

The information baffled her for a moment. 'I have it,' she cried presently. 'You have a rope-ladder in the château?'

I answered her that we had such rings, and thereupon she suggested to me that after nightfall I should descend by it from the lowest window on the eastern side, and swim the moat, bearing the end of the ladder with me; then, having landed, I was to hold it taut, so that it sloped clear of the water. Down this she would descend; and, once she had reached the ground, it would be easy for me to re-enter the castle in the same manner I had left it.

'But you, mademoiselle!' I cried, 'Where will you go?'

'To the Carmelite convent at Bernault; it is a little more than half a league distant, and I know the way.'

I still protested that the descent would be fraught with peril; but she made light of my fears, and so the matter was settled, and the determination taken to carry out this plan of hers after midnight – in the hours when nature would have set the vigilance of our besiegers at its weakest.

It wanted a little to two o'clock in the morning when, having assured myself that all was quiet in the Provost's camp, I made my way down to the courtyard by the light of a lanthorn. As I stepped into the quadrangle I came suddenly face to face with mademoiselle, who had been waiting for me by the door.

'Where are your men?' was the question wherewith she greeted me.

'My men?' I echoed. 'Why, asleep upstairs'; and with a jerk of the thumb I pointed over my shoulder up the steps that I had just descended.

'And the woman Catharine?'

'Is asleep also, I imagine.'

There was a pause. Then, laying her hands upon my arm, and bringing her face so close to mine that I could feel her breath upon my cheek, she said in a whisper, 'It had been better that you had brought Grégoire to guard that door. I am afraid of that woman. I mistrust her. She has been watching me all day, and I have begun to fear that she is spying upon me.'

'*Par Dieu*!' I gasped, ''tis possible. She was a creature of Monravel's.'

'Hist! What was that?' and her fingers tightened on my arm.

'What?'

'Behind you, on the stairs. Did you hear nothing?'

'No,' I answered. Then, smitten by a sudden thought, 'Wait,' I said, and, stepping back, I softly closed the heavy oaken door, and locked it.

196

'Now,' quoth I with a chuckle, 'she may follow us, but not beyond that door. She may knock or shout, but none will hear; the door is too solid. Come, mademoiselle!'

I drew her across the courtyard and through the narrow doorway leading to the eastern wing. We hurried up the flight of steps and along the corridor to the window upon which we had fixed. Softly opening it, I peered out. Nothing stirred; and, although the faintest of crescent moons hung in the sky, the night was dark enough to please and befriend us. Swiftly uncoiling the ladder, I made the hooks fast to the sill; then, drawing off my doublet and my boots, I set myself without more ado to climb down towards the water.

I had gone half-way, and hung but some fifteen feet from the moat, when of a sudden something gave way above me. It seemed to me that the thin streak of moon swept suddenly across the sky; nay, the whole firmament had shifted, and where it had been I now beheld the earth, then the still, black waters of the moat as I splashed into them.

Dazed by my fall, and understanding naught of what had chanced, but still clutching the ladder, I rose to the surface and spat the fetid water from my mouth, thinking that, albeit I was not drowned, 'twas odd I should be poisoned. Too bewildered than to act other than by instinct, I struck out for land. I stretched out my arms to catch at something that might help me from the water, when suddenly I felt it taken in a grasp and found assistance, as unwelcome as it was unlooked for; for as I was dragged out I realised with a shudder that the splash of my fall must have drawn the Provost's people.

Lanthorns began to gleam, and men seemed to spring up around me as by enchantment. I stood up at last with a little knot of fellows surrounding me, and more than one mocking laugh smote my ear. Facing me I beheld M. de Bervaux, and by his side the Provost I had derided. Apprehensively I glance up at the window; but the darkness left me in doubt if mademoiselle were still there or not.

With a laugh, M. de Bervaux inquired what fancy it was had led me to bathe in the moat at such an hour; and I will not dwell upon the score of jests wherewith this was followed by these merry gentlemen. Sick at heart, dripping, and shivering with cold – in truth, very miserable – I was led round to their encampment.

From the dejected state I had been in before, I went beside myself with rage as, upon coming into the clearance that fronts the castle, I beheld what was toward. The postern stood open, and up a plank that was stretched across the moat the Provost's men were filing into the château. How had this thing come to pass? Who had opened the postern? Nor Barnave nor Grégoire, nor yet Catharine, for I had locked them up in the northern wing of the building when I left it with mademoiselle. A light broke suddenly upon my mind, a light by which I saw things as they were; and in that hour I knew that I had been duped – the hooks of my ladder had not slipped from the sill by accident. I bethought me of M. de Crecqui, of his faith and trust in me, and a groan burst from my lips.

♦   ♦   ♦   ♦   ♦

They took me a prisoner to Paris, and in my company went Barnave and Grégoire, whose glances I could not bear to meet. Them they set free; but me they flung into the Châtelet, and there I lay for a week, bitterly reviling myself and my fortunes, and yet more bitterly dubbing the fair sex the 'infamous sex,' with the gallows of Montfauçon looming sinister on my mind's horizon.

On the eighth day of my captivity my sour-faced jailer bade me arise and follow him, saying that Madame de Monravel was come to visit me. He ushered me into a room where I beheld the woman who had brought me to this sorry pass. Beside her stood he whom I had known as M. de Bervaux. From her first words I gathered not only that – as already I suspected – she was none other than Madame de Monravel herself, but also that the gentleman whom she had called her guardian was her guardian by right of wedlock.

I scowled fiercely upon the pair of them, whereupon she came forward with her sweet, scornful smile.

'Nay, not so glum, M. de Pontis,' she cried archly, 'I bring you news of your release and your free pardon for resisting the Parliament's authority. My brother, M. de Crecqui, has lost the Château de Savigny; but I think he recognises how desperate was his case, and I am sure that it will not be long ere he restores you to his favour. The Parliament would have made an example of you, M. de Pontis, but I insisted upon your unconditional pardon. I owed you that, methinks,' she added slyly, 'for the sake – for the sake of Henriette.'

‒ THE END ‒